Choice
OF A
Duchesse

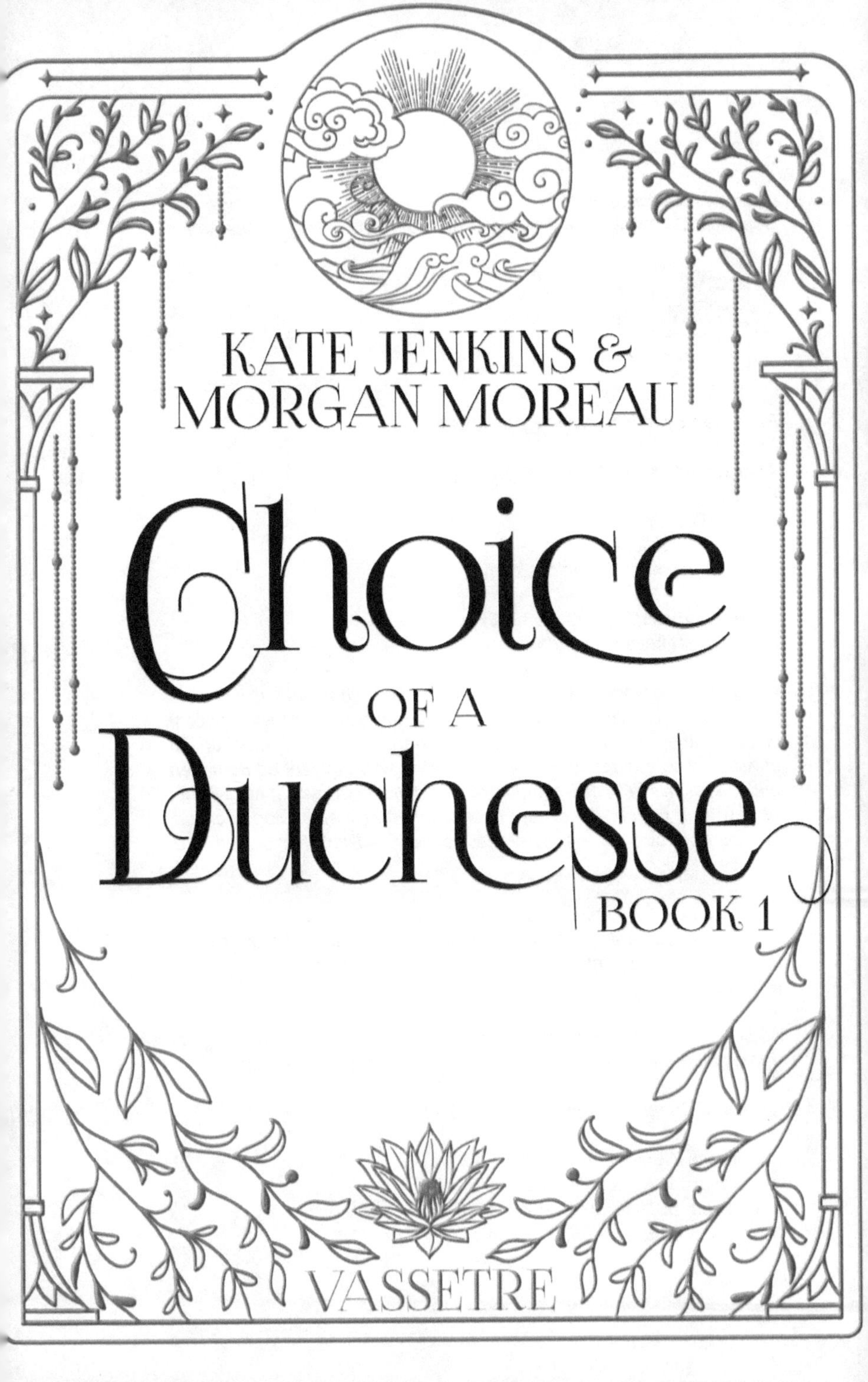

KATE JENKINS &
MORGAN MOREAU

Choice
OF A
Duchesse
BOOK 1

VASSETRE

To Tom Ellis. Without you, there would be no Faron.

~ K & M

To Morgan, for smoothing out my awkwardly
written smut scenes and putting up with my bs.
To Kala, for being so very interested in
reading the smutty scenes.
To Nom, for answering all the weird
texts I sent without asking any questions.

~~ Kate

To Kate, who so happily goes along with the shenanigans.
To Grey, who convinced me writing smut could be fun.
For Jodi Benson, who is the first reason
I adore, and write, mermaids.
And for the cast of *Our Flag Means Death*.

~~ Morgan

Table of Contents

Cast of Characters xiv
Prologue. xvi

Chapter One 1
Chapter Two 11
Chapter Three. 16
Chapter Four. 26
Chapter Five 41
Chapter Six 47
Chapter Seven 53
Chapter Eight 58
Chapter Nine 62
Chapter Ten. 70
Chapter Eleven 75
Chapter Twelve 83
Chapter Thirteen 96
Chapter Fourteen. 102
Chapter Fifteen. 107
Chapter Sixteen 116
Chapter Seventeen 121

Chapter Eighteen 126
Chapter Nineteen 134
Chapter Twenty 148
Chapter Twenty-One 153
Chapter Twenty-Two 157
Chapter Twenty-Three 162
Chapter Twenty-Four 171
Chapter Twenty-Five 175
Chapter Twenty-Six 185
Chapter Twenty-Seven 193
Chapter Twenty-Eight 200
Chapter Twenty-Nine 205
Chapter Thirty 209
Chapter Thirty-One 214
Chapter Thirty-Two 224
Chapter Thirty-Three 231
Chapter Thirty-Four 240
Chapter Thirty-Five 250
Chapter Thirty-Six 255

Author Bios 263
Book Club Questions 267

Azmarin Empire

Other Locations

Azmarin Empire: A country to the north.
Dathria: A country to the east.
Myrefall: County in Coralia.
Quenall: The capitol of Coralia.

Fythias

Vassetre Chateau
Villa du Ciel
la Forêt
Forêt d'Ambre
Île aux Sirènes
Maison du Paradis
Lirac

Cast of Characters

Alain: Human. Deceased king of Fythias.

Alaoin: Human. Child of Eloise and Louis.

Phineas "Finn" Allard: Human. Steward of Vassetre Chateau.

Anaise: Half-Human, Half-Sirene. Member of Sabine's guard.

Tristian Anouilh: Human. Comte du Ciel.

Aphros: Nereid. King of the Nereid People.

Eloise Aresenault: Human. Princess Consort. Wife of Prince Louis.

Grégoire Arsenault: Human. Prince. Middle Child of King Rodolphe.

Louis Alaoin Arsenault: Human. Prince. Youngest Child of King Rodolphe.

Avana: Elf and Dwarf Hybrid. Failed Assassin.

Brielle: Human. Guard Captain of Prince Louis.

Claudine: Human. Caretaker at an Orphanage.

Baron Cyrille: Human. A Minor lord sent by Prince Grégoire to ask for Sabine's suit.

Dion: Human. A Fythian Comte.

Lisbeth Dubois: Human with magic. Personal companion of Duchesse Sabine.

Meri Dubois: Human with magic. Former guard captain, current head cook.

Elodie: Human. Head over the Weavers' Guild.

Faron Istro: Elf. Personal Guard to Sabine.

Glaucus: Sirene. Local Merperson.

Henri: Human. Baron and suitor for Sabine

Jacqueline: Human. Caretaker at an Orphanage.

Marcelle: Sirene. A Vassetre Chateau Guard.

Hugo Onfroi: Dwarf. Retired Guard Captain.

Peronelle: Human. Steward of Prince Louis.

Phindel: Elf. Friend of Faron from Coralia.

Raidne: Sirene. Local Merperson.

Thaumas: Sirene. Local Merperson. Former lover of Sabine.

Sabine Vassetre: Human. Duchesse Vassetre.

Prologue

Faron released the ornate door handle with a low growl, his eyes narrowed in agitation. The giant elf's long black wavy hair fell forward as he pondered the solid door blocking his entrance. Faron knew he shouldn't be upset even though, once again, Her Grace had locked the door to her rooms. Stubbornly, she had not complied with his request to keep the main door to her suite unlocked, no matter the request he'd made on the first day of his job or the subsequent follow-up requests. "It is for your safety. I need unhindered access to your main space," he'd explained. And yet, now the door was locked, and Faron firmly believed her motivated by a heightened desire to vex him.

He might have walked away, grumbling and promising to address his concerns come morning, but a noise—not quite a crash, but more than a minor accident—left him concerned. He pressed his lips together, thinking. The sound might have been nothing more than a dropped book or a stubbed toe as she accidentally collided with furniture. Neither event would justify more action. Just as he decided to wait, another crash, followed by a shout, reached his ears.

"Oh, you fucking bitch! I'm going to kill you," shouted an unfamiliar, high-pitched, feminine voice.

Encouraged by the clear threat, Faron acted. Backing up, he braced himself and put all his considerable strength into kicking the door down. Once, the door barely budged. Twice, the hinges groaned. With a third kick, the door began to give. A fourth kick, and the door was done, breaking at the lock and hinges.

The heavy door crashed against the wall, but he paid it no mind, nor did he detect the sound causing a reaction from the other occupants in the room. Unsheathing his sword, Faron strode into the duchesse's private greeting area, a beautifully decorated room meant for tea with friends, and through the opening to her lounging room. The sounds of struggle grew clearer the farther back he moved, and he sprinted toward the bedroom where she must have been.

Less effort was needed to access this space, and though he barreled through the open door prepared for battle, he came to a stop as he spotted a nearly naked Duchesse Sabine, wearing only the sheerest white chemise, straddling what appeared to be a young child. The poor excuse for clothing did nothing to hide the swell of her perfect pale breasts or the rosy buds beneath the fabric. The fabric of the chemise bunched around her, showing off her long creamy legs.

She held a plain dagger against the child's neck, her other hand wrapped around the child's left hand, which had been trying to go for a dagger just barely out of reach. Sabine used her larger stature and weight to keep the struggling child on the floor.

Faron was about to ask why she was holding down a child when he took in the culprit's ears and face. She was no child. Just an unusually small elf.

"What the fuck?" was all Faron could say.

Chapter One

Hooves rhythmically clacked on the cobblestone street as Faron took in the sights of the village surrounding Vassetre Chateau. Confident in the saddle, the elf did not allow the slight bounce of each step to detract from his interest in his new home. He drew curious looks from shopkeepers and craftspeople as he rode, though he wondered if his substantial height or the presence of a new person was the cause of those glances. In his experience, new faces often drew curious interest. Small villages rarely experienced substantial change.

As he turned down the street leading him directly to the estate grounds, a briny wind tousled his long black curly hair, and Faron inhaled deeply, relishing his new seaside home. The distant sound of waves reached his ears, though the ocean had not yet appeared. Lisbeth promised he'd have his fill of the sea, so he was not especially worried.

Upon hearing of Faron's intention to leave Coralia due to the increasingly unsafe conditions for non-humans, his dearest friend Lisbeth had written him, asking him to join her at the Vassetre Chateau, which sat in the northern part of Fythias. Lisbeth had been sent there a couple of decades prior when her growing magical talents put her and her family at risk in Coralia, and every correspondence confirmed how happy she was in her home.

Years had passed since he'd last seen her, but they had kept in touch. Lisbeth refused to stop writing Faron one letter a month, even if it took him six months to pen a reply. He felt as though he knew all about her employer Sabine Vassetre, the duchesse and most powerful woman in Fythias. He'd also learned of Phineas Allard, the duchesse's steward. More importantly, he knew of Lisbeth's wife Meri, a richly bronzed beauty who won Lisbeth's heart.

Faron could not lie by saying Lisbeth was the only reason he'd come to Vassetre. Her letters about Duchesse Sabine intrigued him. A survivor of the brutal death of her parents, Sabine served her people with care and meticulous attention, something so many nobles neglected. When the need for a personal guard arose, Faron had been offered, and had accepted, the job. Faron couldn't accuse Lisbeth of exaggeration, having never met the duchesse, but he wondered if she would live up to her reputation.

Vassetre Chateau came into view as his horse scaled a small incline in the road. Composed of a light-colored brick and dark red-brown roof, the chateau sat on a hillside overlooking the foamy blue-green ocean below. Two guards stood out front beside a secured wrought-iron gate, both dressed in uniforms of gray and emerald. Faron drew his horse to a stop, then dismounted the creature while ignoring the way the two men looked up at him in disbelief.

Without waiting for questions, Faron retrieved his letter of hire from a coat pocket and held it out to the most senior-looking guard, who plucked it from his hand. A quick browse, and the man surveyed Faron cautiously. "You're Faron Istro?

Her Grace's new guard?" Faron wasn't surprised by the disbelieving tone. He looked like a soldier, in his opinion, but perhaps soldiers in Fythias looked different.

Still, Faron fought to not roll his eyes. An elf, especially a giant, often drew skepticism from those who did not know him. "I have a letter from Phineas Allard saying as much."

"You're early," the man replied, eyes going back through the words as though they might have changed. "Lord Steward Allard said you'd not be here until tomorrow."

"The spirits blessed my travel with good weather and a quick horse," Faron deadpanned. He couldn't help but wonder why they were so keen on him being early or why the older guard eyed him suspiciously. Faron would never truly understand others' fascination with his size. While most elves were usually smaller and lither in stature, his broad shoulders and considerable height weren't exactly abnormal.

"Aye," the guard replied. He handed the letter back over to Faron. "I should still consult with Lord Steward Allard all the same." He turned to the other guard, a younger man with thick eyebrows, though his attention was drawn to two women who leisurely emerged on the distant side of the hill. Both all but forgot Faron and hurried over to aid them.

Impatiently, Faron turned to look at the approaching women. His eyes first landed on a woman with wild ginger hair dripping wet with seawater. Her sea green eyes danced with mirth as she gave a gentle push to the other woman's back. Faron smiled. His friend had grown into a beautiful woman.

Faron looked at the other woman, intending a glance before resuming efforts to be allowed on the ground. He had not intended to be struck dumb by her sheer beauty despite being more than accustomed to beautiful women.

"Your Grace," the older guard said, offering the woman, dressed in nothing but a deep green form-fitting robe which clung to her damp body, a hand until she was on more level ground. "We did not realize you were at the beach."

"I'd not planned it until the last moment," she explained, laughing. Her delicate fingers went to the drenched, light caramel braid resting against her shoulder and began unraveling it. Her sea green eyes, playful and warm, briefly lifted to her useless guards before returning to her task. Faron could not take his eyes off of her.

"Of course, Your Grace," the guard said, offering his mistress a smile. He nodded to Lisbeth, his respect for the young woman evident.

Faron pulled his eyes away from the duchesse, now focused on her visit to the rocky beaches without her front-line guards being aware. It demonstrated a lack of communication in the estate, and he knew he would need to meet with Lisbeth's wife, the former captain of Duchesse Sabine's guard, to begin the process of sorting things out. Assuming he was allowed to make any considerable changes.

"Faron!" Lisbeth exclaimed, interrupting his careful planning. The redhead sprinted over and enveloped him in a hug, giving no mind to her damp dress and skin. "You're early!"

"So I have been informed," he replied with a warm smile as he returned her hug. He chose to ignore his now damp travel clothing.

"Let me guess," Lisbeth said, grinning up at him. "The guards are giving you trouble."

"I think they were just surprised," Faron said as Lisbeth pulled away to look him up and down. Somehow, despite knowing her age, Faron had expected Lisbeth to be no older than when he'd last laid eyes on her. A stupid notion, given she must be well into her thirties by now.

"Because you're early, or because you may be the largest elf any of us have ever seen?" Lisbeth asked.

Faron was not allowed to respond.

"Please allow him to pass, and one of you go fetch Finn so Faron can be settled in his quarters. We do not wish to keep people waiting unnecessarily. Also make sure his horse is taken to the stables, brushed out, and well-fed," Duchesse Sabine instructed the guards. A brief exchange between the men, and the younger one went sprinting to find Finn. Sabine turned to Faron and Lisbeth, taking them in with warm curiosity. Faron was grateful she spoke because he was struck breathless by the intensity of her sea green eyes. "Please, walk with us. Perhaps he'll find Finn by the time we are inside."

Despite the inviting depth of the duchesse's gaze, Faron found it difficult to prevent his eyes from roaming along her body. The robe she wore clung to her every curve, and while the material wasn't sheer by any means, the way it framed her informed Faron of one very important thing: the duchesse liked to swim nude. Inviting though the image was, it left him concerned she'd been left vulnerable in her morning pursuits, given the guard's responses.

"I would be honored to walk with you." He held out an arm to both ladies, Lisbeth latching on right away, her smile wide and beaming.

The duchesse was slower to accept his offered arm, but when she did, he knew he was far too distracted by the curl of her fingers on his bicep. Faron bowed his head to Sabine, ignoring the persistent urge to look more, do more.

"Didn't you tell Marcelle where we were going?" Lisbeth asked as they walked.

"I did," Duchesse Sabine confirmed. "But that does not mean his words were heard when he inevitably passed them along."

"You know he did," Lisbeth replied. "Marcelle never keeps your location secret unless there's a need."

Faron found distraction in Lisbeth and her happy chatter as they passed through the gates along a gray stone path. He was also pleased to hear not all the chateau guards were useless. Still, he would make appropriate assessments once he'd settled.

Inside the grounds, Lisbeth explained each section of the lush garden, her work, and they eventually made it inside the chateau. "My private garden," Lisbeth said, pointing toward a gate. "You cannot see it from here, but when time permits, I'll take you on a tour. Her Grace gave it to me."

"A private garden is quite the thoughtful gift," Faron replied, keeping his expression mostly neutral. Gifts of land were always valuable.

"Not really," Duchesse Sabine insisted. "We had the space, and Lisbeth enjoys it. It made sense for me to give the garden to her. Besides, she shares what she grows, so everyone seems to benefit."

Lisbeth nodded in agreement, though the conversation shifted to another topic as they entered the chateau. The interior provided a warmth Faron had not expected. The walls were the same light brick as the exterior, covered in tapestries and art. Every few feet sat a large window, allowing sunlight to stream in and naturally brighten the space.

Looking down, Faron saw a floor made of small three-inch square tiles in shades of clay. The color was broken up by a rainbow of randomly placed tiles, and Faron detected no pattern or method to the way those had been laid. The older tiles had likely been chosen by a former duc or duchesse, but their excellent shape suggested the duchesse invested time and money into maintaining their appearance.

Once they made it to the end of the entryway, Duchesse Sabine withdrew her hand from Faron's arm. "I will leave you with Lisbeth." She paused as the younger guard approached with a tanned man, perhaps in his mid-thirties, with shoulder-length brown curls. "And Finn," she added, gesturing toward the man Faron knew to be her steward.

"Your Grace," Finn said, lowering his head in respect before looking up. "I heard you were looking for me?"

"Yes," Sabine confirmed. She gestured in Faron's direction. "Lisbeth's friend has joined us, and he is early. Could you make sure his rooms are ready, his luggage is delivered to those rooms, and otherwise ensure he has everything he needs?"

"Of course," Finn confirmed. He seemed to have recognized his mistress had engaged in a morning swim. "You have a visitor later this morning," he said.

"I do," she confirmed. "Which is why I intend to go bathe and dress if it is alright with you?"

Her teasing grin informed Faron she was not insulted by the reminder, and as she walked off without another word, he found himself both relieved and regretful. Working for the Duchesse was going to prove interesting if he couldn't get himself under control. The playfulness in her demeanor alone caused him enough concern.

"Hello," he said, inclining his head to Finn. "I hope my early arrival does not throw off your schedule too much." He doubted it, but his annoyance with the guards at the chateau entrance left him willing to call the men to task as the opportunities to do so presented themselves.

"Not at all," Finn said. "I will go make sure your quarters are ready if Lisbeth would see you to the kitchens for a meal and warm drink. It's early, and I doubt you've had a decent meal today."

"I'd be happy to," Lisbeth chirped before giving the steward a concerned look. "Finn, the guards at the gate were ... acting off about Faron being here early."

Faron patted her arm to comfort Lisbeth, not liking her upset, even slightly, about the whole matter. "I think they were more intimidated by my size," he told her half-jokingly.

Finn let out a frustrated sigh. "They also didn't know you and Her Grace left the palace grounds. I'm more than a little put out with the incompetence. Marcelle knew where she was."

"Marcelle always knows," Lisbeth chirped.

Faron eyed Finn, taking in the tense lines of his shoulders and the firm set to his lips. "From Lisbeth's letters, I know Meri was the captain of the duchesse's forces until her injury. Has her replacement not been up to par?"

"The original replacement was superb," Finn replied. "He retired a few months back, wanting warmer weather for winter months. Finding suitable replacements has proved challenging, and even the competent guards can only maintain certain standards for so long without someone to keep discipline and order."

Faron considered the information, hoping the issues he detected were more recent than the decade since Meri had served as captain. "I could attempt to help with the soldiers when I am not attending to the duchesse," he offered. "I have experience working with guard units, and I'd be willing to step in, even if it's just until someone suitable can be found."

"You would need to consult with Her Grace on the matter," Finn said. "She will likely be amenable, but she keeps a close account of the estate. She's just as aware as the

8

rest of us of the current deficits. I doubt she'll be unhappy with possible solutions."

A willingness to hear suggestion boded well. "I will ask Her Grace," Faron confirmed, and the three walked in silence for a few minutes in the direction of what Faron presumed was the kitchen. He took in the chateau with its inviting, warm colors, the lush furnishings, and the content expressions on Lisbeth's and Finn's faces.

"I am aware why someone in Her Grace's position needs a personal guard, but have there been any recent concerns I should be aware of?" he asked.

"There has been some insistence for Her Grace to consider suit," Finn explained with a nod. "One of her more recent visitors took liberties she did not appreciate, and it was decided she needed someone who would be willing to deal with those who could not show her proper respect."

Faron's grin showed a lot more teeth than was necessary. "I am more than happy to deal with those types of men." The true concern would be showing the right amount of restraint should a similar situation arise again. One of his jobs back home had been protection duty for the working ladies of a tavern. He'd taken their protection more seriously than the offenders had liked, though several of them had been unable to voice those concerns when he'd been done with them. A simple conversation with the duchesse could clear up her expectations and give him boundaries for any necessary responses.

"Her Grace will be pleased," Finn said. They arrived at the entry to the kitchens, a solid oak door separating the group from the interior. "I shall leave you and Lisbeth here to make sure your quarters are ready. I will make sure someone gets you to your rooms and, later, Her Grace's office. Hopefully,

Her Grace will have a few minutes to meet with you before her guest arrives."

"It was a pleasure to meet you, Finn. I look forward to working with you." Faron gave Finn a small closed-mouth smile, feeling confident as Finn nodded in recognition. Faron could appreciate Finn's practicality and willingness to admit shortcomings because it suggested a willingness to address issues.

When Finn turned to leave, Faron stopped him as a question came to mind. "If Her Grace does not have time before her guest arrives, should I simply stand by? I would like to start right away unless this guest is not another suitor."

"They are a suitor," Finn replied with a sigh. "And she'll want you close by. Her request for intervention will not be subtle, should it be needed. I'll let you know what to do if time does not permit a quick meeting."

Faron couldn't help but be proud of the duchesse, knowing she wouldn't just stand there and take whatever misconduct her suitor was willing to perform. "I will be ready to serve as soon as she needs me."

"Good to hear," Finn said, the corners of his lips turning up briefly before he walked off, presumably, to carry out his self-assigned task.

Chapter Two

"I will stop by when I have a free moment!" Faron called out to Lisbeth's wife, Meri, as Lisbeth dragged him from the kitchen. Well, coerced by Lisbeth's pleading, sad eyes rather than dragged. They stood in the corridor outside of the spacious, clean kitchen, with Lisbeth gripping his arm as if he may bolt back inside at any moment.

"We are out of the kitchen. What was the next step in your plan?" Faron couldn't help but ask.

"I had been thinking of taking you to your room so you can freshen up before getting to work," Lisbeth said, but she paused as a confused expression crossed her face. She pressed her heart-shaped lips together in silent contemplation.

Faron hoped she wasn't about to go off on another rant about why he should rest today and start tomorrow, something she went on about twice in the kitchen, much to her wife's amusement.

"I have no idea where your rooms are," Lisbeth said.

"Fortunately, I do," Finn said as he approached the two, his boots softly thudding on the colorful tile beneath his feet. "Your room is ready if you'd like me to show you to it," he offered Faron.

"Yes, please. I wouldn't mind washing up before starting work," Faron said, then laughed at the disgruntled look on Lisbeth's face.

"You do look like you could do with at least a nap," Finn said, glancing up at Faron's face. "But either way, follow me. You can do as you would like once I've shown you where you sleep."

Faron nodded to Finn, looking back down at Lisbeth. "Are you coming as well?"

"No, I need to see to Her Grace. Finn just ruined my plans to get us both horribly lost while searching for your room." Lisbeth winked at Finn.

"We can spend time together later. Go attend to your duties," Faron said, pulling her into a quick hug. "It's good to see you. We will catch up soon, alright?"

"I can't wait," Lisbeth returned before heading off, giving Finn a wave as she went.

Faron smiled at Finn once he and the steward were alone. "I am a bit tired, but I'll be alright. Meri makes a strong cup of tea," he said.

"You might not think so come the end of the day," Finn said. He motioned for Faron to follow along. "Today should be fairly relaxed, though. Her Grace has a meeting with the Weavers' Guild, a visitor later in the morning, and not much else of concern."

Faron nodded. "The visitor is the suitor she mentioned earlier?" He pondered if she would need him for the meeting with the Weavers' Guild, but he assumed not, since he'd been presented with no urgency in the matter.

"Yes," Finn confirmed. "She is not overly concerned with the visit, but she was not with the last one and she had to defend herself, so you never know."

"I will ensure nothing of the sort happens again," Faron said, his hand coming to rest on the long sword at his hip, the only thing he had left of his family.

"Good," Finn replied. "She should not have to resort to throwing things because people do not respect her boundaries."

As they walked, Finn pointed out areas of interest in the chateau, including the duchesse's office and meeting spaces. "She spends much of her day in the office, though when she has groups of visitors, such as the local guilds, she will choose larger spaces," Finn explained.

"Are there certain meetings, like when a suitor comes to call, where I should be inside the room, or does Her Grace prefer her guard to wait outside unless needed?" Faron had worked for employers who had specific preferences, and while he assumed Sabine would not mind him in the room with her, there could be issues with him overhearing anything too sensitive, her being as powerful as she was.

"Generally, if she knows someone well, she doesn't feel as though she needs someone in the room. These suitors being sent by the prince, though, should always be overseen."

Finn paused as he arrived at a heavy, dark wood door. He withdrew a set of keys from his pocket, unlocked the door, and pushed it open, motioning Faron inside. "Here is your suite."

"Thank you. I will keep your advice in mind moving forward." Faron gave Finn a warm smile.

"You're welcome," Finn replied. "You have Her Grace's schedule for today, so you should be set there. She is an early riser most mornings, but she usually doesn't require security until later in the day. You can discuss the details of when you would report to her with Her Grace." He removed one of the keys from the ring and handed it over to Faron. "In case you wish to secure your room."

Faron nodded. "I will talk to Her Grace as soon as possible about my schedule. Thank you again for this." He bowed his head to Finn.

"Of course. Let me know if you need anything for your room. The last occupant didn't like a lot of clutter." Finn gave a final nod of his head and saw himself out.

Faron watched Finn retreat before looking down at the key in his hand. It was simple, made of dark iron, the handle round with what he assumed was Sabine's crest, followed by a long thin neck leading to the biting of the key. It reminded him of the key to his parents' house before everything fell apart. Not really something he wanted to think about at the moment.

Quashing his melancholy thoughts, Faron finished opening the door to his room and stepped inside, stopping almost immediately as he took in not only the quality of the furnishings but the size of the room itself. The furniture looked to be a dark oak, stained and well cared for. The floor, a slightly lighter shade of wood rather than the decorative tile he'd seen throughout the chateau so far, could barely be seen thanks to the large plush forest green rug decorated with vaguely geometric patterns. The shutters on the window matched the furniture. Faron was willing to bet the door to his left led to his bathing chamber, and beside it sat a large wardrobe. His bed was framed by a set of bookcases, a luxury he'd never had before. The large room could have easily fit four small beds comfortably with room to spare, though the large bed situated in the middle could hold him and many others if he'd liked.

Faron wondered if Sabine treated all her employees similarly or if he had been given the extravagant space because he was her personal guard. He made a note to ask Lisbeth later, planning on asking for something more modest if others weren't given the same resources.

For now, though, he removed his boots, not wanting to track dirt on the carpet, and walked to the four-poster bed. The two bags he brought with him from Coralia sat empty in the center, letting him know his clothes and a few personal belongings had already been put away.

Staring at the empty bags made his new position feel a lot more real in the way seeing Lisbeth hadn't. It drove home the truth that he would never return to Coralia, at least, not as a citizen. Leaving Coralia had been an easy choice. Anti-magic users and non-human sentiment had led to increasing violence and a lack of work for himself and others. In the days before his departure, he had been attacked no less than three times by groups of drunkards looking for an elf or magic user to take their frustrations out on, and it would only get worse.

Still, he had lived in Myrefall his entire life, and while he had traveled outside of the province previously, knowing he wouldn't return felt depressing. Sitting on the bed, Faron buried his hands in his hair and let himself breathe, drinking the fact that here, in Fythias, he should be safe.

Chapter Three

The fire crackled invitingly, and Sabine pondered pulling her chair closer, only to immediately dismiss the thought. Her thick light caramel hair was nearly dry, and the sheer volume of it made her think better of getting too close to the fire lest she accidentally catch the lot of it on fire.

The morning swim had been such fun, but the time it took to wash and dry her hair after the fact rendered the activity nearly regrettable in her eyes. The swim had left her chilled, and though normally prone to feeling cold, she knew once her hair was dry and she was redressed, she'd feel more comfortable. If she were being honest with herself, Sabine would admit she was mostly complaining because of the timely efforts her hair now required.

With a sigh, she ran her comb through her locks. With summer approaching, she'd take advantage of the bright warmth, and in doing so, she'd spend many a day in a similar position to now, though her hair would lighten to something more gold and her skin would tan under the increased presence of sunlight.

A gentle rapping from the door alerted Sabine just before Lisbeth slipped inside, her gingery curls now dry and lovely. She gave a quick nod of respect. "I've shown Faron to the kitchens and his room. Do you need help with your hair and dress?" Lisbeth asked as she went to look at the dress she had laid out for Sabine earlier in the morning.

"My hair is almost dry, so hopefully it will tolerate some styling," Sabine said, straightening in her seat. "I'm tempted to remove much of the length with every passing day."

Lisbeth's hand went up to her own shorter length as she considered Sabine's hair. "Your hair is beautiful, but it is rather thick. I know the style is currently 'the longer, the better' for unmarried women, but we could take a few inches off if you wish. For anything more, we'll need Meri."

Sabine laughed as she ran her comb through her hair once again. Deciding it was dry enough, she stood and went to join Lisbeth. "I believe your wife threatened me the last time I discussed possibly trimming my hair. She might have been serious."

"She didn't threaten you," Lisbeth said with a laugh. "She said she should just chop it off at your shoulders so it would be easier to handle."

"She offered to do it herself, as though we all don't know what this," she paused to point at her hair, "would look like short. It was a threat."

Lisbeth hid her giggle behind her hand. "It does get," she paused, looking for the right word, "less controllable than my own."

"It grows big and triangular in shape," Sabine suggested with a wry smile. "For now, will you arrange it for me?"

"Of course." Lisbeth's smile grew brighter as she grabbed the ivory comb, brush, and some hairpins. Arranging Sabine's hair was Lisbeth's favorite part of her job, a product of the other woman not being able to grow her own hair past her shoulder blades without the curls getting too out of control.

Sabine took a seat at the vanity so Lisbeth could work. She watched in the mirror as braids were plated and pinned up. Lisbeth's work was always careful, and never did Sabine feel an overly sharp tug or uncomfortable movement. "Your friend seemed upset with the guards," she commented.

Lisbeth let out a small huff. "They were giving him trouble for arriving early instead of reaching out to Finn as they should have." Lisbeth paused as she started to pin a section of Sabine's hair up, needing to place a pin in her mouth for a moment to do so. "As we walked through the halls, he questioned Finn about the guards and offered to help with them. He is unhappy they didn't know we were at the beach. Even more so when Finn said a suitor tried to take liberties with you."

"Good observations for someone who just arrived," Sabine said. "But then, we knew there were problems, which is why you recommended him."

"Faron has always been observant," Lisbeth remarked. "And intense."

"Then let us hope he can bring some better organization and habits to those he works closely with."

"I think Meri is going to lend a hand. He told her about the guards being surprised to see us, and she almost blew her top. I had to drag Faron out of the kitchen because they were so busy talking about training schedules and such. Meri's mad at herself for not recognizing the lack of discipline in some of the newer guards."

Sabine looked back at Lisbeth with an amused grin. "Tell me how you dragged a giant elf from the kitchens on your own."

"I pouted and told him he would be late," Lisbeth replied with a devious grin. "I also promised I would bring him back to see my wife later since, obviously, he was planning on stealing her from me for her incredible mind and skill at wrangling soldiers. They both looked mortified at the idea. Though he kept turning back around to throw other ideas at Meri as he left with me," Lisbeth said proudly.

"Good thinking," Sabine said with a laugh. She turned to look back at the vanity so Lisbeth could finish her hair. "Perhaps your days will not be filled with managing your friend."

"I don't think Faron will require managing, but one never knows."

"I hope not," Sabine replied. "We need order when it comes to the guards, and we've not had order since Onfroi retired."

Lisbeth made a sound of agreement, another pin between her lips as she used both hands to twist up another section of Sabine's hair. Thankfully, she was almost done, and Sabine would be able to dress and have a quick breakfast before her visitor was expected.

"What does everyone else think of Faron?" Lisbeth asked.

"I think they like him, and I suppose I must be happy if you, Meri, and Finn are," Sabine observed. When Lisbeth finished her hair, Sabine stood to finish dressing in something other than her chemise and stockings.

"I'm just happy Faron's here. It's safer here for him."

"It is," Sabine confirmed as she tightened the ribbons keeping her stockings up around her thighs. She liked the warmth of them and wore them often, even when the weather grew nicer. "Elves are not safe in Coralia from what I hear. Should he need to offer a haven to friends, let him know we can offer a place to stay while new plans are made."

Lisbeth nodded. "I am more than happy to let him know." She walked around Sabine, taking the other woman in, before they began the tedious process of dressing.

A wool petticoat tied around Sabine's waist was among the first items placed on her body: warm and of a fashionable dark color. Her stays were next added. Though they were not tight, as had become the fashion with the teenage girls in the village, they served their purpose in supporting, and partially displaying, her breasts. A front panel, a complimentary green, was next secured to her petticoat.

The gold overdress was added last, the silk fabric adorned with pearls and lace, creating an elegant silhouette for the duchesse. "I'm so glad more rounded necklines have returned," Sabine commented.

"I agree. Rounded is much more flattering on you, though the square cut was also lovely."

"The squared lines always sat funny on my shoulders," Sabine said. She gave herself a once-over in the mirror, deciding she approved. "I think I am ready."

Lisbeth walked around Sabine one last time, straightening and tightening fabric and ribbons before nodding. "You're ready to go."

"Good," Sabine said. "Perhaps I shall have time to eat something before I meet with the representative of the Weavers' Guild. Elodie's last letter suggested she was quite eager for a chat."

"Meri noted you hadn't eaten. She said she would have something brought up for you." A knock at the door, and Lisbeth lit up and swiftly sprinted to the entrance, throwing it open to greet her wife as if she hadn't seen Meri in days rather than mere minutes.

Sabine laughed at the display, though it was hardly the first time she'd watched Lisbeth's enthusiasm for her wife overtake her. She couldn't blame the woman for being so enthusiastic. "Good morning, Meri."

"Good morning, Your Grace," Meri responded once Lisbeth had released her. She slowly pushed a wheeled cart into the room, her limp—a reminder of the atrocities leading to the deaths of Sabine's parents—more pronounced today than normal. Lisbeth made a face, reached to help with the cart, but then pulled back. Meri asked for help when she wanted it. "How was your swim?" Meri asked.

"I hear my outing has caused great outrage amongst the staff," Sabine replied. "And now you and my new guard are plotting away with glee."

Meri pressed her lips but otherwise kept her expression pleasant. "I am very aware you can take care of yourself when needed, but there should have been a guard with you. Those guarding the estate should have been notified in case something had happened. Faron and I were just discussing ways to correct the lapse in judgment and communication with the rest of the guard."

"Did I say the reaction was incorrect?" Sabine asked, noting Meri's annoyance. "I just find it funny you and Faron have decided to reorganize things when I've barely spoken to him, and he hasn't settled in yet."

Meri's cheeks darkened in embarrassment or shame. "Faron is quite serious about his job and your safety." Meri removed her black cane from the cart, balanced her weight on it, and removed the lids from three dishes. One held an assortment of fresh berries and some cream for dipping. Another held thin flat cakes. The third held a bowl of porridge with brown sugar and cinnamon sprinkled on top. A pitcher of juice and a pot of tea rounded out the meal.

"You've done too much," Sabine observed, and she took a seat so she could quickly eat.

"You ate almost nothing before your swim and very little last night. I decided if you were going to have trouble eating, I would make something simple and delicious to encourage your appetite," Meri explained. She allowed Lisbeth to wrap her arms around her from behind and rested some of her weight on the red-headed woman.

"I eat," Sabine replied, though she did not hesitate to begin her breakfast. She picked up a berry and ate it without adornment. "There have been a number of things going on to distract me, like your new giant elf friend."

"Distractions don't mean we don't take care of our needs," Meri lectured, repeating the familiar phrase she'd been using on Sabine for as long as they'd known each other. "Besides, if the giant elf is distracting instead of intimidating, then he's not doing his job right."

"I'm not the one plotting with him in the kitchens or arguing about his arrival time. I just have to address all of it," Sabine replied with a teasing smile before going back to her food. "And you know anyone with his stature will distract. Not much he can do about it, is there?"

Lisbeth giggled as she released Meri and went about picking up the room.

"No, not much at all." Meri placed a hand on Sabine's shoulder while Lisbeth folded her night clothes and readied everything for later in the day. "If you need help with any-thing, all you have to do is let us know, Sabine," she said in a soft voice.

"I know, Meri," Sabine assured her. "And trust me when I say I always get help in areas I can allow."

"Sorry, I just can't help but worry after you," Meri said, giving Sabine's shoulder a slight squeeze.

"I know," she repeated. "And I appreciate all you've done and continue to do. If I had a genuine complaint, I would make it. I promise."

"Please do. We all just want to help," Meri replied. "You've had so much on your shoulders from such a young age, and now the royal coercion to convince you to marry..." Meri took a heated breath through her nose. "It's not right, and you don't need the added stress."

Meri had never been quiet about her dislike of Prince Grégoire, the surviving middle child of the deceased Fythian king. As Meri had expressed, the prince was slimy and scheming, and he had no right to demand the duchesse take a husband.

Lisbeth, who was placing folded clothes into the wardrobe, nodded along with her wife.

"And I will marry when I meet someone worthy of my hand," Sabine assured both. "I am secure in wealth and influence. Any true attempt to force my hand would cause him more trouble than it would cause me."

"He's still enough of a controlling ass to try," Meri pointed out. "But you are correct, thank the Spirits Prince Louis has a better head on his shoulders. I'm glad you're supporting him instead." Meri reached for a small, thin dagger on her cart, gold eyes rising to look at Sabine, who suspected her overprotective former guard captain planned to offer it.

"You must calm yourself," Sabine told her without outright objecting to the silent request.

"You're right. I apologize. I've just been on edge lately, and I don't know why." Meri removed her hand from her dagger then ran it through her short-cropped black hair.

Sabine nodded. "With the uncertainty in the kingdom, I can understand the apprehension, but I cannot tolerate plotting in the kitchens or being treated like a defenseless child."

Meri pressed her lips together, nodded, and looked away from Sabine. "Yes, Your Grace."

Sabine noted the change from her given name to a more formal title. She sighed, mentally adding another item she had to attend to. "Again, I understand, and I do appreciate the concern. I don't begrudge the desire to keep me safe, but no one can unilaterally decide on actions I need to take. I am always open to discussion."

Meri sighed and looked at Lisbeth as she always did when she struggled to explain herself.

Lisbeth smiled. "I'm sure Meri wasn't going to enact any plans with Faron without talking to you first. Right, love?" she asked.

"Yes, exactly, and I feel terrible you think I would. I do want you safe, more than anything. While Faron and I were discussing the situation with the guard, I did tell him he would need your permission and a good plan before we could even consider looking in the guards' general direction," Meri admitted.

Finished eating, Sabine picked up the cloth napkin, cleaned her fingers, then dabbed at the corners of her mouth. "I trust every intention is good, and you will only act if I have signed off. I just need you to recognize I am not inclined to put myself in danger or use poor judgment." Even a near decade later, she missed her parents. Their violent deaths would never stop haunting the halls of Vassetre Chateau.

Sabine rose to her feet after tossing the napkin back on the cart. "Unfortunately, I have the guild meeting, correspondence to attend to, and a financial report to review before my guest is slated to arrive."

"All of which sound delightful," Meri said, grasping the wheeled cart. "I'll clean up breakfast and start on lunch. Any requests?"

Sabine couldn't help the playful smirk. "Are you going to have enough left for the rest of us after feeding Lisbeth's friend?"

Meri made a face. "I mean, he can only eat so much." She laughed. "I'll ask one of the lads to fetch more food from the market to stock us up just in case."

"He's not that big," Lisbeth said, laughing.

"I think you are mistaken, Lisbeth. He's the tallest man I've ever met," Sabine replied. "And I will leave you two with thoughts of his size."

Meri cackled while Lisbeth just laughed softly as she helped Meri get the cart from the room. "Call me if you need anything," Lisbeth called out as they left.

Chapter Four

Dearest Sabine, the Duchesse Vassetre,

It has been brought to my attention you have been less than charitable with some of your most recent suitors. The Baron Cyrille reports an assault by your delicate hands. I struggle to accept the report, as I know you to be a well-mannered, intelligent woman. I hope you to be dutiful to your ruler, as I will inevitably soon be. Surely, your behavior is either exaggerated by Baron Cyrille or a result of ill health.

As old family friends, I am more than happy to come for a visit or send another of our friends to check on you if things are amiss. Please let me know how I can help.

Yours,
Prince Grégoire

Faron yawned as he stood at attention outside the door to Sabine's office. He wasn't bored. He had more than enough to keep his attention at his new home, such as the portrait hanging on the wall across from him which showed Duchesse Sabine at what he would guess was eleven years old with a very beautiful couple standing behind her. Unlike many family portraits he'd viewed in noble estates, this one was filled with brilliant colors and delighted expressions. Her father laughed, while her mother gave the precious Sabine a playfully annoyed look. He thought he might spend hours of his day studying the way the artist captured every small detail.

He yawned again, contemplating Finn's offer to start work the following day. Faron had traveled many, many miles from Coralia, sleeping poorly even when he could find a decent inn to stop at. Even though he was now exhausted, he had never been one to laze about when there was work to be done. The poor work displayed by the guards when he arrived had been something he'd contend with over time. The awaited suitor scheduled to meet with the duchesse today needed immediate monitoring.

The door beside him clicked open, and Duchesse Sabine stepped out, dressed much more modestly than she had earlier in the morning. Still, her figure was hardly concealed by the gold gown she now wore. She paused, not having expected him to be there. "Oh, you've started," she commented. "You weren't here when the representatives of the Weavers' Guild left."

Faron took a second, several seconds really, to compose himself enough not to give the duchesse a long once over. Her obscene beauty still proved distracting, though he managed to keep his eyes trained on her face. "I thought it best to get started right away once I'd eaten."

"Ah," she replied then smiled mischievously. "You are not required to stand guard at the door, you know. I tend to be fairly safe when just those residing in the chateau are present. It's the visitors who sometimes prove suspect."

Faron's cheeks heated. "I was not aware." He really should have asked Finn for more information instead of just asking another of the guards where Sabine would be at this time of day.

"Well, you know, this is what happens when you arrive a whole day early," she teased, looking up at him. Closer now than he'd been when escorting her back to the chateau earlier in the day, he could better observe the green of her eyes. And by the Spirits, they were the most beautiful green he'd ever seen. Not the green of the grass nor the leaves of a tree in spring. They more resembled the soft bluish-green of the sea during sunrise.

He pulled himself back to the present, pushing aside the thought of his new potential favorite color. "If today has taught me anything, it's to never show up early somewhere ever again. Or at least not a day early," he said, returning her joking smile.

She laughed. "Should I make a note of early arrival next time I hire?" she asked.

Fuck. Her laugh was just as distracting as her eyes. "Not a bad idea to notify others. You may want to inquire about their height beforehand as well. Your guards don't take kindly to tall people."

"Oh? Are you tall?" she asked, her shoulder touching the door frame. He found he liked the subtle casualness she was willing to show him.

"Apparently so. I've always considered myself average height."

"Obviously," she agreed with another soft laugh.

Faron smiled down at Sabine. "Makes me wonder how your guards would react to someone shorter than average height. Would they even see them?"

"Oh, I think somehow they'd get along," Sabine replied sagely. "I was going to call for tea. You look like you need some as well."

"Tea would be nice if you have time?" Faron inquired, not sure when Sabine's guest would arrive.

"I'm one of the most powerful nobles in Fythias," she replied, pressing a hand against the line of her clavicle. "My guest cannot make any demands on my time. I will see them when I judge it time."

"I cannot blame you," Faron replied, having not considered her position relative to other nobles. "Do you see guests often?"

"I do," she confirmed. "The people who work in the village have days they maymeet with me to discuss any matters of importance. I meet regularly with the guilds. Other nobles who feel they have business to discuss call from time to time. And as of late, many unsuccessful suitors."

Faron nodded, memorizing the sort of meetings she allowed. Petition days had once been the norm in Coralia before everything changed under Sargarus. Conducting business with others of one's station also fell within the realm of expectation. The unrequested suitors, of course, required more information. "When you say many, do you mean five or five dozen?"

"Nine so far," Sabine replied. "Many of them at least twice my age, and all of them with very different priorities and views than my own."

Nine didn't seem a high number, but he supposed in her position he'd have grown weary long before reaching the number. "Let me guess. The ones twice your age have been married a time or two, and they have strong opinions on how a wife should behave?" Faron asked with a raised brow.

"Oh yes. One of the expectations of a wife would be producing an heir in the first year of marriage."

"Within the year?" Faron asked, though somehow, he wasn't astounded. For all he knew about the more progressive views of Fythias, rich titled men all thought the same. "How would two people form a true, mutually beneficial partnership in such a short period? All forcing you to have a child does is get you out of the way of duties rightfully belonging to you."

"So, you see why I threw a cup at his head," Sabine replied, eyes twinkling with amusement.

Faron laughed. "I can," he agreed. "Have any others made such demands?"

"None quite so brazen as the last, but he presented numerous concerns," she explained. "It was determined I needed a personal guard after the meeting, and here you are."

Faron's face twisted in disgust. "I will never understand why some men feel they have the right to lay hands on another person. It's disgusting, and while I promise to nicely remove any others who try such a thing, know I have broken men's hands in the past for daring to touch what isn't theirs. I am willing to do so again if requested."

His words didn't seem to bother her. No worry lines formed around her mouth, nor did her eyebrows knit together in concern. She simply gave a small bob of her head in recognition. "Let us hope such action is never needed."

"Always, Your Grace."

"Good," she said. "Now, since I am not yet in need of guarding, why don't you call for tea from the kitchens? You can keep me company and tell me things while we indulge."

Faron nodded and stepped away to call for tea. Meri and Lisbeth were nowhere to be spotted on the errand, but the young girl who took his request did so without much question. Sabine, he concluded, must have a very particular way of taking her tea.

He returned, finding her at her desk, though he waited for permission to enter the office. The tile, with its intricate design and random pops of rainbow colors, followed into the space, though an enormous plush rug covered the area closest to her desk. The large desk sat at an angle so her chair, and subsequently the duchesse, sat in a literal corner.

She smiled up at him and motioned for him to enter and take a seat in one of the plush green chairs in front of her desk. He did so, surprised by the easy invitation, as though she were not his employer. "What things would you like me to tell you, Your Grace?"

"Oh, anything. I know your name, your connection to Lisbeth, and you intimidate with early arrivals and height. Surely there is more to know."

"I don't feel like I've lived a very exciting life. Though Lisbeth seems to think so," Faron mused as he considered what was appropriate to tell Sabine.

"She has been quite complimentary of you," Sabine confirmed with a nod. She put a finishing flourish on the letter in front of her, put her pen aside, and moved the letter closer to the edge of her desk where it sat in direct sunlight. "And she was insistent on your selection for the position."

"I'm grateful for her insistence, but she is aware you are the highest-ranking person I have ever served."

"Yes, I was made aware before you were hired," Sabine confirmed.

"I'm glad. I know Lisbeth tends to talk up her friends." Lisbeth hadn't mentioned Sabine's stunning beauty except in passing, a thought Faron quickly bit back. Sharing his physical attraction to the duchesse seemed unwise, no matter how inviting and informal she seemed.

Sabine leaned forward, her arms resting on the desk, the loose parts of her hair falling forward. "Lisbeth is eternally optimistic."

"Until you take the last apple muffin. Then she turns into a feral monster ready to tear someone apart. Unless Lisbeth has dramatically changed during our years apart?" Faron asked.

"If she still possesses such behavior, it has not been demonstrated in front of me."

"We all grow out of bad habits I guess," he said with a small chuckle. He stood to help the young girl who arrived with a tea tray and some finger foods. "These look delicious," Faron told the girl.

"Her Grace's favorites," the girl replied shyly.

Faron gave her a warm smile. "Please tell the cook we appreciate it."

"Mrs. Meri will be pleased." The girl beamed before leaving Sabine and Faron.

Faron made sure to look as if he was studying the tray of sweets and small sandwiches cut into triangles as he set the tray on Sabine's desk. In reality, he was watching Sabine. He noted her interest in the sandwiches holding what looked to be cucumbers. The way her lips pressed together in pleasure when she noted the chocolates on the tray also drew his attention, but the way her smile bloomed and eyes lit up when she caught sight of what looked to be a chocolate and blackberry tart told him what she most favored.

Grabbing a small plate, he asked, "Would you like some?" as he gestured to the tarts.

"Yes, please," Sabine agreed, her green eyes widening in anticipation. She picked up the teapot and poured herself a cup, then a second one meant for Faron.

Faron placed a few of the pastries on a plate while also taking note of how Sabine made tea—a quick pour of milk and three sugar cubes—so he could make it for her the next time. "Are there any sandwiches you would prefer?" he asked.

"I think I'll make my way through the tarts first," she replied before she began on her food. After finishing the first bite, she looked over to Faron. "So, I suppose we should establish expectations, as you are my personal guard."

"I would appreciate it," Faron said with a small smile, still slightly embarrassed about his early mistake.

"I am normally awake by sunrise, but I do not expect the same of you. I usually stay secluded in my suite until later, though as you saw earlier, sometimes I do venture out."

"Do you have a guard rotation set up for while you sleep? In case there is an incident?" Faron asked.

"I do," Sabine said after taking another sip of tea. "When you go to the guard house, ask to speak with Marcelle. He has been overseeing the scheduling since Onfroi retired. He'll be able to provide you with whatever you want."

Faron made a mental note of the name and when he would have time to go meet Marcelle. "What are the plans you have in place in case there is an incident at night? Do you leave your door unlocked? Does the night guard have a key to your room if not?"

"I keep my suite locked at night," Sabine replied. She looked at the tray of food and selected a triangle-shaped sandwich. "And I have not given a key to anyone other than Finn."

Faron did not like her response. It gave a possible attacker the upper hand when the guard didn't have access to Sabine's space. "I would like to request you leave the door to your rooms unlocked, at least until I can get a key to your room."

"I shall consider it," Sabine said before looking to the door when someone knocked. "Come in," she replied.

Finn entered, a sealed letter in hand. "A letter from Villa du Ciel," he explained, causing Sabine to roll her eyes.

"He must have received word from Baron Cyrille," she replied, putting her tea aside before taking hold of the letter. She retrieved a long metal opener from a desk drawer. "Tristian has nothing to do with my feud with Grégoire."

"You did leave a rather large lump on his forehead," Finn pointed out.

"You threatened to leave more if I recall," she retorted.

Faron observed the interaction between the two, taking note of both Sabine's and Finn's reaction to the name of what he assumed belonged to another noble in the kingdom. He would ask Lisbeth about it later if Sabine didn't offer more information. He had to look away as her lips pursed in annoyance while she browsed the letter. By the Spirits, no woman had a right to present such a tempting picture.

"I assume Baron Cyrille is the reason I was hired?' Faron asked, pulling himself together.

"In part," Sabine replied without looking up from the parchment. "He was sent by Prince Grégoire, who has made it his mission to marry me off since my politics vex him. It looks like Cyrille complained to Tristian."

"Tristian Anouilh," Finn clarified for Faron. "The Comte du Ciel. He lives in the neighboring estate less than a day's ride from here."

Faron nodded, making note of the names. "If I may, does Prince Grégoire have the right to try and push suitors onto you if you're not willing?" Faron didn't know much about the nobility, but it seemed wrong to try and force a marriage onto another person.

Sabine replaced the letter opener in her desk drawer. "I suppose the answer depends on your perspective."

"Could you elaborate for me?" Faron asked, interested in learning how her mind worked and what perspective could possibly be alright with such a situation.

"The reigning monarch certainly has the authority to make such demands on their subjects," Sabine began, her eyes twinkling in delight as her posture relaxed against her chair. "Of course, Prince Grégoire is not the reigning monarch, though he is a member of the royal family. One could argue such obedience should extend to him."

"And you've gotten her started," Finn said under his breath, amusement shining through.

"Be quiet," Sabine said, grinning wickedly. "Prince Grégoire underestimates my power and wealth in making his demands, and even were I to comply with a decree to marry, I doubt he would like my selection." Her delicate shoulders rose and fell. "So, we currently play a little game of meeting suitors."

Intrigue, and the way Sabine lit up as she spoke of her situation and surrounding politics, drew Faron further into her grasp. Her lack of respect for the prince was clear, as was her enjoyment in playing this game against him. "He has no idea he is playing a losing game." Faron let out a huff of laughter. "Remind me to never play chess against you. I have a feeling I would be trounced in seconds."

He paused for a moment, grabbing one of the small sandwiches with a green style of sauce and meat he didn't recognize. "What do you get out of playing this game of being forced to deal with men who do not realize your worth?"

"Well," Sabine began, then paused to drink a sip of her tea. "I continue to show something akin to respect for the royal family, despite the chaos of their house. I also delay further decrees which might be harder to circumvent." She motioned to Finn to have something to eat or drink if he wished, and he shook his head, declining the offer.

Faron mentally reviewed his understanding of the situation with the royals in Fythias, which was sadly very little. He knew they had just lost their king, Grégoire's older brother, some months back, though how, he didn't know. "I admit to knowing little of the politics here, but I am more than happy to learn," Faron said, leaning forward in invitation for Sabine to keep going. He truly was enjoying watching her, how obviously in her element she was.

"By birthright, Grégoire should inherit the throne, as our prior ruler died without heirs," Sabine replied. "But the throne sits empty because no one can convince the proper people to proceed with coronation. Grégoire is hot-tempered and a bit stupid, terrible qualities for a leader."

"One of those would make a terrible leader, and both even more so. You mentioned you were delaying decrees. Can he make any while the throne sits empty?" Faron asked before making a face as he bit into the small sandwich. It was a little too sweet for him.

"You've asked another question which depends entirely on perspective," Sabine said before drinking more of her tea. Her eyes looked back at the letter, her expression growing contemplative.

"I hate to make assumptions, but so far, my perceptions match your own, and if they didn't, I believe you could convince me to see your point of view. You're quite the gifted orator." Faron couldn't help the compliment. Sabine truly was as intelligent as she was beautiful.

Sabine smiled at the compliment but made no mention of it. "Personally, I believe he has more legal claim to the throne than his brother, who I would prefer. There is enough pushback to prevent his outright claim, but I owe some obedience and loyalty to the royal family. How I show my devotion matters because Grégoire might claim outright acquiescence as legitimizing his claim."

"Is there a reason he has not already done so?" Faron thought back on his letter from Lisbeth. "The throne has been empty for a while now if I'm correct."

"Her Grace believes Grégoire is afraid to act without powerful support. He knows he cannot receive it from her," Finn shared. "And she is the highest-ranking member of the nobility in Fythias. Grégoire needs her support, or he needs someone to bring her to heel."

"And my steward believes he does not want the throne enough to act," Sabine shared.

Faron considered both sides of the argument. "I think Her Grace has the right of it. Otherwise, why try and marry her off? The prince is likely hoping a husband will be able to override her choices and give him the support he needs. Are all your suitors supporters of Grégoire?"

"Of course they are," Sabine replied, surveying Faron with an expression of what might have been interest.

Faron shook his head. "Grégoire is interested in the throne. Marrying you off is just a way to help him get there with the support he needs." The thought made Faron angry. How could this pathetic prince think Sabine so stupid as to fall for such a trick? He'd known her mere hours, and he could see her intelligence.

"I think I made a good choice in personal guard, don't you, Finn?" Sabine asked, grinning up at her steward.

"You do seem quite pleased with yourself," Finn replied with a returned grin.

"I am," she confirmed.

Faron couldn't help but smile at their banter, even as his desire for the duchesse made itself known. He discreetly crossed his legs. "What concerning decrees has the prince passed or tried to pass?"

The smile faded from Sabine's face. "He sympathizes with Coralia."

Faron barely fought back the curse word wanting to slip past his lips. He didn't think they were on good enough terms, yet. "Then he doesn't deserve the crown."

"He does not," Sabine agreed.

"I'm glad we have someone like you to oppose him," Faron said.

"So am I," Sabine replied. She picked up the letter once again, scanning it as though she hoped to see something different this time. "I suppose I should respond," she said, mostly to herself.

Faron wanted to ask about the letter and its contents, but he held back. "Is the Comte more persistent than the rest?"

"I did throw a cup at Cyrille's head," Sabine reminded Faron. "And Grégoire wonders if I was a little hasty in my actions. Tristian is eager to play the middleman."

Faron shook his head. More and more, the middle prince sounded like the worst sort. "After your meeting, what are your plans for the day?"

"Well, I already went swimming," she said, her mischievous grin reappearing. "So, nothing involving water."

Faron laughed and pushed the image of Sabine from this morning from his mind. "Do you usually go swimming in the mornings?"

"I wish I could," she replied. "My hair takes too long to dry to do it often."

Faron used her reasoning to examine her hair. It was quite beautiful, and he pondered what it might be like to run his fingers through it, but the length and thickness undoubtedly took time and considerable effort to contend with. "Yes, I can see why you might be reluctant to spend most mornings on the task."

"Indeed," Sabine said. "Unfortunately, I do think I should pen my reply before my guest arrives."

"I should ask, other than being here for your suitors and such, are there any duties in particular you wish me to perform?"

"I heard of kitchen plots with Meri," Sabine replied. "Perhaps refine your ideas, make a plan, and present something formal when it is ready."

Faron chuckled. "Less kitchen plotting and more getting a general idea of the state of the guard and possible ways in which to correct the issues. I'm told you haven't had a decent captain since the last one retired."

"I have not," she confirmed.

Faron nodded, respecting her answer. "I will have something for you to review before tomorrow is out."

"I look forward to your recommendations," she replied.

Faron bowed his head, once again fighting against allowing his eyes to slip lower than they should.

"Now, if the two of you will excuse me, I shall compose my response," Sabine said.

Faron nodded, finished his last sip of tea, and rose from his seat. "Will I be alerted when your guest arrives?" he asked.

"I will make sure you are aware and ready," Finn replied. He gave a shallow bow in Sabine's direction and motioned for Faron to exit. Faron, too, bowed to Sabine and followed after Finn.

Your Royal Highness, Prince Grégoire,

As always, I am both honored and flattered by your dedicated attentions. In times such as these, knowing which friends we may turn to remains of the utmost importance. Thank you for your efforts in looking after me. Because we are such dear friends, I do find it important to relate my concerns to you regarding Baron Cyrille.

As you can imagine, I am not a woman who appreciates unwanted advances or presumptuous actions. I am also not a woman of tolerance when others take liberties with me. Cyrille's decision to put hands where hands were not wanted resulted in a dire need to defend myself. As such, not only has an antique tea set become incomplete, but I have been forced to spend my money on a new line of defense.

Because I know Baron Cyrille is your friend, and because I am certain you'd have never sent him to my home had you known the kind of man he is, I will not ask for compensation. If the need for additional security becomes warranted, I will surely let you know.

Yours sincerely,
Sabine, Duchesse Vassetre

Chapter Five

The meeting with the latest suitor, a willowy young man with long braids and bright blue eyes, had been more successful than the meeting with Baron Cyrille. The Baron Henri made for excellent conversation. He liked much of the same music and literature she enjoyed. He raved over the delicate chocolate cakes prepared by Meri, and overall, they had a wonderful afternoon.

When Henri admitted he had no desire to marry, lest his longtime partner, Edmé, might become quite outraged, Sabine breathed a sigh of relief. She wouldn't have to make excuses to avoid marriage, and she could safely report a successful meeting to Grégoire should he ask.

After promising to stay in touch with Henri and seeing him out, Sabine dismissed Faron and decided to take a walk. She'd been locked up in her office for much of the day, and her legs yearned to stretch.

She'd roamed these corridors her whole life, and Sabine believed she must know every inch of the chateau by now. Without looking, she was certain she could guess at every color of the tiles she passed or the old plastered crack hidden behind a painting of some aunt she'd never met. Her familiarity with her home always brought her comfort.

The smell of baking goods from the kitchen, located just around the corner from her current spot, was another.

As Sabine entered the kitchen moments later, she spotted Meri near the wood-burning stove while Lisbeth stood by, presumably providing company.

"I am afraid to report you will not have a new duc from Henri," she reported, feigning great sorrow.

"How sad. He seemed like a sweet one," Lisbeth said. Had Sabine not known her well, she might have believed her to be sincere.

"What was wrong with this one?" Meri asked.

"He's desperately in love with another, to start," Sabine replied. "And I will not do something just because someone thinks I must, as we know."

"Why would he come if he already has someone in mind?" Lisbeth asked, confused.

"Because he has no choice, just as our lady has no choice but to see him," Meri explained as she moved to grab some spices from the nearby rack. "I'm sorry you've had to deal with yet another pointless suitor, Your Grace."

"It is just as well. We had a delightful chat, and I was highly entertained by Faron's scowling," Sabine insisted. "Really, a pleasant afternoon."

"We are both glad you had a good time with him." Meri moved back to the stove and started tossing spices into the different pots.

"Why was Faron scowling?" Lisbeth pondered out loud.

"How should I know? He's your giant friend. I thought you'd have ideas," Sabine replied cheekily as she came to stand beside Lisbeth.

Lisbeth gave a delicate shrug. "I haven't seen him in several years. His face may look grumpy when he's not smiling." She tilted her head slightly in thought. "Though, he never smiled much when I was younger."

"What would there be to smile about, growing up in Coralia?" Sabine replied, not joking now. They all knew Fythias had been a place of refuge for the magical and gifted when King Sargarus rose to power. "Either way, we have an answer to your question."

Lisbeth's gaze took on a faraway quality, and Sabine suspected the other woman was thinking about her old life in Coralia. Meri reached over and placed a hand on Lisbeth's shoulder, seemingly drawing her back.

"Yes, we do," Lisbeth replied, her bright voice strained.

"I wish you'd told us he was so tall, though," Meri said with a huff.

Lisbeth shrugged. "He was a good fighter when I knew him in Myrefall. His height probably helps."

"What is your impression of Faron, now that you've spent some time with him?" Meri asked.

Sabine considered the question. "He seems capable, and an elf of his stature will surely strike fear into those I would need guarding from." She gave Meri a mischievous smile. "Is there some other feature you wish for me to remark upon?"

Meri raised an eyebrow, unimpressed. "Other than looking like he stepped out of one of your mother's more suggestive novels, no." Meri paused, a hand clutching a wooden spoon mid-air. "Maybe he and I should switch places. At least then I won't have to worry about your virtue and you won't have to worry about servants and staff following him around swooning." She winked at Sabine, and Lisbeth laughed.

Sabine snorted. "If you're worried about my virtue, you are about a decade late, my friend."

"Oh, I know. I'm the one who found Thaumas trying to sneak out of your window. The poor boy broke an arm for his efforts." Meri shook her head as she resumed stirring.

"He was not my only friend," Sabine replied.

"No, he was not," Mari agreed. "Just let me know if you decide to add Faron to your list of friends, please."

A laugh escaped Sabine's throat. "What a thing to suggest."

Meri grinned. "I may not be interested in men, but there is something to be said about men who look like Faron."

"Meri!" Lisbeth said scandalized.

"I caught you looking," Meri said with a soft smile, dropping a kiss on Lisbeth's head before going back to the stove and working on their meal.

"Well, there is a lot to look at," Lisbeth responded, blushing.

"It doesn't hurt he's smart as well as observant, on top of his height and build. I think he's going to give the guards a complex, especially if he knows how to wield his sword." Meri tossed out casually, the twist of her lips doing nothing to hide the innuendo.

"Should you hear about those sword skills, you might report them to me," Sabine replied with a smirk.

Finn entered the kitchen, his jaw set and brows lowered in concern. "Thank the spirits you are here, Your Grace."

"What's wrong?" Sabine asked

"Nothing wrong," Finn replied, though he cleared his throat nervously. "But I fear you might be annoyed."

Sabine sighed, pressing the heel of her hand to her forehead. "Just tell me."

"Comte Tristian has arrived," Finn said, fighting to not roll his eyes.

"Why?" Sabine demanded, though she knew her steward would likely not know. "And it's too late in the day for us to reasonably expect him to return home."

"I believe the timing was intentional, Your Grace," Finn said. He rubbed the back of his neck with his hand, brushing against the loose brown curls he wore down.

Meri swore at the news, her language colorful as always. "I did not order enough fish to properly feed the Comte."

"We still have plenty of food to supplement the meal, lovely," Lisbeth soothed. "We will make do."

"Yes, but it means Comte 'does whatever the fuck he wants' might be offended over the meal." Meri pressed her lips together, took a deep breath, and made eye contact with Sabine. "Sorry for the outburst, Your Grace."

Sabine wished to throttle Tristian, but even with her superior rank, the action wouldn't serve her well. "Order fresh fish and other seafood from the market," Sabine decided. "It is early enough you will be able to secure decent quality and quantity and have time to prepare it. Lamprey pie or fish with sauce vert. Pair it with something simple, citrus and greens and breads. Tell Finn what else you will need, and he will make sure it is all promptly delivered."

Meri nodded and began putting away the dishes she'd been working on so she could have a fresh place to begin the new preparations. Sabine looked longingly at the crab and pasta dish, knowing she would not receive it tonight.

"I'll see you later, my star," Lisbeth said, stopping Meri in her dash across the kitchen to see what all would be needed from the market to kiss her on the cheek. "What can I do to help you prepare for our unexpected visitor?" Lisbeth asked Sabine.

"The undercooks need to be called in to help Meri with preparation," Sabine replied. "And someone will need to alert Faron."

"Has Comte Tristian done something to offend?" Finn asked, looking up from the list he'd started composing for Meri.

"No," Sabine said, shaking her head. "Something about him, though… He makes me uneasy."

Lisbeth looked like she wanted to say something before looking away. "I will alert the undercooks and retrieve Faron."

"Thank you. All of you. I am more than aware of how inconvenient his visit is for everyone. Trust me, I am quite irritated." Sabine sighed and shook her head again.

"This isn't an inconvenience for us, but it is for you. We can handle all this, but you were supposed to have a free evening to yourself. Those have been few and far between with everything the prince has been pushing on you," Lisbeth said softly.

Meri gave a "here, here," from behind them as she made a list for Finn.

"Still, you've already done so much work for the evening," Sabine pointed out. "Either way, I shall go to freshen up before greeting Tristian."

"Have the best evening you can," Meri called out as Sabine and Lisbeth left.

Chapter Six

"Surely, you can see why I thought to rush here," Tristian Anouilh, the Comte du Ciel, said after a healthy sip of wine. He gazed placidly in Sabine's direction, eyes glassy from drink as they finished a fruit and cheese course. Meri's skill and impeccable organization had produced a dinner no one could suggest had been planned only hours before. Faron was impressed, even if he thought it ridiculous she had to completely change direction well into the day.

Though Tristian seemed content with the meal, the cutting looks Sabine threw anytime he looked away practically begged him to give some complaint. The duchesse outwardly loathed entertaining Tristian with her eyes alone, much more than she loathed the numerous uninvited suitors who came to call from Faron's observations.

"Oh naturally. Resorting to physical retaliation is never preferable," Sabine replied. "Thankfully, Baron Cyrille was escorted from my home, and I have since hired more security."

"Yes." Tristian chuckled, the hand holding the wine goblet gesturing toward Faron, leaving droplets of red liquid on the floor to his right. Sabine's careful eye followed those as well, Faron noticed. "I see your tall fellow here. He certainly poses a fearsome figure."

"Is Faron tall?" Sabine asked, her green eyes glancing at Faron, glinting mischievously before returning to Tristian. "I had not noticed."

Faron, somehow, managed to contain a smile.

Tristian chuckled, seemingly amused by her words, boyish red curls bouncing with his effort. The wine had him red-faced as well, giving the man an unattractive resemblance to a rather sad tomato.

Honestly, Faron as was done with this whole charade as Sabine seemed to be. His exhaustion from a long day of work, following an early arrival, had him rethinking his decision to begin his duties immediately.

"Either way, Faron seems a smart choice for increased security," Tristian declared, setting his wine glass aside. "But should you need any additional support, my men are less than a day's ride out. We would be here, ready to dispatch whatever service you needed, big or small."

"I will surely keep your offer in mind," Sabine promised, a hand going to one of the loose braids falling across her shoulder. Faron didn't know if her eyes or her hair more strongly held his attention.

Admittedly, Tristian made for a good distraction. Though Faron refrained from rolling his eyes at the offer of additional guards—something they did not need—he knew he'd scowled throughout much of the conversation. The pretense of being here to help, to offer safety, was nothing more than an insult. Meri and he were more than capable of making sure everyone, Sabine especially, was safe.

Dinner passed by without much alarm, though with more than a few extra goblets of wine. Faron assumed

Tristian used his dinners as an excuse to drink, whereas Her Grace took the smallest of already scarce sips. She didn't feel comfortable enough to indulge more with the visitor. Faron's scowl deepened. Even as the visitor's own people helped him from the table and to his allocated quarters, Faron hoped the morning would bring the comte's departure.

"He's not to step foot on the east wing of the chateau," Sabine said as she rose from the table. With only the two of them present now, her pleasant demeanor displayed her exhaustion and annoyance.

"Would you be alright with me stationing guards at the entrance to the east wing while I guard your door?" he asked Sabine.

"I think you need to eat and rest before you think of guarding my door," Sabine replied, the reprimand—as gentle and as amused as it was—clear. "You have been working since your arrival early this morning. You can appoint someone else while you accomplish both."

Faron nodded as he contemplated asking Meri to watch Sabine's room since the other guards seemed too oblivious and inept for the task of protecting Sabine. Perhaps his earlier assessment was unfair, but Faron had been left unimpressed. He would figure out what to do, even if it was relying on someone he trusted a little less while he napped nearby. "Of course, Your Grace."

Sabine laughed to herself. "You're not very good at hiding your thoughts. Were you aware?"

"So I've been told," Faron said with a wry grin. "Does the Comte often stop by unannounced?" Faron offered Sabine his arm. He would at least escort her to her room before figuring out his next moves.

"The Comte has a great interest in my estate," Sabine replied as she took Faron's offered arm for the second time since his arrival. They left the dining room together, the pace of their walk slow and comfortable. "As does the prince he backs."

The comte's estate sat close to Sabine's, only a few hours ride on horse, and a couple more if by foot. He remembered passing it in the early morning hours, and the estate left very little impression on Faron other than the severe difference in money held by each noble. A marriage would merge their lands, titles, and wealth, and Comte Tristian's standing and influence would grow as well. Backing the prince trying to force a marriage on Sabine only proved his poor motivations.

Faron had gotten involved in quite a tenuous situation. He just hadn't realized how much so when accepting the job. "You would think a man with his upbringing would have enough manners to warn a lady before dropping by."

"Oh, I think we both know his lack of notice and his timing was intentional," Sabine replied as they walked.

"Most certainly." Faron wanted to ask if the comte had ever been even remotely inappropriate with Sabine, but in just the few hours Faron had known Her Grace, he'd learned her temperament would have never allowed the man back. "Does he often cross your boundaries?"

"Not like he has done this evening, no," Sabine replied. "His visit has been an escalation. I shall have to act wisely."

"If you ever want me to remove him, I will do so happily," Faron said, and he meant it. A drunkard the man might be, but Faron had not missed how Tristian's eyes had wandered along the planes of Sabine's body. The very thought of the comte even contemplating taking delight in something not offered to him caused a rage Faron had thought long contained to boil to the surface.

"I shall keep your offer in mind," Sabine promised. Her tone gave off little concern for Tristian, but her expression showed some worry about what the visit, and possible future visits, might mean. As Faron watched the worry cross Sabine's face, he fought to not clench his fist, reminding himself he couldn't force Tristian from the chateau tonight.

All too quickly, they made it to the door leading into Sabine's suite. She relinquished her hold on his arm and smiled up at him. "Go enjoy your evening and rest well," she requested. "All shall be well come morning."

"I will ensure it is," he said with a bow. As he rose, his mind contemplated possibilities. He'd identified the areas needing guards, though he doubted Comte Tristian would, or could, attempt anything given his state of intoxication.

He headed for the kitchen first, hoping to seek out something to eat and speak to Meri. If she wasn't free, Faron knew she could suggest the best guards for tonight's watch. He could gather all that information while eating and possibly even send one of the other servants to gather the suggested guards, killing two birds with one stone. Only then would he rest, assuming one could consider a twenty-minute nap resting.

Sabine, my dear friend,

I heard word, through much gossip and insistence of staff, of your encounter with Baron Cyrille. I wish I could say I am shocked at his actions, but we know I am not. Cyrille's inability to keep his hands to himself is well-known in every court. I cannot apologize enough on his behalf, or my brother's. We know Cyrille acted on his orders.

I know you are well because you'd have written were you not. Please, though, think of me should you need anything. Your friendship means a great deal to me and those at my estate. I would deny no request of yours.

Yours,
Louis Alain Arsenault

Chapter Seven

The morning following Tristian's last-minute visit passed without further event. Tristian's early morning departure, and Sabine's continued support from Prince Louis, had the duchesse in better spirits in the following weeks. Recent correspondence with Louis had the young duchesse feeling brave enough to limit the numerous visitors sent by Grégoire. Depending on the hour of arrival, she might let an unexpected group share stable lodging, but she no longer felt compelled to host every single man in the country.

Of course, even with Louis's support, she could not escape every meeting. Planned out visits, encouraged by Grégoire, happened about twice a week, and she was glad to have Faron around for those occasions. Granted, having Faron around proved interesting, even when he did not need to play personal guard.

Sabine now strolled the grounds, taking in the bright colors of flowers blooming along the chateau walls. The ground, still covered in dew, prompted more deliberate, careful steps. A chill hung in the early morning air, and she pulled her shawl closer around her to ward it off. She hated the cold.

The duchesse was flanked by Finn on her right and Marcelle on her left. The three made the habit of taking a similar walk a couple of times a month. It allowed them to survey the property and catch up. Sometimes, the walks led to productive measures, such as repairs and the ordering of supplies. Sometimes, it led the group into the village, where drinks were ordered and stories were told. Right now, the decision of how the day would go had not yet been reached.

"Do you think we should have invited Faron along since he is now leading the guard?" Marcelle asked as they rounded the southernmost part of the chateau. Off to one side, they could just make out the shoreline, though the splashing of waves was just a little too distant.

"You must like him," Sabine replied with a shrug.

"I do," Marcelle said. "A man who recognizes a deficit and steps up to correct that deficit is a good man to have."

Finn nodded. "I agree, though I think he is overzealous in his assessment of the whole of the guard."

"Oh, no doubt. There are finely trained people there, but lax discipline has taken its toll," Marcelle agreed, his inky eyes crinkled in amusement. "And the newer guards required strong leadership while training." As the sun grew higher in the sky, his golden hair shimmered, as did his smooth, dark skin. Sirene always glowed so beautifully in the sunlight.

"Yes, but for members like you—members who are both skilled and highly coveted for their services—I think a little recognition would be appreciated," Finn insisted. His shoulder-length curls hung loosely about his shoulders; a change, as the steward usually liked to keep his hair up during work hours.

"From the training I've watched, I think he does a fine job acknowledging talent and skill when he sees it." Sabine looked at Marcelle. "Would you agree?"

The Sirene nodded. "Absolutely. I'm not saying I agree with everything that leaves his mouth, but Faron looks like a leader, he holds himself to the same standards, and he treats everyone fairly. Having strong leadership matters, and if he thinks we can always improve, no matter how proficient we are at something, why not let him?"

"As long as no one gets insulted enough to leave, I will leave it to you," Finn replied. "Though we are only paying him for his work as your personal guard, Your Grace. Should we pay him for his work with the guards?"

"I think so," she agreed. "You take a look at the household budget and recommend what you think is fair."

Her decree agreed to, they continued walking, bringing the sea into better viewing. Sabine smiled, pondering a visit to the beach. Perhaps later in the day when it was warmer.

"I know you've been having trouble with Prince Grégoire," Marcelle said as they walked. "I think talking to Faron about recruiting more people might be a good idea."

"It would," Finn added. "The prince can't act hastily when it comes to Her Grace, but I wouldn't be surprised if he conjured up reasons to cause problems." Finn's mouth set into a thin line of irritation. He disliked Grégoire and had since long before the prince had any reason to express a right to rule, and he had been the one to suggest an increase in guard presence around the chateau. The suitors the prince sent to her had facilitated Faron's arrival.

"Oh, his escalation is inevitable," Sabine replied with a sigh. "I think we must all prepare for what will inevitably come."

"Surely not war on his own people," Marcelle replied.

"If the trends in Coralia and Azmarin follow, he might not consider all Fythians his people. Faron didn't leave Coralia because of the job here. He left Coralia because it wasn't safe to remain." Sabine was thankful she'd had a spot for Lisbeth's old friend, but she thought of the hundreds, if not thousands, of people who must be in the tenuous position of starting over without much certainty or trying to wait out the death of King Sargarus.

"I can talk with the Sirenes, see if they have anyone interested in joining the guard, or at least, waiting on standby should they be needed," Marcelle offered, running his fingertips lightly along the curve of the chateau wall. He shrugged. "I think it's no secret how much our leader respects you and your family."

"Please do speak with your people when you can," Sabine replied decisively. "And I think Finn should speak with Faron and Lisbeth to see if there are any others they know who need work or help in escaping. Recruiting others can also be brought up."

"Perfect," Finn easily agreed. Convincing Finn to act rarely took much effort. Even when he disagreed with Sabine, he offered his viewpoint and carried out whatever she expected from him.

The rest of their walk around the premises went by with more random chat, though Sabine's thoughts never left the possible futures their estate faced. Were they truly prepared? Could they be? The answer to the first question was no, no matter how much she wanted to claim otherwise. The second question she thought she could be more optimistic about.

"You may invite Faron for the next of our little ventures," she informed Marcelle. "I think he would enjoy the experience, and we would appreciate his insight."

"I will let him know," Marcelle promised. "And I need to head to my assigned duties. I shall let you know what I hear from my people." The promise made, Marcelle bowed to Sabine before he retreated back into the chateau.

"He is not the only one who likes Faron, you know," Finn said to Sabine. "I think you are quite fond of him."

"I think most of us are," Sabine quipped with a grin. "Now, I have things to attend to before my evening with Meri and Lisbeth." She turned and walked back into the chateau, nearly laughing as Finn followed.

Chapter Eight

Hands clasped behind his back, Faron strolled across the rocky beach, his pace leisurely and slow, matching Meri's as they walked. The light breeze gently tossed his hair around his shoulders, though Faron paid it little mind. Not too far from the shore, Lisbeth laughed and splashed with some of the Sirenes who had come to visit. Her gingery curls, soaked from seawater, glistened in the sunlight. She'd certainly be frecklier if they stayed out much longer.

Faron had met a few people, mostly guards, in the weeks he'd been there. Though he didn't recognize the Sirenes Lisbeth now played with, Meri was unconcerned, so Faron was too. No, he was more concerned with Meri's throwaway comment about different kinds of Mers. Apparently, Sirenes didn't drown people, but the shiny green Mers did. He had no idea if she was joking or not, and she'd refused to clarify.

The two continued their walk in silence, turning and heading back toward Lisbeth when Meri had determined they'd gone far enough. If Meri noticed Faron eyeing her gait, smoother and obviously more pain-free today than most days, she didn't say anything.

"It seems like you've settled in well," Meri said, breaking the silence.

"I'd like to think so," was his easy reply.

"Lisbeth said you've added books to your shelves, as well as some knickknacks."

Faron noticed Meri's raised eyebrow, as if having those items meant something important. "Lisbeth likes to bring me little things from the village. Displaying them was the least I could do." Faron shrugged.

"Of course it was," Meri said before patting him on the back. "I'm glad you're settling in. I remember Lisbeth telling stories of when she and her family first moved to Fythias. She said it took over a year before she felt safe here, truly safe."

"Her situation and mine are vastly different," Faron pointed out. "I am a man and a capable fighter. Of course, I was targeted several times because I was an elf, but it was nothing I couldn't handle. Lisbeth, on the other hand, had her house set on fire. She and her parents safely escaping was a gift from the Spirits. Getting away from the awaiting mob threatening to burn her at the stake because she wouldn't endlessly grow crops was another. Taking a lot of time to recover, to believe she could have a peaceful life, makes complete sense."

"She doesn't like to talk about her time in Coralia," Meri admitted. "She had nightmares for years afterward."

"I believe it." Faron still had occasional nightmares about what happened to Lisbeth and her family. What might have happened had he not seen the smoke from the warehouse he'd been guarding? He'd arrived just in time with some friends he'd picked up on the way there, planning to stop the men who'd grabbed Lisbeth and shook her like a doll. Lisbeth had been barely twenty at the time, her powers still growing, getting stronger every day, but not strong enough to meet the senseless demands of the mob. He considered that long-ago night one of the worst moments of his life, and he knew it was the worst night of Lisbeth's.

"Thankfully, time heals most wounds, right?" Meri said, her laugh slightly bitter.

Faron remembered that the anniversary of the attack that injured Meri and killed Sabine's family was coming up. "It does to a point."

"Still, I'm glad you're settling in," Meri admitted as they reached the shoreline.

"You should join Lisbeth. I've heard the waters of the Fythian coast can help relieve pain," Faron said. He had to wonder if the claim was true.

"It does. The locals talk of the water's healing properties. The salt and cooler temperature are likely responsible. I find it works best once I'm past the crest of the waves, where the water is deeper and less choppy. Floating out there on the water, it's the closest thing to painlessness I can get," Meri explained. She carefully removed her shoes then removed the heavier pieces of her clothing.

"It sounds as if you go out there a lot," Faron mused, his eyes carefully diverted, even if Meri revealed nothing of consequence.

"It's one of our favorite things to do in our downtime."

"Oh, I thought your favorite thing would be what I accidentally walked in on in the stables yesterday." Faron couldn't help but tease. Meri and Lisbeth had been in quite a compromising position, even if the two wives had every right to enjoy one another.

Meri blushed for only a moment before throwing a retort back at Faron. "With your superior elf hearing, you should have known what we were doing long before you reached those doors. My wife isn't quiet by any means." She folded her warm coat and placed it down by her shoes. "So, tell me Faron, how was Her Grace?"

It was Faron's turn to blush because Meri was right. The prior afternoon, he and Sabine had been walking together until they'd had to split up. She'd joined some of the ladies from one of the crafting guilds—the Glass Blowers Guild he thought—for a midday tea. He'd been so distracted watching her go that Faron had missed the lewd noises until it was too late and he had the door open. He hadn't seen much, thank the Spirits, before slamming the stable doors shut again.

"That's what I thought," Meri continued with a smirk, obviously enjoying how she'd turned the teasing on him. "Maybe think twice before bringing up activities my wife and I privately enjoy again. I'm not blind after all." She gave a brief wave then carefully stepped into the water, working her way to Lisbeth, who'd seen Meri coming and was happily moving to meet her halfway.

Faron was left standing on the shore, his cheeks still red from the conversation. He swore to be more discreet with his growing feelings for Sabine from now on, even if he didn't want to admit to the feelings.

Chapter Nine

Thankfully, no guests were scheduled to arrive at Vassetre Chateau. Sabine's usual good nature would not tolerate the intrusion. Today marked the thirteenth anniversary of her parents' death. Though she never spent the day actively mourning their loss, she always made sure her time was peaceful. She wanted the same for Meri since the former captain of the Vassetre guard held herself responsible for all the deaths of the long-ago day.

Like many mornings, Sabine started her day by treading down to the beach for a swim. Her time in the water, dotted by visits from the nearby Sirenes, left her relaxed. After returning to her quarters, she leisurely bathed, put her hair up in a loose style, and spent the day reading, writing letters and, eventually, drinking with Meri and Lisbeth in the kitchens.

Lisbeth lined up the shots, pulling out several bottles of what looked to be hard liquor, while Meri manned the stove. Meri had long ago determined only terribly decadent food could be eaten on nights they indulged in spirits; no one had even tried to complain.

"Finn will be joining us in a little while," Lisbeth chirped while pouring something clear into the glasses she'd lined up.

"Didn't you ban him after the last time we drank?" Sabine asked. She'd retrieved a stool from the corner of the room and now sat at the counter.

"Yes, but he bribed me with those." Meri pointed her spoon at a basket full of pomegranates and a small round green fruit the Sirenes were known for growing and rarely selling or gifting away.

"He did visit with Glaucus this week," Sabine mentioned. "I did as well, but you see, Glaucus does not gift me with anything delicious."

Lisbeth made a thoughtful noise. "I wonder if something is going on there?" she mused.

"I don't," Meri said.

"Why don't you?" Sabine asked.

"Because Finn is a private person, and we should respect him," Meri said, her tone proper and curt.

"She was bugging him the other week, and he threatened to cancel the next chocolate order," Lisbeth said dryly, sliding a glass to Sabine.

"I shall ask Thaumas, then," Sabine declared.

"He might answer you," Lisbeth said, grinning as she took a long drink from her glass. She made a face at the liquor's obvious burn.

"Spill the tea if he does answer any questions, please," Meri requested.

"I don't know if I can," Sabine replied, picking up her glass. "He still blames you for his broken arm."

Meri made a face. "It was not my fault." She moved to grab several large plates. "He was just in the wrong place at the wrong time."

"You know he tells a different story," Sabine teased. "Which am I to believe?"

"Considering we were the only people there when it happened," Meri said, plating several dishes, "it's up to you to decide."

"And we know I must decide on the most amusing option," Sabine replied before taking a drink from her glass. The liquor was smooth and warming, and she took another sip immediately.

"Which we all know is my version," Meri said with a sharp grin as she laid out a variety of baked and fried finger foods on the counter. "So, what's today's topic of conversation?"

"Apparently, interesting love connections," Sabine said with a laugh before taking another drink.

"Well, if you say so." Meri traded looks with Lisbeth, but it was Lisbeth who spoke next.

"How much did you enjoy watching Faron train the soldiers today?" She giggled a little as she asked the question.

Sabine smiled, amused by the question, and drank from her glass again. "I admire beautiful things."

"Beautiful shirtless things," Meri muttered, a playful grin on her face.

"How long did it take for him to lose his shirt this time?" Lisbeth asked.

"Do you think I time these things?" Sabine asked. "No. I simply enjoy myself in the moments I have time to do things, like observe the progress of my guard."

"So, you didn't have Finn clear your schedule so you would have a break during their training times?" Meri asked.

"Did it come off right away, or did he wait till almost the end?" Lisbeth said, a calculating gleam in her eyes.

"If Finn cleared my schedule, he did so without instruction," Sabine replied with a playful grin. She could feel the first tendrils of intoxication circling her, though she had no complaints. "And from what I saw, Faron's shirt disappeared fairly early."

Lisbeth refilled Sabine's glass and pushed a plate of fried cheese with bits of apple in it toward her. "So, his shirt is coming off earlier in the training. Did he take it off, or did something happen to it?" Lisbeth shot Meri a look before her gaze returned to Sabine.

Sabine picked up a piece of the food with her thumb and forefinger, examined it, then popped it into her mouth. She shrugged in response as she chewed. "He removed it himself," she finally answered.

Lisbeth broke into a fit of giggles, and Meri put a hand on the small of her back to help her stay on the chair. "I wonder if he knows you're watching or if the weather is too hot."

"The weather has been warm," Meri said.

"Why would he care if I'm watching, hot or not?" Sabine questioned.

"No reason," Meri and Lisbeth said together.

"How's the suitor hunt going?" Meri asked to change the subject. "Any more letters from His Highness?"

"I'm not doing the hunting, so you'd have to ask him," Sabine retorted.

Meri nodded before changing her question. "Have any of the men the prince is forcing you to spend time with been even a little interesting?"

"Not a lick," Sabine said. "But then, I know what I like, and so many of the people Grégoire would choose are not to my liking."

"You mean they aren't tall, dark, and muscular elves who could hold you down with one hand—" Lisbeth cut off with a small squeak as Meri removed her hand from the area of Lisbeth's ass.

Normally, Sabine would have claimed the words to be crossing the line. She was a duchesse, and a wealthy and powerful one at that. She didn't need anyone subjecting her to lewd accusations. However, she was now sufficiently drunk enough to laugh. "I have never been held down by a tall, dark, and muscular elf. I wouldn't know if the person you described was my type or not."

Lisbeth and Meri stared at each other for a moment. It was obvious Meri was debating taking the liquor away from her wife, while Lisbeth was just pouting.

"Lisbeth has been doubling the chores of some of the younger maids to keep them from going down to the training grounds to cheer Faron on," Meri said, turning back to Sabine.

"And why might Lisbeth be preventing the maids from enjoying the show?" Sabine asked coyly.

"Because the man trains for upwards of four hours a day, and the girls weren't getting anything done. The chateau does not clean itself," Lisbeth said, her cheeks slightly red from the drinks.

"Then I shall tell Faron you insist he wear a shirt when working with the guards," Sabine declared. "Shall I call him now?"

"While you're at it, tell him he can also no longer wear anything white when he pours water over himself when he overheats," Meri said seriously, causing Lisbeth to giggle.

"I think the two of you need to have a serious discussion about sharing some time with him," Sabine teased.

"While I find him attractive, it's purely in the sense of enjoying the opportunity to admire rather than do anything with him," Meri said.

Lisbeth nodded. "Same. I have no interest in touching, but he's nice to look at."

"Strange," Sabine said as she got up long enough to reach for the bottle so she could refill her glass. "You two bring him, and his good looks, up quite a bit."

"He's the only thing new and interesting in the chateau. Unless you wish to talk about why Faron bodily dragged Lord Ashton from the chateau two days ago," Lisbeth said with interest.

Sabine rolled her eyes, but she laughed after taking another drink. "It wasn't as dramatic as it seemed. Lord Ashton was a bit patronizing, and Faron didn't appreciate the implications."

"You normally mention when something dramatic happens. We assumed it was nothing big," Meri confirmed. "I assumed it was something about your policies or being a woman in general?"

Sabine nodded. "The behavior has grown tedious, and I can't imagine Grégoire thinks I will respond well to any of them." Thankfully, she didn't even have to respond if she didn't feel like it. Faron would simply put an end to such meetings once a certain tone settled over the meeting.

"You think he would have given up by now, or he'd have started picking better suitors," Meri muttered as she downed her drink.

"The better ones all support his brother," Lisbeth chirped as she unsteadily tried to pour Meri more liquor. "I want to know why he hasn't proposed to our lady himself. He's been a widower for two years now. How much time does he need to move on?"

Sabine laughed. "He isn't looking for a marriage of love, you know. He'll want something more politically advantageous. As I actively work against his wishes, I do not fall into the realm of possibility." She tossed back the rest of her drink. "Thank the Spirits."

"That's what doesn't make sense to me. You are the most powerful woman in this kingdom. You have land and powerful magic users behind you," Meri said.

Sabine could hear the slight bitterness behind the last part of Meri's statement. Veinfire had robbed Meri of many of her gifts the same night Sabine's parents had died.

"If you say jump, more than half the nobles will do so without question. You would be the perfect candidate for the prince to marry, and yet, nothing. Strategically, it makes no sense. He has to have something else in mind," Meri pondered.

"I think you've pointed out why a union with me wouldn't work in Grégoire's favor," Sabine said. Instead of refilling her glass, she picked up another bite of the cheese concoction. "I am dangerous to a man like Grégoire because I would not stand by and say nothing if he acted recklessly."

Meri conceded the point, but the thoughtful look stayed on her face for a few more minutes. Sabine's old guard captain still thought something was off.

"Have you heard from his brother again?" Lisbeth was leaning more to the side, causing Meri to pull her closer.

"I hear from Prince Louis quite often. He is doing well," Sabine confirmed. "And the current state of intoxication you're displaying tells me I should flee before clothes start falling off." She'd had plenty herself, and the warmth of drink could be felt in her cheeks.

Lisbeth's gasp was scandalized before she broke into giggles.

Meri gave her wife a fond look before nodding to Sabine. "You know how she gets," she said with a laugh, which grew richer when Sabine stood and stumbled herself. "I think you've both had more than enough to drink."

"So have you," Sabine replied, realizing she'd lost her shoes. Oh well. "Good night," she bade them before slowly making herself exit the kitchen.

Chapter Ten

Faron raised an eyebrow at the giggling coming from the kitchen. He had been asked, no, ordered to stay out of the kitchen tonight. A brief conversation with Finn left him to understand they were participating in an annual tradition of remembering Sabine's fallen parents.

"I always say I'll show, but I know they do not wish me to," Finn quietly explained after the women disappeared into the kitchen. "Meri and Sabine share the trauma of their deaths. Lisbeth is a benign comfort to them. Everything else, I think, gets in the way."

Faron understood, so he stood in the corridor near the kitchen and listened to the giggling and reminiscing from the kitchen. Over the last half hour, the giggling increased tenfold. He thought the evening might continue with much more laughter and he would be designated as the person to carry each of the women to their beds.

Sabine's voice rang out, and Faron's gaze went to the kitchen door. "Stop, stop, let me leave before you deflower your wife!" Her voice, happy in a way he hadn't heard before, spoke volumes about the amount of liquor she'd consumed.

Quickly, he closed the distance to the kitchen, and he barely had time to catch his very drunk employer as she stumbled barefoot through the kitchen door.

She still laughed, even as he supported her weight. "Oh, there you are," she said through intoxicated giggles. "I should pay you more."

"Oh, should you now?" he asked as he helped her upright. Faron briefly considered just picking her up, but he thought better of it.

"Well, you were right here when I needed you," Sabine explained. "Such attentiveness deserves recognition."

"And you think an increase in the already obscene amount you pay me is the answer?" Faron placed a hand on her lower back to help guide her to her rooms.

"How would you like to be recognized, then?" she asked and stumbled again, which only brought out more laughter.

"Let me think on it," Faron said as he righted her again. "Would you mind if I carried you to your rooms? The floor doesn't seem to like you much."

"The floor shall be my enemy until morning. And you may."

Faron had to laugh as well. She was a funny drunk if nothing else. He swept her up into his arms. "If I could, I would slay the floor in your honor. Since I cannot, we'll make do."

Her arms went around his neck, loose and warm. "I suppose I will allow it."

"You only suppose?" Faron asked, an eyebrow raised. He found it easier to focus on her unguarded words than how nice it felt having the duchesse pressed up against his chest.

"Well, I am drunk, Faron," she reminded him with a smile. "No condition to determine much of anything."

"True." He looked down at her and back up at where he was going. "Did you have an enjoyable evening?"

"I did," she replied. "Sometimes it is nice to just enjoy oneself."

Reaching her room, Faron better balanced Sabine on his one arm before reaching out to open her door, placing the arm back under her once it was open, and kicking it shut upon entry. Striding to her bedroom, he gently placed her on the mattress but did not move to leave.

She looked up at him, eyes glassy with drink and cheeks flushed for the same reason. "Yes?"

"Is there anything I can help you with before I go?" Faron asked, looking down at her, ignoring the stirring their relative positions caused.

Sabine considered the question. "I shall likely need water at some point," she said. Without prompt, she reached up to begin undoing her hair.

"I shall ensure you have one on hand in case it is needed." He watched her delicate fingers undoing her hair. "Do you need help?"

"You may help if you would like," she decided as she removed a pin from her hair. The twist it supported fell and slowly uncoiled.

Faron hesitated, knowing there were only two ways for him to assist, and he was not getting on the bed. "Turn around," he said, holding out a hand for the hairpin she had already removed.

She handed over the pin then turned around, dragging her skirts to follow the change. Again, he caught a glimpse of her bare feet and, this time, an ankle and calf. Faron placed the hairpin on her nightstand. He turned back to the updo and silently thanked the Spirits it was less complicated than her usual styles. Being as gentle as he could, Faron started taking down Sabine's hair. He removed several pins, then ran his fingers through each section as it came loose. The fragrant locks, silky between his fingers, did nothing to quell his desires for her.

"You're working fairly quickly," she observed, her dreamy tone laced with a slight slur on the last word.

"I used to help Lisbeth and some of the other local girls with their braids," Faron explained. "It was not a skill I thought could be useful until now."

"Helping a lady with her complicated hair will always be a useful skill," Sabine insisted. "Just imagine what might have happened had you not been here to intervene."

Faron chuckled. "Oh, you might have fallen asleep with your hair still up and accidentally stabbed yourself on one of your numerous pins. You could have also risen come morning with your hair a mess."

"Both are possible outcomes, and no one would be happy come morning as a result," she agreed, her eyes closed and her shoulders relaxed.

Faron continued to comb his fingers through her hair, allowing himself the moment. "Lisbeth certainly wouldn't have been happy, since she'd be the one tasked with freeing your hair of tangles and pins."

"And we cannot allow for an unhappy Lisbeth."

"No, we cannot. Have you ever seen Lisbeth cry? It's gut-wrenching."

"Especially when she plays it up."

"She still plays up her tears to her advantage?" Faron asked, barely paying attention to his words. He knew he should stop playing with her hair, but he found himself unable to stop. He no longer had the pretense of taking her locks down.

"That feels good," she said, finally acknowledging their connection had exceeded taking her hair down.

"I'm glad you're enjoying it." He leaned down discreetly, breathing in the scent of Sabine's hair. The action forced him to admit how much he wanted Sabine, and more than just physically. Just not while she was drunk.

"I need to sleep soon," she shared, drawing him back to reality.

"I understand," Faron said and reluctantly released her hair. "Let me go get your water."

"Okay," Sabine said. Her hair now released, she turned back around.

Faron gave Sabine a soft smile before moving to where the cup and pitcher waited. He kept an eye on Sabine through the vanity mirror to his right, admiring her form, her hair, and her smile. He reminded himself she was his employer as he poured water and walked it back to her, placing it on her nightstand.

She gave him a sleepy, but thankful, smile. "Thank you. You have helped me tremendously tonight."

Faron chuckled, the sound rumbling deep in his chest. "I only undid your hair and got you water, but you're welcome, Your Grace." He took a breath. "I will be on guard tonight if you need anything."

"You will be the first to know if I need additional guarding."

Faron nodded. "Good night, Your Grace. Sleep well." Without putting much thought into it, he leaned down and brushed a kiss on the top of her head before quickly turning on his heels and leaving.

Chapter Eleven

Faron walked between the pairs of soldiers as they spared with each other, keeping an eye on their footwork as he went. If his eyes happened to wander to the second-story window, fifth from the center of the chateau, where Sabine's office was, no one was stupid enough to mention it.

When he first gathered the guards together, some of them lacked any training. Others could hold their own, if only for a few minutes. Thankfully, several veterans had been trying to get some order going, but without a guard captain, the group had fallen short of keeping order. With a plan written out, and Sabine's permission given, Faron dedicated several hours a day— usually in the early afternoons when he wasn't needed—to training the men.

Training and drills had been rough at first, with the undisciplined soldiers unwilling to fall in line. Meri eventually consented to join him for a few rounds. Meri took no attitude from anyone, and even on bad days when she struggled to walk without pain, she was still able to put a mouthy soldier on their ass. Faron was almost sure Meri could put him down if she truly had to.

Over the following weeks, the soldiers had improved by leaps and bounds. Faron was proud of them, and he hoped Sabine was too. He wanted her to be pleased with his efforts, and not just because she employed him. Admittedly, having her watching them, even from the distance of her office, ended up a distraction he hadn't needed on more than one occasion.

Sabine had proven enough of a distraction he'd been forced to buy several new shirts as different guards managed lucky swipes, which inevitably had him removing his shirt. Allowing the guards to get a strike now and then built confidence and morale, but Faron couldn't deny the selfish motivation to allow more of those lucky moments. Removing his shirt was only one of the ways he'd concocted to keep Sabine's interest.

The desire he felt for her since their first meeting had only grown, encouraged along by the pure want he sometimes saw on her beautiful face. Their mutual attraction had not gone unnoticed. Lisbeth had taken it upon herself to force other ladies of the house back to their duties, though she also provided ideas for other ways he could get Sabine's attention.

"You know, you can use the fence post for stretches. It will show off your muscles so much better for someone watching from the second floor," Lisbeth had advised. On one particular occasion, she'd even offered, "Maybe the soldiers can make it so you lose your pants."

If Faron hadn't remembered how much mischief Lisbeth had caused as a teen, he would have been more concerned. He also may have done a lot of stretches and such, shirtless, on the suggested fence post.

"The twirl you just did may work on the dance floor, but on the battlefield, it will get you killed," Faron yelled out to one of the men who had done some sort of over-the-top twirl as if to confuse his opponent, who was laughing at him. Shaking his head, Faron looked back up to the window and smiled, seeing Sabine was finally there to watch. He opened his mouth to ask if someone wanted to demonstrate new maneuvers with him when he saw Finn headed his way.

"You seem to be having a productive afternoon," Finn greeted as he approached. "Her Grace has been pleased." The steward's long curly hair was tied back, and his more comfortable clothing suggested he'd have a busy, laborious day.

"I am glad to hear she's pleased with our progress." Faron motioned to the men. "They've gotten better with time and practice. I'm sure with more time, Her Grace will once again have the best soldiers in the kingdom." Faron gave Finn a puzzled look. "Looks as if you have a busy day ahead of you?"

"A continuing one, yes," Finn confirmed with a nod. "Her Grace received a letter this morning from the prince. He's hinting at making a personal visit shortly, which means opening up the rarely used parts of the chateau. Her Grace likes to be prepared."

"Which prince?" Faron asked, wondering if he should send some of the soldiers to help. Menial labor was good for the spirit.

"Grégoire," Finn said with a roll of his eyes. "I doubt he will come. He threatens to do so every few months, but it obligates Her Grace to provide a welcoming home."

Faron's lips twisted in displeasure. He did not know the prince, but he disliked him on principle for how he consistently inconvenienced Sabine. His close association with Coralia only added to his dislike. "I can assign soldiers to help if you think it's needed."

"I might take you up on the offer. The household staff is handling things now, but if we have anything heavy to move, help from the guard would be useful."

Faron glanced around the training yard, his eyes landing on a group of six who he knew would take orders from Finn well. "You six, you're on house duty today with Finn. Anything he tells you to do, you get it done. The consequences will not be pleasant should I hear a single complaint." The men complied without hesitation. They gathered their weapons and supplies and marched off to put the items away.

"Their renewed discipline will be useful should Grégoire push his luck," Finn said wryly, though his narrowed eyes showed how little he wanted such an escalation.

"Has he tried to ... push his luck before?" Faron couldn't help but growl out the words.

"He's attempted to force her hand, yes," Finn replied. "Unsuccessfully. Her Grace is stubborn, thankfully."

"Force her hand how? To marry someone or support his position?" Faron's hand twitched. He wished his sword was at hand. He knew if the prince did show up, he would struggle not to strike him down where he stood.

"Both, although he never has directly made an order. He knows he cannot with her."

For a moment, it was as if a storm cloud passed over Faron's face before he shook it off. "If Her Grace ever needs help handling him, I am more than willing to assist."

"I shall pass the message on for you, unless you'd like to tell her yourself," Finn replied.

"I am due to check in with Her Grace shortly. I am happy to tell her myself," Faron said, having to push down the impatience to go to Sabine now.

"Of course," Finn said. "I will leave you to it." He motioned toward the remaining guards before dismissing himself.

Faron nodded and turned back to his guards. "Alright, take a moment to cool down, then you're dismissed. You have the next hour free before you are expected back to your duties." Faron knew he would feel slightly guilty for cutting their training short today, but the prospect of speaking with Sabine before his duties started was too much of a temptation to resist.

Sabine sat at her desk sipping tea when Faron entered the room. Perhaps a quarter of an hour passed since she'd observed her personal guard on the training grounds. In the interim, he'd washed up and changed, though she had no complaints about his freshened appearance. "You finished early today," she commented.

"Finn let me know the prince was considering a visit, and I wanted to speak to you about it," Faron said, moving to stand close to the desk.

"Of course," Sabine replied. She gestured to an open chair after she sipped from her tea again.

Taking a seat, Faron leaned forward, placing both elbows on the desk as he considered his words. "I am wondering if it would be prudent to have the guards more alert and to double the shifts."

"We'd need to hire more guards," Sabine replied, not arguing against his concern. "We have the funds for it, of course, but finding suitable people can prove taxing."

"And we may not have the time," Faron agreed. "I do not like the idea of you being around him without a guard or the idea of him having free rein of the chateau," Faron admitted.

She smiled and reached out, placing a delicate hand on top of his. "I do not like the thought of Grégoire any more than you. I worry what he might think of more guards."

"We could always tell him it's for his protection," Faron said, turning his hands over so their palms now touched.

"We could, and he's arrogant enough to believe it," Sabine said, her gaze dropping to their now far more intimately aligned hands. She did not pull away.

"From the sounds of it, he very much is." Faron's eyes had darkened as he looked at Sabine.

She thought she could very well stay in the moment, despite the serious nature of their conversation. "Why don't you see what you can organize?" she suggested. "I trust your judgment."

Faron nodded. "I'll do you proud, and if the prince steps out of line, I will happily drag him from this estate and toss him out."

Sabine laughed. "What a delightful promise. I almost hope there is a need for it now."

Faron grinned back at her. "I would willingly drag anyone who upset you from these premises, myself included."

"Let us hope you avoid upsetting me so badly," she said with another laugh. "I happen to like you."

"I will endeavor to stay on your good side, then."

Faron seemed reluctant to leave, although the natural conclusion to their conversation had arrived. Sabine felt the same reluctance, although she had no credible reason for him to linger.

"What did you plan on working on for the rest of the day?" she asked him.

"Until recently, nothing of importance. Now I should draw up a plan of action for getting more soldiers or a plan to better utilize the ones we have," Faron admitted.

"Sounds like you have created a busy afternoon for your-self," Sabine replied. "I should not keep you from it."

"How long until the prince may arrive?"

"I will likely know about the time you do."

Faron closed his eyes. Sabine could tell he was thinking something over. "Well, since we aren't sure, I have the afternoon free."

She smiled again. "Good. You can keep me company while I respond to letters."

"I'm happy to do so, Your Grace," Faron said, almost purring the last word as he settled more comfortably in his chair.

Faron stood guard outside Sabine's suite of rooms, doing everything he could to keep his mind focused on his duties and not the woman inside. He found himself failing miserably. After their meeting, Faron had spent the rest of the day with Sabine, first in her office where he'd listened to her as she griped about the pointless letters from her useless suitors. They had enjoyed making fun of some of their more outrageous letters together, at points leaning so close together he found himself surrounded by the sweet smell of her hair.

Later, they had enjoyed a refreshing walk around the chateau grounds. How Sabine felt pressed against his side as they walked through the hedges would follow him into his dreams, Faron was sure. An informal dinner in the kitchen followed, where he'd had to share her time and attention with Lisbeth, Meri, and Finn. They were good company, of course, but Faron had found himself jealous, wishing for her smiles and her words to be his alone.

After dinner, he had excused himself to take a few moments to get back under control. She was his employer, a noble of high standing, and his thoughts were inappropriate. Once he had felt more centered, he had rejoined her for an hour in the library before wishing her a goodnight and taking up his post, which was why he was now wrestling to keep his imagination in check.

A noise, almost like a thump, caught his attention, and Faron tilted his head, listening. But no other noise followed, and so he settled back down. A louder, different noise sounded from inside the duchesse's suite. Deciding to investigate, Faron took the few steps needed to reach the door, grasp the handle, and twist the knob. Nothing happened. Faron released the ornate door handle with a low growl. The elf's long black wavy hair fell forward as he pondered the solid door blocking his entrance. Faron knew he should return to his post. He knew he shouldn't be upset because, once again, Her Grace had locked the door to her rooms.

Chapter Twelve

Both women looked at Faron, who crossed the room to intervene in the fight. He kicked the girl's dagger further out of reach, his sword joining Sabine's blade against her neck. He motioned for the duchesse to move with his free hand, which she did without protest.

Taking the girl in, he scoffed. "By the Spirits, you're a child." He withdrew the blade, knelt to take her by the arm, then pulled the girl to her feet and none-too-gently shoved her against the wall so she had nowhere to flee.

"I'm not a child," the petite elf protested, causing Faron to point his sword in her direction once more.

"You are young all the same," Sabine said, having taken up a space between the two elves while staying out of reach. "And far too young to be doing what you failed to do."

"It's not like I chose to be here," the small elf girl declared. "I didn't want to come here, but my master said 'Go,' so here I am!"

Faron faltered, though briefly, as he reminded himself she might be lying. He opened his mouth to speak when the girl looked over at Sabine in defiance.

"Does your offer of protection expand to the giant oaf?" she asked.

Faron looked at Sabine in disbelief. "You offered an assassin protection?" he demanded. "Why?"

Sabine crossed her arms. "Negotiations where everyone benefits seemed better than bloodshed," she explained, before turning her attention to the girl. "We are all going to have a peaceful conversation. If you try anything, Faron will end you without hesitation."

Faron nodded, more than willing to confirm his willingness to spill blood on Sabine's behalf, even when he was outraged over her decision to practically bribe the elf girl. When the girl nodded, he stepped back, keeping himself between Sabine and the girl all the same.

Sabine pointed to a small table on the side of her bedroom. "Go sit," she directed the girl.

The girl wobbled on her feet, as though internally debating what she wanted to do. She took a tentative step forward, then another, and eventually, she fell into the chair.

"Tell us about your mission," Sabine demanded. "As much as you know."

The girl's eyes flicked back and forth between Sabine and Faron, and Faron realized she must have been hunting for weapons or trying to figure out what trick they were playing. He also noted a rapid tapping of her index finger on the side of the chair, the sound muffled by the fabric.

"I was told to kill you," the girl began. "The man who's been training me gave me your name and location. He said either you die or I do, and what would you expect me to pick with those options? He didn't say anything more." Her jaw set, as if daring either of them to call her a liar.

"Who gave you the order?" Sabine asked, her tone rich, calming, and conversational rather than hostile and threatening as Faron knew his own voice would be.

"I don't know," the girl said, rolling her eyes as though she found Sabine's question stupid. Faron wanted to throttle her. "He always wears a mask and something to cover his hair when he comes to see me. The men he brings to train me are dressed similarly. I've never seen any of them without the mask on."

"And how long have you been with this man?" Sabine prompted.

"My mom sold me to him two days before I turned ten," she said casually, then smirked. "I'm sixty-one now." Faron's brow raised, but otherwise kept his horrified reaction to himself.

Sabine's gaze moved to Faron, and he knew she'd picked up on the youthfulness of their current captive. "And your name? What shall we call you?" Sabine asked.

Again, a pause, the girl's eyes quickly darting to any possible hidden weapons Faron or Sabine might reach for. "Avana." She gave a barely perceptible flinch as if waiting to be beaten.

Sabine nodded, looking down for a moment in thought, and Faron had to fight to keep from asking why the duchesse was still entertaining this. "Are you hungry, Avana?" Sabine asked.

Avana's frantic searching paused. "No, I am not hungry. I have eaten my ration bar, and I don't need anything else."

Her cadence and rapid reply told Faron it was a learned response, and though his wariness did not wane, he had to admit he felt a little sorry for her. And by the Spirits, a glance at Sabine told him she felt the same.

"I would like you to have a bit more before I send you to bed for the evening," Sabine replied, her gaze meeting Faron's. "Faron, please call for Finn. He will make sure she eats and has accommodations for the evening."

Faron refused to leave the room. Leaving Avana alone with Sabine would be an insane choice for anyone to make, let alone her guard. He did go to the row of house bells along a wall near her vanity and pulled the one meant for Finn.

Avana, meanwhile, stared at Sabine, her lips pressed flat in absolute dubiety.

"If you are to stay here, you will need to learn to trust me, though I know with your experience this would be difficult," Sabine said before motioning to Faron. "He growls a lot, and he is useful, but he is not unkind."

"How can I trust you?" The words burst out of Avana's lips before the small elf slapped her hands over her mouth.

"I believe I will have to earn it, just as you will have to earn mine," Sabine said kindly. "But you will note, I did not kill you when you broke in. I have offered you work, shelter, and food. Surely, my offers can be a start?"

Tears formed at the corner of Avana's eyes, which seemed to have grown in size, but the girl didn't move, nor did she uncover her mouth.

"What is it?" Sabine asked.

As if a lever was pulled, the tears stopped and Avana's hands dropped to her side. "Oh, nothing. I was just seeing if you'd fall for the crying child act. I'm not a child, but I am part dwarf, so I'm small enough some people think I am. Then surprise. Knife," Avana said.

"I am not foolish enough to rush to put my arms around someone who wished to kill me a half hour earlier," Sabine replied.

"Some people would be," Avana said with a shrug. Her posture grew rigid as someone knocked on Sabine's door. Faron nodded as Finn let himself inside, crossing through her rooms toward the bedroom in the back in search of the duchesse.

"You called, Your Grace?" he asked, then faltered upon seeing the unexpected guest.

"Good evening, Finn," Sabine said. "Avana needs a proper dinner and somewhere comfortable to sleep. I know Meri might be retired for the evening, but can you see to those things for me?"

"Of course, Your Grace," Finn easily agreed with a bow.

"One moment," Faron said, walking outside of the bed-chamber with Finn. "That girl is an assassin. Her Grace has opted to shelter her in exchange for service. I know you're capable of handling her, but please, do not let your guard down. Do not trust her," he said firmly without giving opposing orders.

"Ah," Finn said and nodded.

They stepped back into the room. "Miss Avana, if you would come with me, I will make sure you are well-fed and given a comfortable room."

Avana warily rose to her feet and joined Finn. "You look like the grumpy type who takes his tea without honey," she observed.

"You might find out if Her Grace decides to keep you," Finn replied as the two left the room.

Now alone with Faron, Sabine fought off the desire to rub her temples, as though the action would ward off the encroaching headache. She rolled her eyes as she caught sight of

Faron's expression. "Don't make that face at me," Sabine said.

Fear and a bit of anger radiated from Faron, the look in his eyes more intense than Sabine had ever seen it. "You negotiated with an assassin *while* she was attempting to kill you," Faron said, a forced calm in his deep voice which he seemed to have little control over.

"What would you have had me do exactly?" Sabine asked. "She's practically a child."

"Childlike or not, she came at you with a knife," Faron said, his hands moving to run through his hair. "You don't negotiate with people trying to kill you." His voice took on a hint of desperation.

"She did a rather poor job of killing me," Sabine replied. "I made the smartest possible decision here, given the circumstances."

"The smartest possible decision would have been to kill her."

"She is young. Were I inclined to have someone die on my behalf, it wouldn't be a near child."

"You didn't know her actual age. I look like I'm in my late twenties when I'm closer to seventy years old. She could have been my age or older." Faron took a step toward Sabine, as if being closer would help her understand what he was saying, only to take several steps back a moment later.

Sabine rolled her eyes again. "You aren't the first elf I've ever come across, Faron, and she most definitely was not. I do appreciate the deeper understanding I now have of your perception of my judgment, though."

"Sabine, no. That's not... I... I didn't mean it like that," Faron said, his frustration evident in how his hands moved back to his hair, the way he paced for a moment before he turned back to Sabine. When he stepped toward her, he didn't back away. "For Spirits' sake, Sabine. I heard the crash. I heard the assassin say she was going to kill you, and when

I tried to get to you, your door was locked. I had to break your door down to get to you." He motioned toward the entrance outside of her bedroom. "I asked you to keep the door unlocked. You could have been dead by the time I was able to get inside," he said, his voice desperate.

"I was not dead," she reminded him as calmly as she could, standing her ground against the much taller man. "And I never agreed to leave my door unlocked."

"You're right. You didn't. You also never agreed to give me a key despite my requests for one, and now your door lay in ruins. If the assassin had been more skilled, you'd have been dead in the time it took for me to get to you. I will just have to figure out a way around your refusal," Faron said, his lips pressed in a firm, unhappy line.

"And how exactly do you plan on working around my refusal?"

"I'll sleep outside your window or on the floor of your greeting rooms. Depends on the weather, I think," Faron said in a serious tone.

"You will do neither, Faron," Sabine warned.

"How else am I to keep you safe?"

"You'll have to figure something out."

Faron nodded his head, looked at the open window, the broken latch, the discarded knife, and then in the direction of the now broken door. He closed his eyes, the fear seeming to overtake the anger and frustration. "Your safety must come first." Faron closed the distance between them, and in one quick movement, he lifted Sabine and gently placed her over his shoulder. Turning on his heel, Faron moved swiftly from the bedroom, through the living quarters, and into the main corridor of the chateau.

Sabine only saw the briefest glimpse of the shattered door before Faron turned a corner, leaving her quarters behind.

"What are you doing!" she shouted as she was hit with the realization of what was happening. "You don't get to pick me up like this!"

"Of course, Your Grace," Faron replied, though he did not put her down.

"I am capable of walking," she tried again.

"I am aware," he said as he turned the corner, barely moving to the left in time to avoid running into Meri.

"What are you doing?" Meri sounded slightly outraged or maybe that was more concern.

"Taking Her Grace to a safe location since her rooms have been compromised," Faron replied as he continued toward his destination.

Meri's brows furrowed and she nodded to herself, killing any hope Sabine had for intervention.

"Good idea. Hello, Your Grace."

"Meri!" Sabine said in outrage before turning her ire back to Faron. "This is not funny, and if I am not put down at once, I will throw every conspirator from this estate."

Meri nodded as if she understood why Sabine was upset. "I know you're upset, but your safety must be our top priority. There was an assassination attempt on your life. Finn says your door is gone, which means your room isn't secure." Meri chewed on her bottom lip before continuing. "And while Faron may be going about this the wrong way," Meri paused as Faron grumbled in disagreement, "he is taking you somewhere safe. Please, Your Grace. Let us protect you."

"I do not care!" Sabine shouted. "Put me down, now!" She might as well have not spoken for all the good it was doing her.

Faron came to a stop in front of a dark wood door, opening it and stepping inside. Only then did he put her down. "Your accommodations for the night, Your Grace."

Meri joined them, standing just behind Faron, nodding in approval of the space.

Sabine took in both members of her household with an anger she could not adequately describe. She knew she was firing both, perhaps even pressing charges for how she was physically handled. She stood there, glaring at them both for several long beats before she lifted her hand and slapped Faron with all her strength. Faron staggered back at the blow, rendered silent from the shock of it. The resulting red mark on his face hardly satisfied Sabine.

"How fucking dare you," she snarled. "The way the both of you treated me just now is unacceptable." Each word came out louder and angrier, and she knew every soul in the chateau could hear her.

Meri looked down, her cheeks glowing with shame. "I apologize, Your Grace. I should not have allowed him to carry you."

"You were certainly quick enough to justify his actions, weren't you?" Sabine replied, shouting now.

"I gave in to my fear, Your Grace, after speaking with Finn about the elf girl. I won't do it again." Meri bowed deeply, her bad leg shaking from the strain as Faron stood, still silent.

"How do I know you won't do something like this again?" Sabine demanded of her. "How can I possibly trust either of you with anything after what you did tonight?" She gestured to herself. "I am practically naked!" she screamed. "And you two thought it was a brilliant idea to physically haul me across the estate where everyone we passed could catch a glimpse of my fucking body!"

"What is going on?" a male voice asked from the doorway.

Sabine turned to the door, spotting an alarmed-looking Finn. Sabine crossed her arms, the effort better concealing her chest since the chemise was insufficient. "I'm about to fire these two, so you will need to organize their immediate departure."

"What?" Finn asked, blinking in surprise. "What has happened?"

"Meri decided to enable Faron to carry me against my will across the chateau while I was dressed in nothing but my undergarments," Sabine explained, sounding far less rational than she wanted to. "They were both ordered to desist numerous times. They chose to ignore me. I want them gone."

Finn looked at Meri and Faron, eyes wide, though his lips were pressed together in cross irritation. When he returned his attention to Sabine, his expression was much more civil and respectful. "Are you certain you would not like to wait until you are calmer, Your Grace?" Finn asked. "There is no excuse for what either has done, but knowing you as I do, you will not want to make such a decision while angry and hurt."

Faron's face showed disbelief and regret for a moment before it became blank. "I regret my actions caused you discomfort, embarrassment, and anger. I only wish for your safety. If you wish to dismiss me from my post, I will be gone by morning."

Meri stood there flabbergasted, her mouth opening and closing, but no words issued forth.

Soft footsteps could be heard running from the opposite direction before Lisbeth slid to a halt in front of the group, her red hair more disheveled than usual, a green robe thrown over nightclothes. She took in the entire scene, her eyes scanning each person's face and body language before turning on Meri. "What did you do?" she demanded, her normally soft voice raised in anger, causing the other woman to bodily flinch back.

"They physically forced Her Grace from her quarters to this room despite her protests and direct orders," Finn replied since Sabine was ready to push Faron from the building and Meri was too stunned or afraid to answer. "In her current state of dress," he added, making sure his eyes never dipped too low. "Her Grace has dismissed them from the estate."

Lisbeth's head swiveled toward Finn, then back to Meri and Faron, her tanned skin flushed crimson. "You, you... How could you do something so stupid? What were you thinking?"

Faron opened his mouth, only for Lisbeth to poke him in the chest. "I wasn't asking you."

Faron's mouth shut with an audible click, and Lisbeth put her hand back on her hips, just staring her wife down.

"I just wanted Her Grace safe." Meri's rich voice was softer than Sabine had ever heard it.

"There were better ways to go about it!" Lisbeth almost yelled. "Go to your rooms, both of you. I don't want to see either of you right now." Flushed even redder, Lisbeth turned to Sabine. "As long as that's alright with you."

"We are standing in Faron's room," Finn explained.

"Then he can sleep with the horses because that's where he belongs right now," Lisbeth said in a more proper tone and volume.

Finn sighed and turned to Sabine. "Your Grace, if it is still your wish to dismiss Meri and Faron, I will oversee it all. However, I do beg you to reconsider your stance when you are less angry. Meri has served you and your family well." He glanced at Faron. "Lisbeth recommended him for the position, and I trust his usual judgment was clouded in fear."

Sabine's brow rose, unimpressed. "So, I am to forgive when one has been warned repeatedly and the other is not the least bit contrite?" she asked, voice cold.

"Not forgive," Finn said reasonably. "But allow them to continue serving you despite serious misjudgments on their part, and as your steward, be assured I will personally make sure nothing like this ever happens again."

"And I will help," Lisbeth added, glaring at her wife and friend.

Sabine was tempted to ignore the suggestion and stick with her original decree. With Finn and Lisbeth obviously wanting her to reconsider, she briefly questioned if irrationality and anger clouded her judgment. She did not think so. "I will make a decision come morning."

"Thank you," Faron said, meeting Sabine's eyes. She saw the remorse there, remorse not tied to fear of job loss.

Lisbeth's shoulders relaxed, though Meri's did not, and Sabine gave neither Faron nor Meri any additional attention.

"Since I have been forcibly sequestered to this room for the evening, I am going to bed. You should start dealing with their insanity," she informed Finn. "And make sure eyes are kept on Avana."

"Of course," Finn said, bowing. "We will give you some peace." He straightened and instructed Meri, Lisbeth, and Faron to leave.

Lisbeth stepped forward and took each by the arm. "Let's go now. We have a lot of talking to do."

Finn followed behind the group, leaving Sabine alone in the strange room. She'd known it belonged to Faron, having agreed to Finn's assignment before her personal guard had arrived. She closed her eyes, forcing herself to breathe and calm. Anger would rob her of peace and sleep, and she needed both.

She went to the fireplace, stoking the fire into something brighter and warmer. She tended to feel cold in the evenings as the weather grew milder, and given what she was reduced to wearing, she would need it. Only then did she crawl into bed and settle beneath the thick covers, finally allowing herself just a moment to grieve over the evening.

Chapter Thirteen

Faron felt Lisbeth's small hand on his forearm, heard her admonishing words as she marched him and Meri away from Sabine.

Sabine, who had been in danger just twenty minutes before.

Sabine, who could still be in danger even in the safety of his room.

He felt his breathing quicken and had to fight his body's instinct to gently pry Lisbeth from his arm. It wasn't like she could stop him. He'd only allowed her to lead him away because of his shock. He wanted to run back to Sabine, to make sure she was safe. To show her where he kept weapons hidden around his room.

But he could not. He'd crossed enough boundaries with her tonight, and even if his actions were motivated by fear, there was no excuse for what he'd done. Her slapping him, threatening to fire him, it was the least he deserved. If anything, Sabine should be calling the guards to have him arrested. By the Spirits, he had never acted so stupidly before in his life.

Faron knew Sabine was a bright, intelligent woman. He had witnessed her quick thinking and ability to handle problems during the last few weeks in the chateau. While she may not be as skilled with a blade as he would like, Sabine had been more than capable of defending herself until help arrived.

Was it possible Avana was just a test to see if someone more skilled was needed? Yes, but Faron honestly didn't think so. With more training, Sabine wouldn't need to fear another assassin. Maybe he would try and broach that subject later, assuming he still had a job. He had, after all, promised to remove any threats to her person, himself included, and he wouldn't go back on his word.

Even in his worry, Faron recognized another part of him couldn't escape the idea of Sabine sleeping in his bed, enveloped in his scent and wrapped in his bed linens. His desire to return was only partially motivated by safety.

"In here," Finn commanded when they reached the second-floor landing where he kept an office. Faron had only visited the spacious office since his arrival, and his third visit promised nothing positive.

Finn saw himself behind his desk, a heavy oak-stained dark wood cluttered by parchment, books, and an assortment of other items. He took a seat in an old but well cared for chair, taking in Meri and Faron with a critical eye. "I don't even know where to begin with the both of you. I can't even promise she'll change her mind by morning."

Faron looked down and away from Finn, embarrassed. Regret and anger radiated from his person. He felt Lisbeth release his arm but, from the corner of his eye, saw she didn't remove her hand from Meri's, offering comfort and rebuke at the same time.

Finn sighed and leaned back in his chair. "One of you has to say something. The last thing I want to do is remove you from the grounds, but I don't have a lot of room to argue here."

"I reacted out of fear," Faron admitted, the confession only making him feel worse, driving home even further how stupid he'd been. "I heard the assassin say she was going to kill Her Grace. The threat, on top of finding her door locked, and the following argument about negotiating with the assassin instead of just outright killing her put me in a fear—and anger—driven mindset. I became worried Her Grace would decide to sleep in her own rooms and reacted badly. I am aware she would not have made such a choice, but at the time, I couldn't think past my fear for her. It's not an excuse. I am not excusing my actions. If she chooses to fire me, I will accept her decision. I was in the wrong."

"She wouldn't have slept in her rooms," Finn agreed. "She's also got eyes on Avana, and she knows if one assassin appears, others inevitably will." Finn looked to Meri now. "What about you?"

Meri looked up at Finn, her eyes full of pain and loss. "I saw Faron coming down the corridor, and for a moment, I considered stopping him, but then all I could see was her mother's body in that same hallway. Her uncle bleeding out after doing everything he could to keep Sabine safe. I decided Faron was making the right choice in keeping her safe. I should have stopped him, told him to put her down, but I didn't. I went along with it out of my own fear and loss."

Meri shot Faron an apologetic look, and he mustered what smile he could, knowing she wasn't trying to blame him, just explain her thoughts. "I keep thinking, 'What if there was another assassin?' I can't lose her, too," Meri admitted.

Finn let out a long sigh as his fingers steepled together in thought. "Meri, she remembers the night she lost her mother and uncle probably better than anyone else in this room. She would be aware of the threat Avana posed, no matter her ineptitude," he pointed out. He pushed himself from his chair and grabbed a decanter and glasses from behind him, placing them on the desk and filling each. "Drink," he instructed the group.

Each one of them picked up their glasses. Faron and Meri with more hesitation than Lisbeth, who treated the drink like it was a small shot of liquor rather than a half-full glass and downed it in one go. She put the glass back on the table with more force than was necessary, causing Faron to wince before making grabby hands at the decanter. "I'm going to need more."

Meri cast a glance toward Lisbeth, but instead of addressing her wife's need to drink, she opted to address Finn instead. "I know it haunts her even more than me. Their deaths. I don't see how it couldn't."

Finn obliged and refilled Lisbeth's glass. "Then you don't get to use the excuse, unfortunately. Not when we all agree she would be most aware of potential danger." He slunk back in his seat, nursing his drink for a moment. "I will do what I can to smooth tonight over with Her Grace. She may be more receptive to discussion come morning. I hope Lisbeth will be willing to do the same."

Lisbeth, whose anger had cooled slightly in the face of their confession and her first drink, turned to face Meri and Faron with a sigh. She stared at them in silence for a few moments, taking another sip before speaking. "Yes, if only because I don't want to have to travel from work to home if Meri gets fired. I know we keep a house in town, but I like living where I work."

Meri winced.

"Okay," Finn said before taking another sip. The four drank in silence for several long moments before Finn placed an empty glass on his desk. "In the morning, proceed as usual as much as possible. Her Grace probably will not want to see either of you first thing," he said, waggling fingers in Meri and Faron's direction. "But you'll have enough to get on with without coming into her view. I will speak with Marcelle about guard placement for tonight and tomorrow. Lisbeth can bring her breakfast."

Faron and Meri nodded, though Faron noted Lisbeth's thoughtful expression before she pointed at Meri.

"I know you're going to want to make Her Grace's favorite foods as an apology, but don't. The gesture will be taken as bribery and not an apology." Lisbeth paused, pressing her lips into a straight line for a moment. "Just make what you normally would. Nothing special." She waited for Meri to nod in acknowledgment before asking Finn, "Should Faron go to the training yard to continue working with the guards and stay in his quarters the rest of the time or, I don't know, guard the back gates? Any of that should keep him out of Her Grace's way until she's ready to see him."

Faron wanted to protest, even if he understood the need to keep him away from Sabine while she debated their fates. It wasn't the training of the guards he wanted to protest. He enjoyed doing the work, but it only took up a small portion of his day. There were other more useful things he could be doing then staying in his room or guarding the rarely used back entrance. They could allow him to guard the assassin instead. As soon as he thought of the task, he knew they wouldn't allow it, not right now at least. He did pose a danger to the assassin, and it would put him in Sabine's path. Much as he hated to admit it, Lisbeth was right in her suggestions.

"I think I agree with keeping Faron busy with tasks other than guarding Her Grace," Finn said. "She's been pleased with the work you've done with the younger guards. Start with them in the morning, and I'll figure out the rest of your schedule after."

"They've been very eager to learn and listen. Well, most of them," Faron replied unthinkingly.

"Good," Finn said. "You'll continue being productive, then." Finn gave another sigh. "Well, I'm going to make some guard assignments for the evening and turn in. Try to get some sleep. We won't know anything until morning."

All three nodded. Lisbeth helped Meri from the room, turning the two of them toward their bedroom once they reached the corridor. Faron followed along behind them, turning to follow only to remember Sabine was currently occupying his room.

He thought to ask Finn or Lisbeth if there was a spare room he could use when Lisbeth called out, "I said you were sleeping in the stables, and I meant it. We both know you've slept in worse places." She shot him a menacing grin from over her shoulder before she and Meri turned the corner. Lisbeth was right, he had slept in much, much worse places. They'd met while he'd been staying in one of them. Oh well, at least he knew Sabine's stables were kept warm and clean.

Chapter Fourteen

When Sabine woke the next morning, she couldn't exactly claim less anger. As she became aware she was not in her own bed, surrounded by her own things, the remaining cinders of the night before renewed in a flash of shame and anger. Throwing the covers off, she got out of bed then hissed as her feet touched the freezing floor.

She looked around for a source of relief then paused as she realized there would be nothing for her in Faron's bedroom. Well, nothing but a throw blanket, which she wrapped around her shoulders, both for warmth and concealment of her body that had been forcibly put on display for the whole chateau.

She saw no one as she emerged from the room and thankfully passed no one on the way back to her chambers. Admittedly, the weak light trickling in through the windows suggested she'd risen earlier than normal, which suited Sabine fine.

Her suite met her with the remnants of her shattered door. Most had been cleaned up sometime in the night, but the frame and door leading into her sitting area would need replacing. Faron would not receive a key, assuming she decided to keep him. She strolled into the sitting area and headed toward her bedroom. When she was safely secured in her bedroom again, Sabine found a pair of her fur-lined slippers and a robe to warm herself. Then she turned to the fireplace to resolve the ongoing issue of the cold. A light knock sounded at the door once, then twice more, a knock she associated with Lisbeth. "Come in," she called out.

Lisbeth opened the door just enough to slip in before closing it behind her. She hurried over to Sabine, a surprising feat given how exhausted and upset her pinched expression suggested. She held out a hand for the fire poker. "Let me?"

"I've got it started," Sabine replied quietly.

"I know, but if I don't do something, I'm going to go back to yelling at Meri. So, may I please help with this and draw you a bath?"

"Sure," Sabine replied, handing the poker over. She didn't have a desire to convince Lisbeth to let her be.

Lisbeth tended to the fire until it glowed bright orange, throwing a few more pieces of wood on as the flames grew. The silence between the two women stretched on in a way it hadn't before: uncomfortable and heavy.

Sabine resumed her seat on her settee, enjoying the warmth of the fire while Lisbeth worked. "How is Meri? I assume not well, as you were yelling at her."

Lisbeth kept her eyes focused on her task. "She wasn't doing well before I started yelling, and once I started, I couldn't stop. I'm just so disappointed in her," she said with a sigh. "I understand Meri's issues with her guilt and feeling of failure, but she cannot treat you like she did last night. We aren't even going to touch on Faron right now. I know where his head is, but for Spirits' sake."

"Faron's behavior was quite unfortunate," Sabine agreed. She was only just starting to embrace how much harm his actions had caused. The increasingly casual, and somewhat intimate, relationship they'd built felt lost.

"And much like with Meri, I understand why he reacted as he did, but it doesn't make it right." Lisbeth finally looked her way after putting the fire poker away. "As much as I hope you don't fire them, I completely understand why you would."

"I don't want to fire anyone," Sabine said, meeting Lisbeth's gaze. "I'm just not sure how to reconcile feeling unsafe in the hands of two employees while making sure everyone else is happy that they do not have repercussions from the incident."

Lisbeth brought a hand up to her lips and paced a moment before stopping at the wardrobe to pull out Sabine's clothes for the day. "You could suspend Meri for a month. We have a cottage in the village; it would need airing out, but she could see to it."

Lisbeth laid out the dress and other garments Sabine would need before going into the washroom. The sound of pouring water sounded, followed by the scent of lavender, before Lisbeth emerged again. "As for Faron, you could remove him as your personal guard for a week, a month, or permanently. Put him with the guards and make training his main duty. Obviously, these are just suggestions."

"I'm not suspending Meri," Sabine decided as she rose from her seat. She'd known Meri too long, and she wasn't the main culprit from last night even if she'd refused to intervene.

"Alright," Lisbeth said. "What about Faron, then?"

What about Faron? Sabine found herself conflicted. "I don't know. I haven't known him for long. I had no complaints about him until last night, and he traveled far for the job."

Lisbeth opened her mouth to say something, closed it with a small snap, held up her finger, and walked quickly into the washroom to turn off the water. When she returned, her lips were twisted. "You could always talk to him about his actions and why he did them. You could also just demote him, especially if he no longer makes you feel safe, though I do believe your safety was the only thing on his mind."

"Not listening to me and acting irrationally in what he deems as a crisis doesn't bode well for my safety.

"No, it does not." Lisbeth paused. "Sometimes, not often, but sometimes, when someone Faron cares about is in danger, he will do what he deems necessary to protect them. If you talk to him, it should help, though. From the way he was last night, I'm sure he knows what he did was wrong."

"He did not seem especially contrite when he made his apologies in front of Finn," Sabine pointed out. "He looked at me like I was stupid."

"No, he was ashamed and realized he'd just royally screwed up. He's upset, but he's only upset with himself." Lisbeth motioned for Sabine to head to the washroom when she was ready. "If his words and the way he acted when we reached Finn's office are any indication, he knows he doesn't deserve to be kept on."

"He doesn't," Sabine agreed as she walked to the washroom. She stopped in front of her vanity to quickly pull her hair up into a bun. Once accomplished, she stepped out of her slippers and undid the tie on her robe. "How did he act?"

"Well, he told Finn you should fire him, his reaction was unwarranted, and he knows you can take care of yourself. He also didn't argue with me while I yelled at both him and Meri on the way to Finn's office. The moment we left you, he had this look in his eyes... I don't think I've ever seen so much self-loathing and regret from him before." Lisbeth made a thoughtful face before adding, "Oh, he also slept in the stables last night without complaint."

Sabine both appreciated his understanding of the harm he had done and hated his worry. She sighed again, knowing she would be firing no one. "He seems to understand his offense, then. Perhaps he won't make another mistake like this."

"One can hope."

"I suppose I will let them both stay on," Sabine decided, even if she still felt uncertain.

"You don't have to," Lisbeth insisted. "If you truly don't feel like you can trust their actions, the kindest thing for all would be to let them go."

"I intend to make my opinions known," Sabine replied, giving Lisbeth a tired smile. "And issue a warning about further behavior."

Lisbeth nodded. "I fully support any decision you would have made here, but I am glad you're not firing them. I'll leave you to your bath. Unless you need help with anything else?"

Sabine shook her head. "Can you let Finn know my decision?"

"Of course. I'll be back to help with your hair." Lisbeth bowed and left. Sabine heard her adding wood to the fire before the bedroom door shut a minute later.

Chapter Fifteen

Morning passed in much the way it always did. Sabine dressed, allowed Lisbeth to arrange her hair, and ate breakfast. She then hid in her office, where she relayed her daily tasks and requests to Finn before reviewing accounts and correspondence. A few hours into her day, she took a light tea then went for a stroll around the grounds before her midday meal.

The conversation with Lisbeth played through her head whenever she had a free moment. She still felt quite hurt by the events, but she also felt more settled with her decision to keep on Meri and Faron. In time, she would forgive them, assuming their contrition felt genuine.

Finn arranged for her to meet with Avana in the afternoon, a conversation she was both interested in having and also moving beyond. She thought Avana might make a fine addition to the chateau, assuming she proved herself trustworthy. Avana would need to find a way to trust them, though, and Sabine knew it would take time.

For now, she saw herself into the kitchen after she returned to the chateau. It seemed a kind gesture to check in on Meri. Voices sounded as she entered, belonging to Meri and Lisbeth.

"If I bake you your favorite pie, will you let me join you in bed again?" Meri asked her wife.

"No, but you're still baking the pie and doing all the other things you promised, and in another week, I'll consider it," Lisbeth responded.

"I can live with that," Meri said in a soft voice.

"Did I interrupt you two?" Sabine spoke up as she stepped forward.

"Not at all," Lisbeth said cheerfully despite the lingering exhaustion.

Meri ducked her head and continued to plate the light luncheon she'd made. "Good afternoon, Your Grace."

Sabine nodded. A twinge of guilt surged through her for how she'd treated Meri the night before, but honestly, Sabine had been much kinder than warranted. She didn't have the luxury of simply overlooking offenses of disobedience and coercion. "Good afternoon, Meri," she replied.

"How has your day been?" Lisbeth asked when the silence went on for a beat too long.

"Busy," Sabine replied. "And I still have to meet with Avana."

"If it helps, she's been behaving. She has given neither me nor her guards any problems, though she has requested she be allowed to go to the gardens," Meri let Sabine know.

"If we allow her in the area near the greenhouse, with an escort, I see no reason to deny her," Sabine replied. "At least, we could potentially allow her the liberty after I've spoken with her."

Meri nodded. "I will let the guards know. A few of them are worried she's only behaving to put them off their guard. With the way she's acting, though, I don't think so."

"I think with her age, she will be easier to sway to us, no matter her intentions now," Sabine said in agreement. "And if we can give her a chance for something better, we should."

"She is just a small little thing, especially for an elf," Lisbeth said as she grabbed a plate.

"She is, and I bet she uses her stature to her advantage," Meri told her before sliding a plate to Sabine.

"Oh, I know she does." Lisbeth looked over at Sabine. "Are you taking Faron with you when you talk to Avana?"

"I have not yet resumed speaking with Faron," Sabine replied.

Lisbeth nodded. "I can understand your decision." A noise from outside the kitchen caught their attention, and Lisbeth made a face. "I will go check on the disruption." She gave Meri a piercing look before almost fleeing the kitchen.

Meri sighed. "My wife is not subtle." She looked down at her hands which were playing with a napkin. "I am so sorry."

Sabine took a breath and nodded. "I know. I knew last night. Admittedly, part of the reason I have been as calm as I have been today is because of how long we have known one another."

"Still, I should have stopped Faron. I shouldn't have allowed myself to panic. You were obviously fine, and yet..." She held out her hands in front of her as if to encompass the list of her sins.

"We have a history which informs how you behaved," Sabine said, her voice gentler than she actually felt. Eventually, she knew she would also feel much kinder toward Meri, and in the meantime, she wasn't going to treat her poorly.

Meri shook her head. "No, Lisbeth is right. I let my guilt over the death of your parents and uncle cloud my judgment when it comes to protecting you. I... I just don't want to lose you too, but you held off the assassin. You protected your-self. I have to remember you are a capable and brave woman and not the sixteen-year-old grieving your entire family."

Sabine smiled sympathetically, and she reached out and placed a hand on top of one of Meri's. "A near decade has passed, and we've all grown since."

"We have, and yet, I struggle to let my guilt go, and I need to, and I will try." Meri turned her hand over and linked their fingers. "I will do better."

"I know you will. None of us are perfect, and all we can do is keep trying."

"Thank you," Meri said. "You are too kind, Your Grace."

"I am pragmatic, which is less a point toward my char-acter, but valuable all the same," Sabine argued. She picked up a utensil so she could start eating.

Meri laughed. "You are so much more than just prag-matic." She turned back to the stove. "Ten coppers say Lisbeth set up whatever the racket was in the hallway so we would have to talk."

"I would not be surprised, though it would mean she had someone waiting for me when I decided to come here," Sabine replied. She took a bite of her food, finding it deli-cious as always.

"Lisbeth is rarely sneaky or devious, but she can be when she thinks something needs to be handled. She also knew I wanted to apologize."

"And I appreciate the apology," Sabine confirmed. She finished her food in a few more bites, knowing she still needed to chat with Avana.

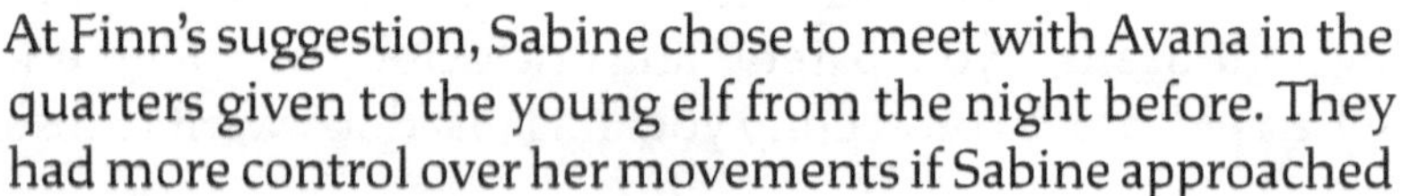

At Finn's suggestion, Sabine chose to meet with Avana in the quarters given to the young elf from the night before. They had more control over her movements if Sabine approached her, and though the duchesse wanted to be generous, she intended to remain cautious all the same.

She smiled as she approached the door, seeing Marcelle standing guard. Marcelle stood a couple of inches taller than Sabine, his wild golden hair pulled back by a chord. His dark skin shimmered a faint green all over, and Sabine couldn't help but be reminded of the horrors certain Merfolk currently suffered under Coralian rule. Thank the Spirits Sirenes had no scales.

Marcelle smiled in return, his ink-like eyes exuding an extremely calm warmth she knew only Sirenes possessed. No signs of feathers or fins showed on land, but she'd witnessed Marcelle and other local Sirene in their true form on many occasions. "Good day, Your Grace," he greeted. "I hope you are well."

"As well as I can be," Sabine replied more brightly than she felt. "Please tell me you have not been here since last night."

"I just returned to the post only an hour ago," Marcelle assured her. "Finn has made sure we are all well cared for."

"Good," Sabine said, letting out a sigh of relief. "Has Avana caused you any trouble?"

Marcelle shook his head. "Surprisingly, she's been rather pleasant."

They both turned to look as Finn joined them. He nodded to both. "Are you certain you wouldn't like a guard to go in?" he asked after all proper greetings had been exchanged.

"I think more guards will make it less likely Avana will speak with us," Sabine said. "We should go inside and see what we can determine. If it goes poorly, well, I took her down last night on my own."

They proceeded into the room after knocking to let Avana know they were coming in. Sabine had provided the young elf with a guest suite—small and windowless but otherwise spacious—and every possible luxury someone could want. The suite consisted of two spaces: the bedroom positioned at the back of the suite and the sitting room, bright and colorful, at the entrance. Not spotting her, they proceeded farther into the space until they saw her.

Avana sat on the bed, surrounded by pillows and reading a book. She glanced up when they entered, waved, then held up a finger to ask for a moment before going back to her book. After a moment, she closed the book and gently set it down. "Sorry, I wanted to finish my chapter."

"Understandable," Sabine replied, watching the curious little elf. "I see you have found ways to entertain yourself."

"I told Meri I was bored and she brought me books. I've never had books like these before. They're fun," Avana replied as she climbed off the bed. Standing barefoot on the ground in loose, simple clothing, she looked even smaller than before.

Honestly, Sabine was surprised to learn the young elf could read, given what information she was able to gather the evening before. "I'm thrilled to hear you enjoyed them," she said. "Have you had enough to eat?"

Avana twisted her lips and glanced over to where a tray sat, covered and untouched. "There was a lot of food, I couldn't eat it."

"You wouldn't be expected to eat more than what's comfortable," Sabine assured her.

"It's just, I ate my morning meal which was a lot of food. I wasn't expecting another meal a few hours later." Avana shrugged. "I didn't want to tell Meri she had the meals wrong. She seemed nice."

"Ah," Sabine said, understanding now. She exchanged a glance with Finn before looking back at Avana. "We tend

to eat three separate meals here. And tea if it is desired. You are welcome to eat as much or as little as you like of each."

"Oh!" Avana said, eyes wide with surprise. She glanced back at the untouched tray. "Is there always so much food?" she asked, her voice quieter than before. "I don't normally get so much."

Sabine knew Meri would have served Avana the same thing she fed the rest of the household, and usually, midday meals were lighter. She didn't have to look to know there wasn't much food on the tray. "Meri tends to provide consistently sized portions," Sabine replied.

Avana just nodded, but Sabine could see her trying to process the information.

"Do you mind if we have a seat?" Sabine asked.

"It's your room," Avana said, but not rudely. She wore an expression of confusion as she spoke, and not only about the seating.

Sabine took a seat in one of the armchairs, and only once she was settled did Finn do the same. "I know we talked about some of this last night, but can you go over the events leading you to the chateau?"

"There isn't anything more to tell you. I was told to kill you, given directions, and sent out. That's it." Avana shrugged.

Sabine caught her glancing at the door, but her body language didn't give away an intent to run. "Expecting someone?" she asked.

"Just your giant elf deciding to burst in again. He doesn't seem the type to leave you alone for long. Not with the way he looks at you." Avana wrinkled her nose.

"Faron has other assignments today," Finn spoke up, prompting Sabine to nod.

Avana shot Finn a suspicious look and opened her mouth as if to say something before her eyes went wide. "Okay," she said, her eyes darting away from them.

"What is it?" Sabine asked her, curious about the reaction.

"Nothing. Nothing," Avana said quickly. "Did you have more questions for me?"

Again, Sabine and Finn exchanged looks. "I do not believe you when you say 'nothing,' Avana. I would very much like to trust you, but it will require you to be consistently honest with me."

Avana gave her a flat look. "Look, I understand you're trying for the nice and sweet angle, but I'm not stupid. I would prefer not to get beat for speaking out of turn." Her eyes went wide, and she scooted back on the bed. "Sorry, I didn't mean it like that."

Sabine couldn't deny raising a hand when angered, considering she was certain she might have left a bruise on Faron's face. "I have no plans to beat you. Anything I did last night was in self-defense."

"Of course it was. I tried to kill you," Avana replied as if it was obvious. She didn't address the first part.

"You did," Sabine agreed. "And I think you upset my staff more than you upset me."

The confusion on Avana's face spoke volumes. "That's good, I guess."

"It's been a bit of a headache, to be honest," Sabine said with a sigh. "Either way, you needn't worry about violence while here." She gave the young girl a kind smile. "I understand you're not inclined to speak with me, and I can understand the view. I shall not force anything, but you understand you will be limited in your movements within the chateau while we build trust with one another, yes?"

"What do you mean by limited movements?" Avana asked.

"Well, I don't think we want you roaming around alone," Sabine said practically. "But there are spaces you may go. I understand you inquired about visiting the gardens. There is a space near our greenhouse that is lovely, and you may visit unimpeded."

"Wait, you're going to let me go outside?" Avana's voice was a mix of hope and disbelief.

"Of course," Sabine replied. "If you want to leave the chateau altogether, you may, of course. But given the reason you came, I cannot imagine it would be safe to leave for some time. I hope having some time in the fresh air might help prevent feeling locked away, even if self-imposed."

"You're going to let me go outside, to a garden, and possibly go to the village?" Avana's body language moved quickly from excited to tense in seconds. "What do I have to do to earn my privileges?"

"Prove yourself trustworthy," Sabine answered. "It is as simple as that for me. If I cannot trust you, then you cannot be here. If you are here, I would like you to have the same freedoms as everyone else, but I must know you will not act against us."

Avana's eyes narrowed, but she nodded her consent anyway. "Of course."

"Good," Sabine said as she stood. Finn did the same. "I shall let you return to your reading."

Avana gave no reaction other than picking up her previously discarded book and flipping to a page somewhere in the middle. Sabine simply nodded to Finn, and the two left the room, eager to get on with more of their day.

Chapter Sixteen

Faron sat hunched over in one of the taller chairs in his room. The dark green chair didn't provide the same comfort as the smaller matching one, but it was a better fit for his size. In his hands was a crumpled letter summoning him to see Sabine, a meeting scheduled for twenty minutes from now. It had come in the early hours of the morning, giving him time to bathe, groom, and dress presentably, even if he was relatively certain she was going to end his employment.

Was Faron certain of the outcome? No, but a day and a half had passed since he crossed a very large boundary. His fear and dread lingered, not just because he had thrown her over his shoulder basically naked, but also because he had then ignored her insistent protests several times. Faron deserved to be fired for his actions, and he could not muster the willingness to defend himself even half-heartedly. As for the rest of the household, Finn was the only person speaking with Faron outside of his assigned duties, and his communication focused on job assignments while Sabine determined what she wanted to do. So Faron was relegated

to training guards, guarding the back entrance of the chateau, or otherwise remain in his room.

A knock sounded at his door, and Faron called out for
the person to enter. Unsurprisingly, Finn appeared, his curly
reddish-brown hair pulled back from his tanned face. His
relaxed expression did nothing to alleviate his worry. "Her
Grace is ready for you," he shared.

Faron nodded, rose from his seat, and strode to the
door. "Thank you, Finn. Is she in her office or is the meeting
elsewhere?"

"Her office," Finn said. He smiled up reassuringly at
Faron. "Don't look so worried. She'll be fair."

"I know she will, which means I will be leaving the chateau before the day is out," Faron replied, trying to muster
a smile for Finn.

"Only one way to find out," Finn said. He motioned for
Faron to leave the room.

Faron nodded and stepped out, he wasn't sure what the
protocol for this was. Did he wait for Finn to lead him there,
or did he go on his own? "Are you escorting me?" he finally
asked, then winced at how it sounded.

Finn shook his head. "I am certain you can find Her
Grace's office, and she does not feel you need an escort."

Faron nodded and began his walk, leaving Finn behind.
Although the distance between his room and her office was
short and his pace brisk, Faron couldn't ignore the knot of
anxiety growing in his chest. When he reached her door, he
took a deep breath and knocked.

"Come in," Sabine said, her voice only partially muffled
by the closed door.

Faron closed his eyes, giving himself a moment to
enjoy the peacefulness of the chateau one last time. Then
he steeled himself. He wouldn't be able to hide the circles

around his eyes from the lack of sleep, but the least he could do was put on a brave face and not make Sabine feel guilty for firing him. He was in the wrong here. He deserved this. Grasping the handle, he stepped into the office, though he did not close the door. He had stood over her that night and, without meaning to, had used his height in a way that could have been seen as intimidating while he tried to get his point across to her. Maybe leaving the door open would show her he had no intentions of ever making her feel intimidated or unsafe around him again.

Sabine sat at her desk, her light caramel hair mostly down, an odd sight, and her gaze focused on several sheets of parchment arranged in a line on her desk. She only glanced up briefly to look at him before looking back down at her work. "Explain yourself."

Faron did not sit down as he'd grown accustomed to since his arrival. Instead, he remained standing, making sure he stayed several feet away from the desk, hoping his distance would allow Sabine some comfort. "There is no excuse for what I did two nights ago. Was I worried about a follow-up attack? Yes. Was I upset over never considering the possibility of an attacker coming through your windows? Yes. However, those fears do not justify my actions or demands in any way. I should have spoken to you, told you my concerns, and presented my solution, not haul you bodily across the chateau, especially once you said no." He paused, taking another steadying breath. "I once told you I would remove anyone from the chateau if you asked, myself included, and I am more than willing to do so now if you tell me to."

"How am I to be certain you will not repeat this type of mistake in the future?"

Faron hung his head. "The terror I felt, knowing you were not safe, is a feeling I've rarely experienced. It is hard to restrain myself, but I have in the past, and I will do so again now."

Sabine did not respond right away. Instead, she picked up her quill and jotted down a note he could not read on one of her parchment sheets. She replaced the pen in its holder, and finally, Sabine looked up at him, her bright green eyes showing the hurt and irritation she felt with him, even if the rest of her face remained neutral. "I will have you thrown out if you ever cross another line, and I will do so without hesitation. Am I understood?"

Faron felt the vise which had taken root at the thought of never seeing Sabine again loosen. "Of course, Your Grace."

"Good," Sabine replied. She rested her hands on her desk, loosely clasped together. "You may resume your normal duties, then."

"Thank you, Your Grace." Faron turned to go stand guard outside her office door. He paused at the threshold. "I am so sorry, Sabine."

Something in her carefully guarded expression broke, allowing him to see just how much his actions hurt her. He hated himself for causing her pain.

"I know," she replied softly.

He nodded, hating himself even more. "Would you like the door open or closed?" he asked gently.

"Open," Sabine replied. "I'm about done for the day, I think."

Faron nodded. "If you need anything, I'll be outside," he said before taking his position outside Sabine's office door. He had a lot to make up for, but at least he was being given the chance to do so.

Lord Tristian,

Thank you again for your continued offers of support. In times such as these, knowing who we may rely on continues to maintain importance. Thankfully, I have full faith in my guard and staff. Their efforts continue to amaze me, and I could not be more thankful for their efforts. Should my circumstances change, I know who I might call upon for aid.

Yours,
Sabine, Duchesse Vassetre

Chapter Seventeen

In the days following Sabine's decision to keep him on and allow him to resume his duties in full, Faron had done everything he could to show support for Sabine, even when she made decisions he didn't always agree with, such as making the assassin feel welcome and at home or visiting with her regularly. He made sure to keep his face neutral when around the assassin. When directly asked by Sabine how he felt about the elfish woman, Faron responded as diplomatically as possible. He could never lie and say he trusted the assassin, but he trusted Sabine. It helped he was allowed to be there when Sabine was spending time with the assassin, even though he'd been told he wasn't allowed to bring his sword. Apparently, it made the girl nervous.

Another good thing was being allowed to spend a majority of his day once more in Sabine's presence. Though their usual comfortable conversation remained somewhat stilted, she was talking to him. Faron hoped they could eventually return to their former relationship, but he knew it would take some work.

Faron followed behind Sabine as they traveled down the corridor to her office, doing his best to keep his eyes off the sway of her hips or the way the light made her hair shine even brighter than the last time he looked. Faron truly had believed he was going to be banished from her side, and now he found himself soaking in her presence, enjoying the beauty of her smiles, and drinking in her laughter, the few times he'd heard it recently.

Pulling his thoughts away from her beauty and his need to be around her, he was struck by another thought. Before he could think better of it, he found himself asking, "Your Grace, I was wondering, do you carry a dagger or keep one nearby?"

"I do," Sabine replied, casting a glance behind her. "Why?"

"Personal curiosity. I never realized you were armed. You're very good at hiding any weapons," Faron said as he considered the best way to phrase his next question without offense. "You handled the attack on your person extremely well, but I haven't seen you train since I arrived and was wondering if you needed a new sparring partner."

"I generally don't train," Sabine replied with a shrug. "I know just enough to hold off most until someone can intervene."

"Would you like to train?" he asked tentatively. Faron pushed away the mental image of her broken door, choosing not to say how getting to her would be easier if she'd just keep the damn thing unlocked.

"It sounds like you want me to say yes," Sabine replied. "Even though I'm pretty sure I could have you on the ground without much effort."

Faron laughed. He couldn't help it. "I believe you. Still, a little practice never hurt anyone. Well, except my pride in this case, I assume."

"People are surprised by my ability to land them on their back," she confirmed.

"One should never assume their combatant is less skilled than they are. If anything, assuming the opposite keeps you alive longer." Faron knew his tone was darker than needed, but he'd had to teach one too many people what such mistakes could cost. Allowing his thoughts to go in a darker direction was better than thinking about how Sabine would feel on top of him.

"You think someone in my position wouldn't know as much, Faron?"

"I do believe you do, and I'm sorry if my words sounded condescending," Faron said.

She shook her head, caramel hair swaying with the effort. "Not condescending," she assured him. "But I am a woman in a powerful position who lost the entirety of her family at a young age. People try to take advantage of my position, and they consistently underestimate me."

Faron's eyes darted to her hair, watching the way the light played across it once more before pulling his eyes back to their surroundings. "Why do I feel like the prince is one of those?" he asked with a roll of his eyes. From everything he'd been told about the middle prince, he was surprised the man hadn't done more to get Sabine under his thumb while she'd been grieving so many losses. However, with the people she had surrounded herself with, he was willing to bet they had helped her in every way they could to thwart whatever plans the prince had tried to enact.

"I present a danger to him," Sabine said simply. "But I've told you as much."

"You have, but to prey on a young woman suffering loss? Are you sure I could not arrange an accident for him the next time he visits?" Faron half joked.

She laughed. "I am afraid such tragedies happening on my estate would bring misfortune to all living here."

"Might be worth it, though," Faron replied. "So, would you like to train with me? For fun?"

"I see how much fun my guards have with you," Sabine pointed out. "But if you insist."

"You are different from the guards," Faron pointed out.

"True," she agreed.

Faron once more thought over how smart it would be to ask the next question before deciding he would take the rebuke. He had to know. "How is the assassin handling things?"

"I believe she is having a difficult time believing she is safe. Whoever had her before she came here did not treat her well."

"They probably thought her disposable. People who view others in hierarchical groups rarely treat anything they view beneath them well, as I'm sure you know," Faron said with a sigh.

"Sadly, I do," Sabine said. "My uncle was a shifter, and nearly all of his people were killed off centuries ago. I've heard of the atrocities Coralia and Azmarin committed against Merpeople. I know of the horrors Lisbeth has told me."

"It's only gotten worse since she's left." Faron let out a harsh breath. "People aren't disposable, but it's going to take the assassin time to learn as much. It sounds like she's behaving though, not attacking anyone or trying to escape."

"I did tell her she could leave if she liked, but I pointed out it would be dangerous for her since she hasn't completed her assigned task. I think she knows she's got a good situation here."

"I hope she does." Faron couldn't help but think there was a chance the assassin could consider waiting until they became more comfortable with her before trying again. He just couldn't act unless, or until, he had something solid.

They reached the door to her rooms, now repaired from Faron's frantic plow through. She turned to look at him, surprising Faron given the state of their current relationship.

He managed to keep himself together. "Whenever you wish to train, please let me know. I'll make myself available immediately." When she nodded, Faron moved to stand beside her door, a position he'd increasingly grown accustomed to.

She went inside her rooms without another word, and he listened for the click of her lock. When it did not sound, Faron blinked, surprised. She'd actually listened to his suggestion, and he smiled despite himself. He knew then, without question, he would encourage her to take up some training with him. Nothing hazardous or overly strenuous, but enough to sharpen whatever skills she had. He frowned almost immediately. Training meant touching, skin touching skin. Spirits, it might even mean full-body contact. Assuming she agreed, he'd be in so much trouble.

Chapter Eighteen

Faron gave Meri an exasperated look from across the center kitchen counter where she was plating a tray for Sabine's dinner. He caught the hint of a smile playing on her lips and did not like it at all. "How do you stay so calm knowing Sabine is alone with the assassin again?" Faron asked, aiming for dark and menacing but missing the mark by a wide margin.

Meri, knowing what he'd been attempting, gave him an unimpressed looked. One of her hands picked up a medium-sized chopping knife. She began to play with it, twirling it between her fingers, as if he needed the reminder that she could take him in a fight. "Finn's there and Marcelle is standing guard. Sabine is a grown adult capable of making her own decisions, and if she feels safe seeing Avana, then she's allowed to."

Faron barely resisted rolling his eyes. He'd never seen Finn with a weapon, and while he felt comfortable assuming the steward's training was minimal at best, for all he knew, Finn could be the most dangerous person in the chateau. He also knew he was doing a disservice to Marcelle, who was a fine warrior in his own right. With him there, and the assassin's lack of skill, Faron knew Sabine would be fine.

"She keeps asking me if I'm alright with the assassin being here and Sabine spending time with her. I've been truthful with her, but how can I be expected to be alright with her taking her own life into her hands? All it would take is a moment. How are you alright with this?"

Meri flipped the knife into her hand, catching it by the handle and pointing the blade at him. "I never said I was okay with it," she hissed out. "But you and I have done terrible damage to our relationships with Sabine. We are lucky to have our jobs, and I'm lucky to still be married with how upset Lisbeth had been." She set the knife down and looked away from Faron. "However unhappy the situation makes us doesn't matter. It matters that Sabine has taken the girl under her wing, determined to win her over, and Avana is reacting well to Sabine's care. Getting upset and confronting Sabine will just reinforce the belief we don't trust her judgment. There is a difference between expressing our opinions when asked and shouting them for the world to hear."

Faron nodded, knowing Meri was right. "I knew I could vent and you would smack sense into me." Faron and Meri exchanged small smiles. "Has Sabine always been like this?"

"What? You mean stubborn, independent, compassionate, sensitive, and loving? Yes," Meri answered quickly. "If you were thinking anything else, you're wrong. Unless it was beautiful." She gave a one-shouldered shrug.

Faron rolled his eyes. "I just want her to be safe."

"We all do, but as Lisbeth says, we have to trust her to ask for help when she needs it." Meri looked to her left and glared at a medium-sized box made of a metal Faron didn't recognize and the puddle of water surrounding it. "The heat needs to break soon," she muttered. Raising her left hand,

Meri twisted her wrist as far as it would go before lifting her hand above her head.

Faron watched in amazement as the water lifted from the ground and surrounded the metal box before freezing solid.

"Sorry, but if the box doesn't stay cold, I'm going to lose a lot of meat," she explained. "But Lisbeth is right. Neither of us has shown we trust Sabine, and in doing so, we've broken her trust in us."

Faron continued to stare at the now frozen box before turning back to Meri. "Lisbeth wrote your magic was gone."

The unimpressed look was back on Meri's face, one eyebrow lifted. "The topic of Sabine is more important but..." She held up her wrists and tapped the two snugly fitting metal bracelets together. They were gold with strange designs carved along the edges. "My magic isn't gone. It's just completely out of my control. I took a Veinfire arrow to my lower back the night Sabine's parents were murdered."

Meri sighed as Faron looked at her, confused. "Veinfire affects magic and stops wounds from being healed by magic. It's fast-acting and, in most cases, deadly. For me, I was lucky because it missed anything vital. It was just embedded in me for so long that by the time help arrived, the poison had robbed me of control over my ice magic." She motioned to her leg. "My nerves have also never been the same. Honestly, I'm lucky to be walking."

"So, what about the bracelets?" Faron asked.

"Oh, they had to be made so my magic wouldn't kill me. I can still use it for little things like the ice box as you saw, but it isn't useful the way it used to be." Meri shrugged as if one small arrow hadn't changed the course of her whole life.

"Now, back on topic," she ordered.

Faron went back over the conversation in his head. "You're right. I need to continue showing Sabine she can trust me and she's safe with me. Being upset with her choices won't help build mutual trust."

Meri gave him a soft, approving look. "Exactly, and I'm worse than you are about overreacting to danger. So, anytime you get the urge to be overprotective, come see me, and we'll talk it out. Unless her life is in immediate danger, then think, 'How angry will Sabine be if I do this?' and go from there. The lower the chances of Sabine being upset, the better the choice is."

Faron had to admit the advice wasn't bad, and talking to Meri did help. He just had a feeling being reasonable when Sabine was in danger or possible danger was going to be extremely difficult for him. "Thanks," he said, resolved to do better with Sabine. He wanted to do well in the position Sabine hired him for, but honestly, Faron knew he had other motivations and desires he still refused to examine too closely. At least right now.

"You're welcome," Meri said with a bright smile. He more than understood why Lisbeth fell for the former guard captain. "Now get out of my kitchen."

◆———————◆

Sabine popped a piece of chocolate in her mouth as she studied her cards, eyes moving from one end to the other. She chose one with delicate fingers and placed it on the table between herself and Avana. The two sat by an open window in the sunroom, food and drink beside them as they played cards. "Okay, so what would you pick from your hand?" she asked the young elf.

She glanced to the corner where Marcelle stood. The Sirene guard had chuckled on and off since she and Avana decided to play a card game, and for every gesture of amusement, Sabine's would-be assassin shot the man an annoyed look. "Ignore him," Sabine instructed.

Avana bit her bottom lip as she glared at the cards in front of her before she cautiously pulled out a card and put it down. "This one."

A smile bloomed on Sabine's face. "Good. You're improving," she said as she laid down another card. "And your response?" she asked.

Avana made another face. For all that she seemed to enjoy reading almost any type of book, games like cards or chess seemed almost beyond her. "This one," Avana said.

"You just won," Sabine replied, putting her cards on the table. She nudged the bowl of chocolates forward. "You pick up on things pretty quickly."

Avana studied the cards on the table and then the ones in her hands, her eyes going back and forth between the two for a solid minute before putting the cards in her hands on the table. "I don't understand how I won, but okay," she said. Her small hand moved to hover over the bowl of chocolates, her head lowered like she was still studying the cards, but Sabine noted Avana's eyes on her, waiting for permission.

"Go ahead," Sabine encouraged.

Avana kept her eyes on Sabine the entire time it took for her to grab and place the chocolate in her mouth. However, once the candy hit her tongue, Avana visibly relaxed, and while her face remained almost blank, her eyes gave away her enjoyment.

Sabine smiled to herself. She imagined her own delight at good chocolate probably read as obviously in her own expression. "How have you been enjoying your time with us?"

Avana took her time savoring the chocolate before answering. "It's different. Not a bad different, but different."

"I imagine it would be given what you've told us," Sabine agreed.

Avana's nose crinkled for just a moment before her face cleared again. "Well, you let me outside so..." She shrugged and with the hand opposite the chocolate bowl, she picked up and twirled a card.

"I feel like a person should have the right to pursue whatever brings them pleasure. You seem to like exploring, being outside. There is no reason you shouldn't." Sabine motioned to the chocolate again. "Help yourself. I can tell Meri to send you some with your meals if you like."

Avana shook her head even as she took another piece. Sabine noted that more than one piece was gone. Avana's sleight of hand skills were much better than her ability to assassinate people. "You are the only person I've met who feels that way. Well, you and the others who live here. I keep waiting for you to ask for something, but..." Avana stopped talking for a moment, popping a piece of chocolate in her mouth to buy her time. "I don't think you're going to."

"How did you arrive at your conclusion?" Sabine asked, curious. She doubted there was anything she could not secure for herself or have someone with more skill carry out, but Avana embracing the truth was of interest.

"Because you haven't yet," was the simple answer. "It took three days for the man who bought me to start making demands of me. The most you've done is try and make me want to be here while having a complete understanding I could leave at any time. I tested that yesterday by the way. That one." She nodded her head in Marcelle's direction. "Didn't do anything to stop me. I said, 'I'm leaving,' and his response was, 'Have a great time. I'll be here when you get back.' What type of answer is that?" She turned and glared at the Mer in question as if personally offended he hadn't chased after her.

"The answer I'd expect someone to get who wishes to leave," Sabine said, shrugging. "I told you; you are free to go if you choose, or to remain. If you are here with us, obviously, you are going to be treated as I treat everyone else." She picked up another piece of chocolate. "If you do want someone to chase you, you could ask someone. I hear some people enjoy it."

Avana's eyes went wide, a blush covering her cheeks before she replaced it with a mischievous grin. "Does he like to chase people?" She motioned to Marcelle once more.

"I have no idea," Sabine replied over Marcelle's booming laughter. "Perhaps you should inquire when you two are alone."

Avana's blush was back, but her grin didn't falter. "Maybe, maybe I will," she said it like it was a challenge.

"You'll have to tell me how it goes," Sabine said, prompting Marcelle to laugh again.

Avana shoved another piece of chocolate into her mouth as if to stop herself from saying something else.

Sabine laughed softly in response. "Well, either way, I've had fun playing cards with you this afternoon," she said, and she instantly wondered if Avana had ever been in a similar position for leisure activity before. "When I go back to my office, perhaps Marcelle will continue on in my stead."

Avana's lips twisted, and Sabine felt Avana didn't really want Sabine to go. "If he was willing to let me leave, he'd more than likely let me win. Where's the fun in that?" she said as she reached for the cards, shuffling them badly.

"Perhaps we should continue playing and invite Marcelle to join. Meri will be bringing dinner up soon. We can eat as we play," Sabine suggested.

"I... I like that idea," Avana said.

Sabine was pleased to see Avana had gone this entire time without flinching.

"Do you think Meri would want to play too?" Avana asked.

"She might," Sabine said, then she laughed and shook her head. "She will, actually, and from experience, she will win every hand."

"I am not as good as Her Grace, but I can play well enough," Marcelle said. "Still, it would be a fun time, all of us playing cards. Meri tells good stories."

Avana gave him a small smile and turned back to Sabine. "Show me how to shuffle again?" she asked, holding out the cards, which she'd made a terrible mess of.

Chapter Nineteen

The warm, sunny weather demanded Sabine's attention. She'd never really enjoyed much of the tedium of her position, which often kept her locked inside an office, and though she normally allowed her more practical side to determine her choices, she found it impossible today.

During her daily morning meeting with Finn, she informed him of her decision to walk down to the village, and her steward promised to make all of the necessary arrangements. As no guests were scheduled, arrangements mostly consisted of telling Faron he would also be walking with her. She'd gone to the village alone many times in her life, but Avana's appearance had her feeling cautious. More assassins might appear, and she did not want to be vulnerable if such an event occurred.

After making sure she was appropriately dressed for an afternoon in the village, Sabine left her suite and walked down to the entryway where she was to meet Faron. Footsteps sounded, heavier than anyone else's in the chateau, alerting her to Faron's approach. He looked handsome as always, neatly groomed and well-dressed.

Faron stepped beside Sabine. "Your Grace," he said warmly with a bow of his head.

"Faron," she acknowledged with a nod. She still harbored some less-than-kind thoughts where he was concerned, but those were fading in intensity each day. "Aren't you pleased to have more to do than stand by my door?"

"Well, I don't mind guarding your door, but it will be nice to see more of the village," Faron admitted as he held the door open for her.

She thanked him and walked out into the sunshine. "Have you not used any of your free time to visit the village?"

Faron's eyes slid from Sabine to the path, letting her know his answer before he even opened his mouth. "I have been spending my free time learning the layout of the chateau, spending time with Lisbeth, or training the soldiers."

"You ought to be using your time for something a bit more leisurely," she said.

"I've never been particularly good at leisure."

"I insist you figure it out. You miss a great deal of life's pleasures if you are always tasking yourself with something viewed as more productive."

"I'll try," Faron promised before a grin grew on his face. "Maybe I'll go visit the beach. Lisbeth says it can be refreshing depending on what you wear for the swim."

Sabine smiled despite herself. "Oh, it can be rather refreshing under the right circumstances."

"What circumstances do you consider correct?" Faron asked.

"Oh, I'd refer you back to the day you arrived," Sabine said.

Faron made a thoughtful noise. "It's best then if I don't invite anyone else for a swim those days."

She laughed this time. "Given how I take my swims, I'd agree."

"Which is why I have yet to follow you on guard duty."

"Perhaps I'll invite you next time I go swimming," she offered.

"I think I would enjoy an invitation," Faron said, his lips quirking up in a smile. "After all, I'm not the best swimmer. Maybe you could offer pointers so I don't drown."

"Oh, you plan on joining me?" she teased. Sabine had no idea why she was being so playful with him given how she felt about being carried across the chateau against her will. Something about Faron simply demanded she play along.

"Only if invited," he replied with a smile.

"We shall see next time I decide to go for a swim." The two descended the small hill down into the village, the crunch of gravel beneath their feet. Small shops and homes came into view, bright yellows and oranges welcoming them. In the distance stood the little market in town, and to the far right, the harbor where Meri purchased fresh fish and other seafood.

"When I rode through the village my first day, I thought it rather pretty and much calmer than the villages in Myrefall," Faron admitted.

"I'm surprised to hear that," Sabine said. "Coralia is known for being a beautiful country. It's just unsafe for most these days."

Faron tilted his head to the side. "Coralia is beautiful if you can ignore the ugliness festering in its people, on its streets. They've a king who preaches the Mother in all the worst ways, bans all other religions, and kills those with magic as well as the non-humans. Is that ugliness all over Coralia? No, but it thrives in Myrefall and most of Quenall, even as other towns try to stand against it."

She nodded, and though she had not experienced it for herself, she'd read more than one letter or report confirming those words. "It's trying to spread here."

"It's already in Azmarin from what I saw traveling through there. They just hide it much, much better," Faron said darkly.

"I think it's honestly everywhere to some degree," Sabine said. "There are people with terrible opinions no matter where you go. Coralia allows those people to move from thought to action. Azmarin is following the trend. If Grégoire gets his way…" She trailed off, shaking her head.

"We could always stage a coup and behead him before he can cause trouble," Faron suggested, his playful tone suggesting he wasn't serious. The deadly grin more than informed Sabine he would follow through with any encouragement.

"He's already causing trouble," Sabine pointed out. "Which is why I'm working with his younger brother."

"What is the younger prince like?" Faron asked as he looked around, taking in the shops on the outer edge of the village.

"Idealistic, I think. Still, he seems to understand the threat his brother poses."

"Good. There's nothing wrong with being idealistic. But if it prevents you from seeing when people wish you harm or wish harm on others, it can be a problem." He paused to look over a few knives displayed on one of the first carts they approached.

"He listens to advice when given, so I feel positive about his potential."

"I'm glad you have faith in him," Faron admitted as he stepped away from the small display. "Was there anything in particular you were looking for?" he asked as they stepped into the town square. Vendors were selling all manner of things, from baked goods and colorful fabric in a material Faron hadn't seen before to weapons and small trinkets. He took it all in as they went, appreciating the different carts and stalls. As they walked, merchants would bow or lift their hand in deference to Sabine.

Sabine shook her head. "I didn't want to stay inside today. The village is a good way to ensure I didn't have to."

"I understand. Especially with all the time you spend in your office," Faron said. "Finn made it sound like you wished to do some afternoon shopping."

"I might if I come across something I like," Sabine replied. She carried money with her, and she liked to support the endeavors of those on her estate. "Do you plan on buying anything while we are down here?"

"I don't know. I think it will depend on if I find something I like as well." He glanced toward a stall selling what some people might consider torture devices and others something else entirely.

Sabine watched as Faron browsed, and an amused, knowing smile formed. "And what would you find interesting?"

"I've seen a few things here and there." He gave her a sharp grin even as his eyes moved back to the stall.

"You should go inquire," Sabine pointed out. "You could even blame it on me if you like."

Faron's brows rose, perhaps showing surprise in her teasing understanding of where their minds were. "The blue would complement your eyes," Faron mused, a hand lazily pointing out the silk blue rope.

"Yes, but I find silk isn't always as sturdy as one would like. Someone with skill is needed when it is utilized."

"True, and it's less likely to damage the skin of someone who can't quite keep still. If one knows their knots well enough, it can be very hard to slip out of or untie, especially when … distracted." He looked back at the vendor. "Would you like to join me?"

Sabine nodded. "Sure."

Faron's grin broadened, and the two strolled over to the booth to look. "Up close, the blue rope is not an option. The lighter green, however…" Faron mused, glancing at and meeting Sabine's gaze. "What else should I consider purchasing?"

She didn't answer at first as their eyes met, and Sabine had to acknowledge the primal longing she felt somewhere in her middle. She couldn't recall wanting anyone or anything more than she wanted Faron. She turned her gaze to the table, forcing herself to focus on something there. "Depends on what you like, I think."

"I find myself open to almost anything. For me, it's more important what my partner enjoys. I have my boundaries, of course, but the point stands." Faron's voice was lower than normal, his body closer to Sabine's as he leaned over to inspect what looked to be a paddle.

"Good to know," she said, though she had no idea why she would need the knowledge. Still, she enjoyed knowing all the same.

Faron glanced at a few more items before purchasing the rope and thanking the merchant for her time. "Has anything caught your eye?" he asked Sabine when finished.

She shook her head. "Not today."

"Should we continue our stroll?"

"Yes," she confirmed, nodding again. Her distraction with Faron so close to her had her missing the offerings of other vendors.

As they walked, Sabine felt Faron place a hand on the small of her back, helping her to avoid a small child who darted out in front of her.

"You seem distracted," Faron said close to her ear, his voice almost drowning out the noise from the ever-increasing crowd.

She looked up at him, turning her face so it was closer to his own. "Just thinking about some things," she explained.

"Like what?" he asked, his voice lowered and his hand still on Sabine's lower back as he guided her through the crowd to a more secluded area.

"Many, many things."

Faron turned them onto an empty street, then into a well-lit but more private alley. "Anything you wish to speak of? You've been very distracted."

Sabine had no plans to confess to her thoughts. "Not particularly, though you do seem quite curious."

"Well, you have been distracted since we left the merchant selling rope." Faron leaned closer to Sabine, not quite backing her into the wall behind them. "Which item are you thinking about? The paddle? The rope? Or something else?"

She looked up at him, feeling cornered in by the tall elf in a way she found delightful rather than intimidating. "I think you are the one preoccupied with the rope."

The left corner of Faron's lips lifted in not quite a smirk, but something more confident, hungry almost, even as his eyes never left hers. "Very much so. I've been told I'm good with rope and even better with my hands once everything's secured."

"Really?" she asked, her expression growing similar. "And how, exactly, has your very unique skill benefitted you?"

"Well, it has helped me to make some very good friends. Friends who needed someone to take away the stress and pressure of their positions. To help them clear their mind for a while and just be." Faron had leaned closer, saying the last sentence in a low growl into her ear.

Sabine felt the cold stone of the wall against her back now and the almost-there touch of his fingers against the skin of her wrist. She couldn't speak for a couple of breaths. The promise in his voice assured her she wouldn't have to do much of anything to show how appealing he was or how compliant she would be under such a scenario, even with the anger and hurt she still felt from his actions the night Avana arrived. "And what is the technique which makes you so successful?"

"There isn't one technique in particular. Each person is different, has different limits, and enjoys different things. Though, I have had much success with tying a person's hands above their head." Here, Faron did touch Sabine, his hands wrapping around her wrists and slowly raising both arms above her head. Once both hands were above her head, he grasped both wrists in one of his large hands, while the other moved down to grasp her hip firmly. "And then using my mouth to make them come over and over again until they beg me to stop or fuck them."

Her skin burned at each point of contact, even though layers separated his hand from her hip. She kept eye contact the whole time, unable to object, to tell him to take a step back. She didn't want to, though. No, she very much wanted to encourage him, to plead with him to go further. "And what is the longest you've found yourself in such a position?"

"Most people don't make it past three rounds, but I have a feeling you'd do much, much better." Faron closed the distance between their bodies, letting her feel his want against her hip, his lips close to hers. The hand on her hip moved down her leg as if to lift it, to give him better access, but he didn't, at least not yet.

She took in a breath, perhaps to calm herself or to prepare herself for something she could not deny wanting. "We might have to test your theory sometime."

"We should." Faron leaned in closer, his nose barely grazing her cheek. "I could unravel you here. We are secluded enough. No one would see. Or we could wait to get back to the chateau, though we might not get so far. I could take you to one of the outbuildings, and I could make you scream loud enough the Spirits would pay attention." He hooked his hand behind her knee and lifted her leg to his hip, pressing against her center, his eyes still keeping contact with hers. "I could tie your hands above your head, the rope thrown over one of the wooden beams or a large sturdy nail. I'd hook your legs over my shoulders and make you come no less than three times with only my mouth. From there, I could use my fingers to bring you over again and again, and only when you're sobbing with need would I fuck you. Deep and long, as hard or as soft as you want for as long as you want."

Sabine knew no other thought would possibly penetrate her head for a long time. She was so tempted to suggest they head back so he could demonstrate his words. "How long have you considered this?"

"Since the first moment I laid eyes on you," Faron admitted. "But adding a rope, testing your limits? Since we left the booth."

"I don't think I'm patient enough to get back to the chateau," she said without pause.

"Well then." Faron tightened the grip he had on her wrist. "I want you to keep your hands above your head until you

can't anymore, and if possible, keep your voice down. Unless you like being watched."

"You should know better," she remarked, though she made no change to what they'd agreed on.

"It is always polite to ask." He looked down at her, intent radiating from his gaze. "If you say stop, I will, but is there anything else I should listen for?" Faron asked as he lowered himself to his knees.

"Stop is fine," she said. "If you need something different later, we can figure it out."

Faron nodded and gathered Sabine's skirts, pushing the layers of fabric up around her waist before tucking it behind her. Placing both hands on her hips, he lifted her enough to guide her to place both legs over his shoulders, giving him access to her bare center. "Beautiful," he murmured as he studied her for a moment before looking back up at her. "Just say stop and I will," he repeated before leaning in and licking at her center.

She gasped at the first contact, only half conscious of her volume. Her fingers curled down into her palms, though her hands remained positioned above her head as she had been instructed.

Faron made an approving noise which vibrated against her clit as his tongue flicked up and down, exploring Sabine and what she liked.

The back of her head rested on the stone wall, and she closed her eyes, letting the whole of her existence focus on the teasing of Faron's tongue. The smallest of moans left her lips as his tongue slowly circled the sensitive bud at her apex. Faron teased at her clit lightly, slowly increasing the intensity before finally sucking the bud into his mouth. Sabine almost moved a hand to her mouth to cover the sound she couldn't contain but stopped herself at the last moment, barely managing to keep her lips together. She could feel Faron's grin against her even as his tongue stimulated the small nerve caught between his lips. She could feel the electricity building low, and she barely issued a warning cry before she reached the delicious surge.

Faron didn't stop his efforts as her body calmed, though he did release her clit from his mouth, replacing it with the flat of his tongue, moving up and down. As promised, Faron continued on his quest, and though she surpassed the third round of intense pleasure, the fourth had her lowering her hands to hold on to his shoulders as she came. Only then did she ask for him to stop.

Faron pulled away slowly, kissing down her thigh until he reached her knees. He whispered soft words of praise for how good she'd done. Slowly, he lowered one of her legs to the ground, then the other, placing both hands on her hips to help hold her steady. He did not rise, instead letting her use him to catch her breath. "I can massage your legs. It may help return some of the blood flow."

She nodded as she breathed, knowing she wouldn't be steady on her feet just now. Faron started at Sabine's ankles, massaging his way to her hips. His eyes followed his fingers, stopping at the apex of her thighs. "Hmm, let me clean you as well." He reached down into one of the pouches on his belt and pulled out a handkerchief. "May I?"

She almost objected, unsure she could stand even innocent touches just yet. Still, she nodded again, knowing she definitely couldn't stand Faron's hands leaving her.

Faron kissed her upper thigh then very carefully cleaned his saliva and her wetness, careful of her sensitive center. By the time he'd finished, she'd caught her breath. Sabine couldn't believe what she'd agreed to, though she had no regrets about it. She let her skirts drop, covering her once more. "You are a terrible influence."

"Am I?" Faron asked, his tone amused. He stood, brushed off the knees of his trousers, and offered an arm to Sabine.

"Indeed," she confirmed as she took his arm. They stepped out of their secluded spot and back into the sunlight. "But I suspect you knew as much without my declaration."

"Lisbeth makes the same declaration sometimes." Faron grinned as he spoke. "I don't know why she's so positive with her accusations."

"Why do you think one would attribute poor influence to you?"

"I honestly have no idea." Faron led her back toward the main hub of the market where they browsed much more innocent items. Sabine knew many of the sellers, and she chatted with them, asking about specific parts of their lives, including jobs, partners, and children. Many of the booths hosted the Sirene, and one sold a collection of exquisite pearls and other finery.

"Your collection is quite impressive today, Thaumas," Sabine observed as she picked up a rosaline pearl.

Thaumas stood at a height between Sabine's and Faron's. His bronzed skin seemed to glow in the bright sunlight, the orange reflections just one indication of his Sirene origins. His inky eyes twinkled with delight, and he tucked his tight black curls behind his ear as he spoke. "It's good to see you, Bine. You know I wouldn't display anything you wouldn't like."

Sabine felt Faron tense slightly from behind her before he relaxed again. When she glanced back at him, she didn't notice anything off. She turned her attention back to Thaumas, smiling. "You've said as much before." She handed over the pearl she'd been observing. "I would like this," she indicated.

They discussed price, and Sabine retrieved gold coins from the silk purse tucked away in a skirt pocket. Money and products were exchanged. "Do you think Teles would be interested in fitting this in a necklace for me?" Sabine didn't often see Teles, at least not in the past few months. Thaumas's sister preferred to travel rather than come to the shores of her estate, though she always seemed happy to see Sabine.

"I'm sure she would be delighted," Thaumas said. He motioned to the pearl. "I can hold on to it if you would like."

"Thank you," Sabine said, handing the item back. "It's good seeing you again. You should stop by for a visit soon. I know Meri would love to see you."

Thaumas scoffed. "I think Meri would sooner see the backside of me. I promise to visit soon, Bine."

They said their goodbyes and Sabine and Faron moved on. "Are you friendly with all the Mer in your land?" Faron asked with a smile and raised brow.

"Many of them, yes," Sabine confirmed. "Thaumas is an old friend."

"It's good to have a close relationship with them. I always found Merpeople fascinating." Faron paused to look at one of the stalls for a moment, this one filled with various shells. "I didn't know you had a nickname."

"The Merpeople who live off my coast go by Sirene," she explained. "And Thaumas is the only person who calls me 'Bine.'"

"Oh," Faron said.

Sabine thought she detected a hint of jealousy or a question. She smiled. "Childhood love connects people," she explained. "Thaumas and I will indefinitely be friends. Especially since I am godmother to his children." She noted his shoulders relaxed ever so slightly.

"How many children does he have?"

"Three."

"Three is a good number, provided they all get along," Faron conceded.

"They are sweet, though I don't have to discipline them."

"Do you want children? I know your thoughts on the nobles thinking you must have one immediately after marriage, but how do you feel about children?"

Sabine gave the question some thought because she knew her response could be complicated. She managed to provide something concise. "I think if I found the right partner, children would be wonderful," Sabine replied. "What about you? Do you see children in your future?"

"I didn't for a long time, but after turning fifty, I considered maybe having children wouldn't be a terrible thing," Faron admitted.

"Perhaps you shall. You look like you could handle three or four."

"I might." He shrugged. "If it happens, I will give thanks. If it doesn't, I will still give thanks."

She nodded. "Shall we head back?"

"Are you sure you're ready? We could take a walk down the shoreline?" Faron offered.

"I find I am in need of a nap before getting on with my day. I cannot imagine why," Sabine joked.

"It's the sun. It tires people out," Faron said as if he wasn't giving Sabine a knowing grin.

"Must be," she agreed with a laugh. Still, they began the short trek back up to the chateau. Sabine knew she would have to give more thought to what had just happened between herself and Faron, but she wasn't terribly worried for now.

Chapter Twenty

Faron stared down at the plate in front of him, picking at the food more than eating it as the sounds of conversation between Meri, Lisbeth, and Finn washed over him without quite making any impression. The four had gathered to share an evening meal in the kitchen, though Faron doubted he even tasted his food.

His thoughts firmly remained on Sabine and how she had tasted, how she'd felt during their stolen moments in town. His mind swirled and danced around newly forming questions, such as how his name would sound moaning from her lips, how she'd feel around his cock, how she would look tied up on his bed as she screamed and screamed her pleasure throughout the night. He was completely unaware of the satisfied smile on his face or the fading conversation as the three others watched him with knowing looks.

Faron's thoughts continued along the same path, his mind occupied with Sabine and all the things he wanted to do with her, surprisingly not all related to sex. He was only roused from his thoughts when Meri placed a teacup down in front of him with enough force that he found himself surprised none of the dark brownish-green liquid inside managed to spill. Only then did he look up and see the other three staring at him.

"Yes?" he drawled, upset they had interrupted his thoughts.

"You're going to drink every drop in the cup and not bitch about the taste once," Meri ordered.

Not liking the look in Meri's eyes, Faron lifted the cup and sniffed at it, then winced as the odor informed him it was going to taste even worse.

"It will be worse if you let it get cold," Lisbeth chimed in.

"And I won't let you heat it up," Meri said, her lips twisting into an unpleasant grin.

Faron rolled his eyes and downed the cup as quickly as possible, gagging and choking at the taste. "That is vile!" he exclaimed.

"And you will be drinking it once a day from now on." Meri's tone brooked no arguments even though Faron had no idea why he was being subjected to such a vile substance masquerading as tea.

Finn laughed then drank from his wine. "You brought it on yourself."

"What is it?" Faron asked, still gagging.

"It's a tea to prevent littles," Lisbeth said.

"Why would I need that?" Faron asked, his eyes widening as he wondered what gave it away.

"Have you and Her Grace not crossed certain lines?" Finn asked.

"No..." Faron trailed off as he stared at the three of them.

Lisbeth burst out laughing so hard Meri was forced to put a hand on her shoulder so she didn't fall off her chair.

"It was really a matter of time," Finn said with a shake of his head.

"Sabine has been happier than usual since you returned from the village, and you've had this goofy grin all afternoon and evening." Meri's look was unimpressed. "All the household staff have felt the tension between the two of you."

"Even when she was angry enough to fire you, I think we all assumed she would back down because of the thing existing between you," Finn said.

"Truly?" Faron said, confusion on his face. Until today, he thought Sabine was friendly but not interested in him the way he was her. He had also been sure she'd planned on firing him the evening Avana arrived. He was still certain any more mess-ups would yield the same result.

"Of course," Finn said after another drink. "Her Grace is kind, but what must have happened between the two of you certainly goes beyond kindness, do you not think?"

"Yes, but Sabine is also pragmatic, and I thought she had just decided it wasn't worth trying to replace me," Faron admitted.

Finn looked over to Meri. "You hear the part he's focusing on."

Meri had her head in her hands. She lifted her head enough to look at Faron, Finn, and Lisbeth. "The brains didn't come with the body," she said.

"Excuse me," Faron said, but he still couldn't help but laugh.

"Just do as Meri has instructed and continue staying on Her Grace's good side," Finn suggested.

"I have been trying to stay on her good side," Faron insisted.

"Then there is nothing to worry over," Finn said. He finished his wine and placed the empty glass back on the table. "I should check in on the status regarding Avana."

"How's the assassin doing?" Faron asked Finn.

"Her name is Avana," Lisbeth interjected.

Finn laughed and nodded. "Surprisingly, I think she's beginning to trust Her Grace. She's listening to instructions, which is good."

"I'm aware," Faron told Lisbeth, catching the roll she threw at him before gently tossing it back to her. "It's good news, her willingness to comply," he said to Finn, though Faron knew his lack of trust was evident in his tone.

"Her Grace thinks so," Finn agreed. "Obviously, we aren't letting Avana run around without supervision anytime soon, but the decision to keep her here seems to be working well enough. Now, we just have to wonder when the next assassin might show up."

"And she says she saw no others being trained at wherever they kept her?" Faron asked.

Finn shook his head. "If she knows more, she hasn't shared it. Perhaps she doesn't, or if she does, she'll feel more comfortable soon and will divulge." Finn took another sip of his wine.

"Here's hoping," Faron agreed. He turned to Meri to compliment her on the meal which consisted of a pink fish with lemon and a small salad with nuts and fruit. He paused when his stomach gave a strange lurch.

Meri gave him a knowing look as Lisbeth said, "The tea can make you sick the first time."

"Thank the Spirits I sleep with men," Finn said as he rose. He walked over to a series of cabinets and pulled out a decanter. He opened it, poured a clear liquid into a glass, and sat it in front of Faron when he returned. "It's bubbly, minty, and should help."

"Thank you," Faron said before taking a few small sips. It tasted better than the tea and, as Finn promised, fizzed as he drank it. He glanced over to Meri and Lisbeth. "You two are horrible."

"No, we aren't. We're practical. No point in Sabine having to go through childbirth later down the line. You should do what you can to spare her the pain," Lisbeth said brightly.

Faron had to concede her point. Childbirth, from what he'd seen, was rather terrible.

"You three have a good rest of the evening. After I check in on Avana, I have the evening off," Finn shared with a grin.

"We'll see you come morning," Lisbeth said with a giggle. "Tell Glaucus hello for us."

"I'm sure I don't know what you mean," Finn said, still grinning as he left the kitchen.

Chapter
Twenty-One

Sabine smiled at Thaumas and passed a bowl of citrus fruit to the Sirene. They shared a blanket down on the rocky beach, watching the sunrise together, much as they had when they were younger. The chateau, appearing champagne-colored in the rising morning sun, sat behind them.

In a few years, she would be thirty and more than a decade would have passed since she and Thaumas amicably agreed to end their relationship. Still, she kept up with her old friend as much as possible, loving to hear about his life and his family. On some of these early morning meet-ups, Thaumas would bring his wife and children, but today, it was just the two of them.

"You're lucky you have me and your wife to keep you fed," she teased as her friend took the bowl. She pulled a thick wool blanket over her lap as the breeze pierced her bones. She never had liked the cold, and she somehow thought she never would.

"I think I'd manage on my own if I had to," Thaumas said with a chuckle. He wore no protective layers, even as his clothing remained damp from being in the water recently.

He ate a few bites of fruit, the salty wind tossing his hair back and forth, though he gave it no notice. Thaumas remained every bit as carefree as he'd always been. Well, regarding most things. He looked over to Sabine, who was enjoying a small chocolate tart. "Your elf is sweet on you, Bine."

"My elf?" Sabine asked, though she didn't need the clarification. Currently, only one elf was in her employ, and that same elf had met Thaumas during their visit to the village.

"Ah," said her former lover. "You are sweet on him."

Sabine didn't argue the assertion, although she thought the situation a little more complex than Thaumas suggested. Faron had a way of acting impulsively, and she did not like it. After all, she had ended up over his shoulder at one point, angering her to the point of contemplating firing him. Other than the indiscretion, she had to admit she liked chatting with him. Flirting with him.

What he could do with his tongue...

"I barely know him," she said, which was sort of true given the lack of depth in their conversations thus far. She didn't know a whole lot about him, not really. Nor did he know much about her. What they had shared thus far, though... It did seem promising.

"I think you know enough," Thaumas said. "At least, enough to have an opinion about him." He nudged her shoulder. "It is perfectly acceptable for you to be attracted to him, or more. You have the right to find happiness and companionship."

"You are very invested in my romantic life," Sabine pointed out as she selected a berry from their food options.

"Your romantic life is a damn sight more positive than some of the other things we could talk about." His gaze turned out to the sea. "Our empress has agreed to take on more Nereid refuges."

Sabine's mood shifted and her expression grew darker. "I take it they are fleeing from Coralia?"

"Azmarin, too, although they say they have no stance on the Merscale trade." He gave a short, bitter laugh.

"Having no stance is the same as an endorsement when it comes to maiming people," Sabine said. "Is there anything I can do to help?"

"Same thing you always do," Thaumas suggested, his inky gaze still directed at the splashing water. "Though I will ask the empress when I see her. I know she appreciates all you do for us."

"What, treat you like people?" Sabine asked.

"The sentiment is slowly becoming less believed by certain humans," Thaumas said with a shrug. He finally looked back at her. "I have a family to protect. I would not be surprised if Mers of all kinds decided to go after places like Coralia."

"Not just Mers would be interested. You know what humans have done to many, like the shifters and the elves."

Thaumas nodded. "I miss your uncle, too. Alain was a good man, even when he decided to be a grumpy deer." He cast a smile at Sabine. "He's half the reason I broke my arm coming to see you. Unlike Meri, he laughed."

Sabine shook her head, amused. "I like how the story of your broken arm changes every time it's told." She also liked the change of topic. She felt powerless in a world that demanded to be cruel to others for the sole reason of what they were.

"I have to keep it all interesting, Bine." Thaumas sighed and leaned back on his elbows. "You'll be expected back by your many admirers before long. Your elf might come out here and accost me for whisking you away, you know."

"Faron is being a good boy," Sabine replied. "He knows what I will and won't accept in terms of treatment from others." Admittedly, there was a particular kind of attention she rather thought she would enjoy quite a lot.

"I know what you're smiling about, Bine," Thaumas teased. "And I know you're probably freezing out here. Why don't you head back up to the chateau? I'll gather everything and have it returned to you. The last thing I want is for Meri to come after me for not returning her dishes."

"You're a wise man, being afraid of Meri. Of course, she was not up when I borrowed her things." Sabine rose from the blanket and brushed out her skirt. "I shall see you soon," she said. Thaumas reached out and squeezed her hand, a gesture they always exchanged whenever they had time to meet up.

When their hands dropped, Sabine made the short journey back to the chateau, finding it quiet as she let herself back inside.

She rubbed her hands together as Thaumas's prediction about how cold she was had been right. She'd go up to her rooms and warm up by the fire.

Chapter Twenty-Two

Faron stood, feet shoulder-width apart, hands clasped behind his back as he watched the soldiers train. All the while, he did everything he could to ignore the itching between his shoulder blades. Taking a deep breath, he mentally shook off the need to turn and stare back at the person watching him. He didn't trust himself to keep his mouth shut, to refrain from doing something to get himself in trouble with Sabine.

He relaxed his arms and strode toward the soldiers, the eyes on him sliding off as he walked between them, correcting footing here, explaining the best way to grasp a long-sword and a broadsword to another. It was a comfortable routine, and he fell into it easily for several long minutes until he reached the end of the line of soldiers.

"The group at the very end starts to screw around every time you're distracted with another soldier. I think they're bullying the smaller soldier." A firm, feminine voice told him.

Faron was not ashamed to admit he visibly flinched, not having seen the assassin get so close. "What was that?" he said through gritted teeth.

"Every time you're busy helping someone, the group of four at the end stops working and starts screwing around. I'm pretty sure the brown-haired woman is picking on the smaller red-headed male next to her who's been struggling with his footwork and his grip," Avana clarified.

Faron's attention shot to the group at the end of the line. Immediately, he knew these individuals were the ones who struggled the most with the basics of swordsmanship and archery. The rest had been broken up into other smaller cohorts, consisting of veterans and students, for more advanced training. Faron wondered if it had been a good idea if he truly was missing something like bullying in the ranks.

The worst part of the whole thing was the unwillingness of the other soldiers to speak up. He'd have to rely on the assassin to help catch them in the act. He hated the thought.

"Why are you over here? I thought you were supposed to stay in the flower garden with your guards," he said.

"They figured I couldn't cause too much trouble, since you and these so well-trained soldiers were here. I think they're gossiping about Finn and a Sirene. They gossip more than they watch me. Well, except for Marcelle. He just teases me and points out where the exit is."

Faron didn't grind his teeth. It was close, but he managed. The assassin had been there only a handful of weeks, but just because she behaved, they were willing to let her go around unwatched? Yes, the flower garden was on the other side of the hedge directly behind the training field, but the order had still gone unobeyed. He wondered if Sabine would let him assign the assassin new guards. Well, except for Marcelle. He wasn't about to touch whatever was going on there.

"How long have you been watching us?"

"I assume you mean how many days?" she asked.

"Yes," he said, giving her an unimpressed look. She knew what he'd meant.

"Since they first let me out here," she said, as if it was no big deal.

Faron pinched the bridge of his nose. He had told her guards to keep her away from where they were training. "And how long has the group at the end been acting up instead of practicing?"

"Three days. I think something happened during the off-hours. The olive-skinned man used to practice with the red-headed male, then suddenly, the brown-haired female was just not letting it happen."

Faron glanced at the group, noting she was right. Usually, the two men practiced together while the other three, a brunette woman and two Sirenes, practiced together. Now, pointed out by the assassin, the tension they were trying so hard to hide from his attention could easily be seen.

"Okay. I'm going to walk the line. The moment they start acting up, tap your upper arm twice. I'll try and catch them."

Avana nodded and took a few steps away from Faron.

Moving through the soldiers, Faron once more tried to lose himself in the task of training, but the tension of having the assassin watching and knowing something was wrong with the soldiers didn't allow him to.

Faron helped three soldiers and ran through another two sets of drills before the assassin tapped her arm. Spinning on his heel, he saw it. The brunette woman tripped the red-headed male while he was sparring with one of the Sirene, who had a vicious smirk on his lips.

"What was that?" Faron roared as he marched over to the group. The instigator, Adeline, if he remembered correctly, backed up quickly.

"H-he tripped, sir," she lied badly.

"Over your leg, you mean. Do you think me stupid, soldier?" Faron demanded. "Fall in line," he snapped at the rest of the group, and all five stood shoulder-to-shoulder. "I have it on good authority four of you have been giving Jean a hard time." He motioned to the red-headed soldier. "Do we have a problem?"

"No, sir," all but the olive-skinned man, Pascal, said.

"Is there a problem?" he asked the man. The soldier eyed the others.

"Jean accidentally spilled an entire tray of drinks on Adeline at the tavern a few nights ago because he was distracted. She's decided to try and make him look bad in front of you. Those two are too stupid to tell her no." He motioned to the Sirene, who looked ashamed.

Faron turned on the female. "I'm recommending you be placed on stable duty for the next two weeks. Bringing stupid grievances to the training yard could get someone killed if we were working with real steel. If I find you doing this again, I will ensure you're removed from the guard and sent home. Do I make myself clear?" Faron asked calmly, anger shining in his eyes.

"Yes, sir," she said.

"Go, now, and take those two with you. They're on stable duty as well." He watched the three walk away before turning to Jean and Pascal. "Next time something like this happens, you bring it to me immediately. Do you understand?" he said kindly but firmly, receiving a, "Yes sir," in response.

Taking a step back, he faced the group as a whole. "Alright, everyone," he said loud enough his voice would carry to each soldier. "Start running, and don't stop till I say so. You saw what was happening and said nothing. You stand up for your fellow guards the way you stand up for your family.

Someone could have been injured, and it would have been on all of your heads. Start running the entire courtyard now!" Faron waited for them to obey before turning to the assassin, who was unsurprisingly behind him.

"You were fair," she said, surprised.

"No one got hurt. Thanks to you, we caught it in time. Thank you, Avana." Faron walked away, a smug smile on his face at the look she had given him for using her name.

Chapter Twenty-Three

Faron walked down the hallway to Sabine's office, the letters Lisbeth gave him in one hand, the other resting on the pommel of his sword. He hadn't seen Sabine since morning, before he'd gone to train the guards, and he found himself missing her something fierce. Between Avana becoming comfortable enough in her freedom to encroach on his training, the childish bullying he'd had to address over a spilled drink, and then being informed Sabine didn't need his services for the rest of the day, making the possibility of spending time with her slim, had left him tense and snappish. So much so, Meri had banished him from the kitchens and Lisbeth had been giving him pointless errands to run all day. His current task allowed him to see Sabine, a privilege he did not take lightly. Reaching her office, he rapped lightly on the door, waiting for her allowance to come in.

"Enter," Sabine called out.

Faron walked in, making sure to close the door gently. He took a moment to stand there, just watching Sabine. Spirits, he had missed her today.

She lifted her gaze from her work, bright green eyes focusing on Faron. The corners of her lips turned up. "Thank goodness you've come to rescue me from tedium," she declared.

Faron couldn't help but return the smile as he strode to her desk. "Sadly, it appears as if I have been tasked with the delivery of more tedium." He held up the letters. "I could, of course, just throw them into the fire, and we can both pretend they never existed." He motioned to her ever-roaring fireplace, watching her lips to see if she would smile at his jest.

"You could, but then I am afraid I might be accused of not knowing the business of our kingdom or the surrounding ones," she explained. She smiled again. "Tell me why I am supposed to care about Coralia's king finally producing a legitimate heir."

"Because you're expected to send a gift to welcome the new baby?" he guessed, though honestly, he had no idea why Sabine should care. "Or tell them they named the child something pretty?" He moved closer to Sabine, noting the tense lines of her shoulders and the small dark circles under her eyes.

"I suppose a gift is customary," she replied, pondering the notion. "And it's better than me trying to find which sheet of paper tells me the name. It was something silly either way."

Faron chuckled. "Most royals do like to name their child silly, symbolic things with meanings important only to them." Faron placed the letters on her desk and moved closer to Sabine, still an arm's length away but close enough to catch a hint of fragrance he could never quite place.

"If ever I have children, I suppose I will have to be sensible to ensure no one has this same conversation about them," she said, turning full attention to Faron. "Meri had you running errands?"

Faron nodded. "She did."

"Might it have something to do with petty grievances amongst the guards and you having to speak directly with Avana?" she asked with a teasing grin.

"I'm thinking of extending their stable duty. Those guards got upset at each other and made an even bigger mess in the stable," Faron said before grudgingly admitting, "Avana was helpful in handling them."

"I'm not surprised. Avana seems to have a good head on her shoulders, even if she acts like a feral cat." She smiled at him. "And I knew you'd eventually get along. At least well enough to co-exist."

"Co-existing is stretching it, but I am trying, at least. I will also be allowing her to spend time training with the soldiers, though I will be her partner." It had been something Faron had been considering but hadn't voiced until then.

"Great," Sabine said with genuine pleasure. "It sounds as though you have things well handled."

"As well as possible. The entire group of soldiers is in trouble, but it will sort itself out." He sighed, deciding he would focus on more interesting things. Like Sabine. His eyes slid down Sabine's form, taking her all in. "You look stressed today, Your Grace. More than usual."

"I am always stressed," she replied with a shallow shrug. "I do not feel more so today than any others."

Faron made a noise of concern. "Are you sure? Are you not sleeping well?"

"I slept well enough," she decided. "Perhaps not as long as I might have liked."

"You've told me before you don't usually have trouble sleeping. Are there any concerns I might be able to help alleviate?" Faron asked, even as an idea started to take root in his mind.

"How do you plan on alleviating any potential concerns?"

"Depends on the type of problem. I could stab or beat someone to death. I could burn upsetting messages and you could claim you never saw them. Remove Avana from the chateau if you're worried for your safety. If you are stressed, I know ways to relax your body to help you sleep," Faron said.

"You seem set on action."

"I only wish to help, but I am a person more prone to action than anything. However, you just need a listening ear. I am willing to listen."

"You may help," she decided as she watched him. "However you think it is needed."

Faron took the last step needed to close the distance between them, certain what he was about to do would be well received given what they had shared in the village. Pushing lingering vestiges of doubt aside, he gently grasped Sabine's chin with his left hand and made sure they had full eye contact. "If at any time I do something you do not like or want, stop me." Then he brushed his lips against hers once, twice, and a third time before dropping to his knees. He found he liked looking up at her from the position as his hands moved under her skirt, caressing her ankles before slowly moving up her calves to her upper thighs.

Faron made a satisfied noise in the back of his throat when, after several long seconds, she didn't stop him. He moved his hands higher. Keeping eye contact with her, he motioned for her to part her thighs, and delightfully, she obliged. His fingers made it to her warm center and started to rub gently, finding her clit with little exploration.

She inhaled slowly as his fingers first caressed her, fingers grasping onto the arms of her chair as his caresses continued softly up and down, incrementally increasing the pressure and pace as he went, his eyes on her face the entire time.

She gasped softly, her breathing growing more frequent with each stroke. Her head tilted back and her lashes lowered. Letting her reactions guide him, Faron pressed firmer, impatiently anticipating the victory of seeing her come apart.

A small sound of pleasure left her mouth, stifled though it was behind closed lips, letting Faron know she was close. Even when she cried out in pleasure, he did not let up until he wrung every bit of pleasure he could from Sabine. He only stopped when she sat there panting, eyes closed and shoulders drooping in bliss. Still, he pushed her skirts up. "Lift your hips."

"What?" she asked as though she must have misheard.

"Lift. Your. Hips," he said slowly, firmly, a hungry look in his eyes as he watched her. She obeyed without further question, and he moved her garments out of his way, hands finding those delightful hips and easing her forward. He nudged her thighs further apart, fully revealing her delicate center, slick from the first round of pleasure. Without a word, he buried his head between those creamy thighs, feasting on her like a starving man. His tongue lapped at the sensitive bud as his hands held her thighs open.

She moaned openly now as his tongue and lips teased and petted her. Faron sucked her clit into his mouth. He felt the chair move, though his steadfast hold on her thighs kept her in place. As she came, Faron only pulled back and settled himself on the ground, licking the taste of her from his lips. "You taste divine," he told Sabine as his hand moved up to her center. He slid his index and middle fingers along her entrance, coating them in her juices, making them nice and wet. "However, you still look a little stressed." His fingers entered her, but he kept his eyes on her face, watching to make sure she didn't want to stop. She gave no sign other than a desire for him to continue, her hips lifting and falling to meet the relentless pace of his fingers.

Faron couldn't help the satisfied smile as Sabine drew closer to her second climax, and he couldn't help but wonder if he should give her time to gather herself between climaxes in order to draw their time together out more. However, it was quickly drowned out by the way Sabine tightened on his finger and his insatiable need for Sabine, which was so much worse than when he first arrived now that he'd tasted her.

He barely registered the knock at her office door, so enraptured by the way she responded to him. By the second knock, which he did hear, Sabine could not answer as she was covering her mouth to keep from crying out.

"Ask who it is," he said, his command firm and teasing. She moaned again in response, prompting him to rub his thumb against her clit. "Answer them."

She took a breath, then another. "Yes?" she called out, her voice strained.

"Good girl," he purred, slowing the thrust of his fingers.

"Your Grace?" Finn could be heard from outside.

"Yes?" she called out again, sounding a little more like herself. "Something you need?"

Faron knew he should stop, he knew should—manners demanded it—and yet, he didn't.

"I'm here to notify you of an invitation to dine with Lord Tristian at his estate later this month," Finn replied through the door. "His steward said it was urgent."

Faron listened carefully as he continued to slowly tease her, angered by the intrusion of the wretched man he knew Sabine barely tolerated. Without much thought other than the need to drive the names of any other man from her head, Faron's thumb moved up and pressed on Sabine's clit, making small slow circular motions.

"Ahhh..." Sabine said, the obvious distraction from Faron echoing in her voice. "We will discuss it later. I have more urgent business to see to."

"What shall I tell Lord Tristian's steward?" Finn asked.

"Just what I said," Sabine called out.

"Of course, Your Grace," Finn replied before the sound of his footsteps walking away from the door could be heard.

"By the Spirits, what do you think you're doing?" Sabine demanded breathlessly.

"Helping you destress," Faron responded simply as he increased the speed of his fingers once more. He felt her tightening around his fingers, and soon, she was quivering in another beautiful climax. He withdrew from her, put his fingers to his lips, and licked the taste of her from them. Only when he was finished did he ask, "May I fuck you?"

"After everything you just did?" she replied, her breathing still heavy.

"Yes," Faron replied. "I know you can handle it." He expected her to decline, or at least tell him to wait. She did neither.

"Please."

Faron gave her a pleased smile. "I'm going to lock the door. I don't think we want any more disruptions." Faron rose, strode to the door, and locked it before coming back to Sabine. He stared at her for a minute before holding out a hand for her to take. He grasped her hand when she offered it and pulled her to her feet. He turned them so her back was to her desk. Releasing her hand, he lifted Sabine onto the desk, her skirts pooling around her thighs. Faron kissed her again as he undid his trousers so he could free his cock.

Faron stepped forward, rubbing his cock against her center. She moaned in response, prompting him to repeat the process, needing to see and hear her need for him. He did this until he couldn't stand to wait longer. Lining himself up, he gently pushed the head of his cock into Sabine. He pulled out and, with one long, demanding stroke, entered her again, filling her until his hips were flush with her. He groaned with pleasure at the feeling of her wrapped around his cock.

"Alright?" he asked.

She nodded. "Yes," she breathed out.

Faron kissed her again as he started thrusting slowly, then quickly picked up speed. Sabine continued holding on to him as his hips moved against hers, her mouth seeking his in desperate need. One of his hands slid between their bodies, finding her clit. He broke away from their kisses so his lips could trail along her jaw and down her throat. He nipped teasingly at her skin before lightly biting into her shoulder.

"Like that," she said. "Just like that.

Sabine's enjoyment of the rougher side of things sent a thrill through Faron, making him feel like he could let his control slip more than he usually would. The hand on her hip gripped her tighter, and he bit down slightly harder on her shoulder.

Faron groaned against her skin as he felt her tighten around him and held back from his own release by sheer force of will alone. "Good girl," he said as she trembled through another intense orgasm, crying out in pleasure against his shoulder.

His thrusts became wilder, less rhythmic, as his own climax drew closer. He moaned loudly as he came, spasms of pleasure running down his spine and through his limbs.

Even as his body relaxed, Faron remained close, enjoying the feeling of her around him even as his cock softened inside of her. "I knew you could handle it," he told her softly.

"You flirted with a line," Sabine replied, sounding spent but amused.

"Flirting isn't too bad." Faron's tone was teasing. "Besides, elves have almost no recovery period. You could take the rest of the day, and I could truly help you relax."

"No," she said with a real laugh. "In fact..." She scooted back on the desk enough to separate them.

Faron couldn't help the disgruntled noise passing his lips as his half hard cock slipped out of Sabine. He accepted her rejection easily, but he couldn't help shooting her a playfully disappointed look.

"Later could be a possibility, though," she said.

"I can work with later," Faron said, brushing his lips against hers.

"Good," she replied then kissed him again.

Chapter
Twenty-Four

I am certain you have heard of the joyous news coming from Coralia. The heir, Princess Collette Venora Josselyn Gaillane, was born to King Sargarus and Queen Adorra. I am certain you feel much joy for our ally, and I know you look forward to any opportunity to demonstrate Fythias's excitement.

Make plans to travel to Coralia in the coming months to attend the official presentation of the princess and provide royal gifts on my behalf. The Vassetre line has always been a proud family for Fythias, and I know you will make me proud.

I do realize you have many people of different origin on your staff, and you have not always agreed with Coralian policy regarding the magical and non-human. If it pleases you, I shall arrange for others to escort you to Coralia so you do not have to worry about your own people.

Grégoire, Prince of Fythias

"I am not going to Coralia," Sabine said, the flat of her palm hitting her desk on the word "not."

"No," Finn agreed with a nod, quill poised over the book he held. "Coralia is not safe for anyone right now, and it would not be wise for you to leave the country for such a long journey given the uncertainty of who will be ruling."

Sabine sighed and sat back in her chair, her fingers tapping on the chair arm. She highly doubted Grégoire cared about the birth of a princess belonging to another country. He hadn't cared about the birth of his own nephew some time back, and though she knew the middle prince admired Coralia's humanitarian crimes, he had no great love for anyone or anything beyond himself.

If she had to guess, the edict to visit Coralia had more to do with getting her out of the country than anything else, and if Grégoire wanted her out of the country, it made her wonder what plans he had. "You know... I think he counted on Avana taking me out. Demanding I randomly travel to Coralia seems ... hasty."

"Are you going to make the accusation?" Finn asked her, his brow creased in concern. Finn, she knew, supported her with his whole heart and soul, but he was smart enough to consider actions from every angle. He'd think an outright accusation rash.

Sabine shook her head. "Even with my rank, I think doing so would go too far, at least for now. I am curious, though, why he's escalated."

Finn closed his book and placed it on the desk. "He could be tired of waiting on what he thought would be an easy path to sway you."

"Perhaps," Sabine said, and she sighed. "I'll chat with Faron about the security concerns. I'll have to be bodily dragged to Coralia, and I doubt anyone in the chateau would allow Grégoire the opportunity." Faron alone, she knew, would have his sword swinging the second a hand was laid on her.

"Not a chance," Finn confirmed. "Might I suggest extending your concern to Prince Louis? Perhaps he would be willing to speak up on your behalf."

"I intend to inform him," Sabine confirmed. She knew getting him to act more definitively might be a little more questionable. Both princes were happy to remain in their cold standoff, but maintaining the current stance would be unlikely for much longer. "We'll see what he says. In the meantime, the household needs a plan in case things turn more hostile."

"Of course. I know you have some meetings this morning with the local Blacksmith Guild. I can arrange some time in your schedule to have an actual formal meeting with Faron," Finn said.

Sabine smiled. "As opposed to all of our informal meetings?" she asked.

Finn chuckled. "Indeed. No one has missed the peculiar friendship you've formed. Personally, I'm happy to see the two of you getting on again."

"You're happy you don't have to find replacements for Faron and Meri," Sabine countered, though time and distance from the event had softened her stance a little. She certainly had not wanted to bring on new people either, no matter how angry she remained.

"You are not wrong, Your Grace, though I'd have not blamed you had you decided otherwise. Their behavior was unacceptable, and you have too much else resting on your shoulders to have to deal with on top of having to deal with staff who won't listen."

"You know your arguments the night they lost their minds are the only reason I didn't fire them that evening," Sabine said. "And Lisbeth helped the following morning. Neither of you wanted me to fire them, and I think you would have been unhappy had I followed through."

"We would have been," Finn acknowledged. "But you would have been more than justified had you made the choice." He stood from his seat and picked up his book. "You have more than earned the respect granted to you by your title and position, something we all agree about. Your graciousness is appreciated and responsible for their continued employment. We all know the loss of a job would have been the least of their worries in another household."

Sabine nodded. She knew Tristian, whose estate was less than a day's journey from her own, would have had Faron arrested for what he had done, and possibly Meri as well. Possible charges would have included assault, attempted kidnapping, and more. Faron's status as an elf, and an especially large one, would have potentially put him in terrible danger in any other home, which was another reason to silently promote Louis's claim to the throne.

"Remind them of my graciousness next time they start to slide into old habits, and we won't have too much to worry over."

Finn smiled and nodded. "Of course. I will be on my way, Your Grace." He gave a small bow and left the room, leaving Sabine to ponder what she might do when it came to Grégoire.

Chapter
Twenty-Five

For her own peace of mind, Sabine decided she would write to Prince Louis the following day. The order to go to Coralia did come with a sense of urgency, but she felt as though she would have nothing productive or even rational to say in any letter she composed that afternoon. She could see herself making demands of the youngest prince, of commanding him to do something about his brother, even if it was a warning to leave her and her estate alone. Going down that route would serve no one, especially herself. Sabine had spent the afternoon pursuing leisurely activities rather than anything else she should've been attending to.

The evening arrived with a quiet, luscious dinner in her quarters, a hot bath, and long hours curled up in her favorite seat near her fire, book in hand and chocolate and wine within reach. She couldn't remember the last time she'd been so indulgent, but she had no complaints.

A glance out of the window, newly reinforced with the sort of locks Faron insisted upon, told her it was late, though she hardly minded despite her tendency to rise early. Sometimes, she required longer, slower evenings. Evenings where she could move and change direction as it suited her. Thinking about Faron as she observed the darkness of the sky was her most current directional change.

In truth, she thought about her personal guard with some frequency, especially when he was nowhere in sight. She knew she had but to summon him, but Sabine tried to be respectful of his time, especially since his mornings also came early.

A knock sounded at her door, the same familiar rhythm Lisbeth used anytime she came to Sabine's room without being called. The duchesse closed her book and put it aside. "Come in," she beckoned.

Lisbeth stepped into the room, holding the door open for Meri, who was pushing a cart with her. From her vantage point, Sabine could see several covered trays as well as what looked like chilled bottles of wine. "We thought Your Grace might like dessert or something to drink," Lisbeth said with a smile.

"I do not oppose good food and drink," Sabine said, looking over the quantity of food being ushered toward her. "I have been snacking on chocolates this evening, so I suppose you will have to help me consume all of this," she said, gesturing toward the trays.

"Only if you want the company," Meri said before Lisbeth could respond. She wheeled the cart to within reaching distance of Sabine, ensured it would stay put, and began uncovering the different dishes.

"I am not opposed," Sabine replied. "You must have been feeling quite sorry for me to have gone through so much trouble so late in the day."

"Not sorry—" Meri started only to get cut off by Lisbeth.

"Meri's been stress-baking ever since she heard the *prince*," Lisbeth basically spat the word, "is trying to order you to Coralia."

The low rumbling growl coming from Meri startled Sabine, but she didn't find it unexpected.

"We also thought, despite your trip to the market yesterday and the other … activities you've done to reduce your stress levels, this might help a bit more. We are both glad you decided to take the rest of your day for some much-deserved downtime." Lisbeth gave Sabine a bright smile.

Sabine chuckled to herself. Truly, she wasn't the least bit surprised by the spread of gossip or the way Meri and Lisbeth chose to handle the news, both about Coralia and her ongoing situation with Faron.

"Well, no one under this roof is going to Coralia," she said simply. "So, you might as well find a seat and help me eat everything."

"We assumed you would say no. We also assume the prince will somehow try and take you to task for it. Though really, we all know he'll just send a strongly worded letter about how disappointed in you he is and how you obviously don't care for Fythias as much as you claim. Get a husband, blah, blah, blah." Meri's voice changed into a deeper mocking cadence, speaking as if she were Grégoire.

Lisbeth giggled as she pulled two smaller chairs over for them to sit in.

"I'm hoping the response I receive will follow along those lines," Sabine confirmed. "But we shall see. I think Grégoire's patience with me is running thin."

Meri's eyes took on a calculating gleam as she sat down and grabbed a small plate, loading it with chocolate covered strawberries, a crepe filled with a blue fruit, and several other items before handing it to Sabine. "I want him to come here.

I am positive Avana will be able to identify him by his voice. If she can, you can have his head for attempted murder."

Lisbeth rolled her eyes as she uncorked a bottle of what looked like honey mead. "Her Grace couldn't take it that far, but she could pressure his brother into an active investigation."

"His title would protect him, even if you're right," Sabine pointed out as she settled the plate in her lap.

"One can dream," Meri said with an exaggerated sigh.

"Dreaming is nice," Sabine replied with a sigh. "But we cannot forget he has more legitimate rights to the throne than Louis does. I cannot overplay my hand." She picked up a strawberry and took a bite.

"He may have the legitimacy, but he doesn't have the support. At this point, I think only the minor nobles who dream of wealth and power support him. Everyone else, including the people, support Louis. I fear we may have a civil war on our hands if that prick tries to take the throne anytime soon," Meri groused before she took a bite of a tart with red filling. Sabine guessed it was sour, but for some reason, Meri liked her sweets with a kick.

"You're not wrong, and we don't want war if we can prevent it." Sabine rather thought things could turn violent without much prompt, but she'd prefer to avoid it if possible. She just didn't know if she could ensure such things. "Eat, Lisbeth," she said.

Lisbeth gave Sabine a mischievous grin as she handed out glasses of the mead before making herself a plate of fruit with some cream. "Everything with the prince is such a chore. Someone should just assassinate him already," she said lightly.

"And who do you think should take on the task?" Sabine asked, knowing full well she was legally bound to turning

Chapter Twenty-Five

Lisbeth in for treason. She opted to disobey that particular law.

"Meri should do," Lisbeth said without thinking. "But obviously we'd blame some assassin from Coralia."

Meri opened and closed her mouth several times before saying, "And why am I doing it?"

"Oh, because you can disguise the poison I give you by baking something yummy for him," Lisbeth explained.

"Makes complete sense to me," Sabine joked. "Your food is delicious. I'm certain your offerings would be all we'd need."

Meri grinned. "Doesn't he like vanilla? I could send him a three-tiered cake and decorate it very nicely. We could send it as a special delivery. No one would be able to prove I actually sent it."

Sabine laughed and shook her head. "Somehow, I think we are better served sticking to jokes about this topic rather than any actual follow through."

"Of course, we would never, ever follow through," Lisbeth said, giving Sabine a look of such innocence, the duchesse would have thought the redhead had never done a bad thing in her life if she didn't know her as well as she did.

"Now, talk to us about why you've been so happy lately," Meri said as she and Lisbeth exchanged knowing looks.

"Given that I know you've been making Faron a specific kind of tea, I wonder why you'd have to ask that question." Sabine put her plate down and took a drink of her mead, finding it fruity and sweet.

"He told you, did he?" Meri asked with a smug grin. "I thought it was better he took it rather than you."

"We just... We don't want details, but we're still curious," Lisbeth said, blushing.

"You see a need for tea to prevent children, but you don't want details," Sabine summarized coyly. "It seems as though you know as much as possible within those parameters."

"She doesn't want to know," Meri said, shooting Lisbeth a look as the other woman made a noise and hid her face. "I, on the other hand, want all the details. You look too relaxed for him not to be good." Meri laughed and tried to avoid the hand Lisbeth was using to swat at her.

"Oh, I see," Sabine said before taking another drink. The mead provided warmth and encouraged a wagging tongue. "Well, he is quite thorough."

Meri grinned. "Thank the Spirits. The last one you were spending time with just made you look grumpy. I'm glad you found a man who knows what he's doing." She downed her drink and motioned to Lisbeth to give her the bottle, which the blushing woman did without complaint.

"I can't abide by poor sex," Sabine said, then she held a hand up. "I will amend my statement. Most people can learn. Those who cannot are the ones I cannot abide."

"And you shouldn't," Lisbeth said, refilling her own cup before handing the bottle to Sabine.

"Are we right to assume Faron is toward the top of your list of friends when it comes to after-hours activities?" Meri asked.

"He's currently the only person I'm sleeping with," Sabine confirmed with a shrug. Her glass refilled, she placed the bottle back on the cart.

Meri laughed, but the shake of her head told Sabine she was going to take the answer for what it was. "Well, I'm glad you're enjoying your giant," she said fondly.

Lisbeth nodded and she popped a cream-covered berry into her mouth.

"Is he my giant, now?" Sabine asked with a laugh. "I don't think anything so official has been decided."

"Of course not," Lisbeth said, and she and Meri exchanged grins. "We are happy to see you relaxing and smiling, though. With everything going on, we were worried about you."

"You two worry about me regardless," Sabine pointed out. Truly, she was thankful for their concerns. So many households were filled with indifferent staff, and she would be content to call Meri and Lisbeth friends.

"True, but it's out of love," Lisbeth said, resting her head on Meri's shoulder.

"I know," Sabine assured them. "And there's not nearly enough of it in this world."

Lisbeth held her glass between her hands, studying it carefully. "You know, Faron is a good man, no matter his impulsiveness. You would be able to have a mutually respectful relationship if it was something you wanted."

"Your people would accept it," Meri added, her words bolder than Lisbeth's. "They accepted your mother, you know."

Sabine did know, and the thought had reverberated through her mind as of late. She nodded. "I'm aware."

"You should consider it if it makes you happy," Lisbeth said with a soft smile.

"You're aware more than one person is involved, yes?" Sabine replied.

Meri raised an eyebrow and Lisbeth laughed. "If you told Faron you were getting married tomorrow, I'm pretty sure he'd say yes without question."

"I think you are much more romantically minded than I am," Sabine replied. "But given the length and happiness in your marriage, I am not surprised."

Lisbeth laughed. "We work hard to keep our romance alive. It's too easy to get comfortable and stop thinking about the other person the way you should," she said as she reached out and took Meri's hand. "But I do think Faron would agree if you asked him."

"And you, my dear friend, have consumed too much mead if it has you suggesting I propose," Sabine said. She would not give the notion thought. Not tonight. Perhaps not ever.

Lisbeth giggled. "Well, it doesn't take much." And it was true. Lisbeth was very much a lightweight.

"I know," Sabine replied with a laugh. "Which tells me Meri should take you back to your rooms for the evening."

"I'm going to leave the food and drinks in case the large shadow that was hanging around decides to come say hi." Meri winked at Sabine as she gathered Lisbeth into her arms.

"Uh huh," Sabine said. "You two have a good evening." She would have no problem with Faron deciding to join her. She just wouldn't count on it.

When she was alone again, Sabine poured herself another smaller glass of mead to sip from as she settled back to read. She was several pages in when a knock sounded at the main door. She lowered the book and looked back toward the door. "Come in."

The door opened and Faron stepped in, a small smile on his face. "I'm glad they brought you food and drink, but Lisbeth and Meri took forever to leave."

"They did," Sabine confirmed, smiling up at the elf. "Were you anxious to have them leave?"

"I'm glad you got to spend time with them, but I wouldn't have complained if they'd dropped off the food and left," he said with a shrug.

"It's just me now," she pointed out.

"And I am hoping you don't mind company for the remainder of your night," Faron said, his grin making his intentions clear.

"Of course not," she replied.

Faron moved across the room to where Sabine sat and took in the delicacies and alcohol on the cart. "Meri thought you would be this hungry?"

"Meri thought I would have company this evening," Sabine corrected. "So far, she has not been wrong."

Faron laughed. "Am I becoming too predictable? Should I start coming through your window instead?" he joked as he took the chair Meri had been occupying just minutes before.

"I think taking the window would just delay the inevitable," Sabine decided. "But you are welcome to if you find it fun."

"I prefer just using the door," Faron admitted. "Are you still hungry?" he asked.

Sabine shook her head. She'd not been especially hungry when Meri and Lisbeth stopped by, but she wanted to avoid wasting the food. "You should eat, though. Meri might be offended otherwise."

Faron nodded and picked up a tart, his middle finger getting some cream on it. He kept eye contact with Sabine as he licked it off. "Is your book good?" he asked.

Sabine's gaze did not leave Faron's mouth for a moment, her mind reminding her of how he so expertly used it on her. "I suppose," she replied.

Faron raised an eyebrow. "Your answer makes it sound boring. Maybe you would rather do something else? We could find you another book. Talk over some..." He paused to look at the alcohol Meri and Lisbeth had brought. Mead. "We could take a late-night stroll through the gardens, or," he paused again, this time dipping his index finger into the cream with purpose, "we could move on to other pursuits."

"And what other pursuits are of interest, Faron?" Sabine asked.

"Spending time with you in any way you'll allow, but maybe with fewer clothes."

"With fewer clothes," Sabine replied, allowing her words to trail off. "Perhaps you should do something about that."

Faron's playful grin turned into something darker as he stood and moved around the tray to where Sabine lounged comfortably, lowering himself to his knees once there. "Maybe I should."

"How do you think you'll start?"

"I think I'd like to start at your ankles and work my way up if that's alright with you, Your Grace."

Sabine nodded. "By all means."

Chapter Twenty-Six

The letter sent to Prince Louis did nothing to quiet Sabine's nerves. She could not be forced to go to Coralia, but Grégoire could make life difficult for her if he so chose. Once again, she was thankful to have a reason to leave the chateau for the first part of the afternoon. This time, instead of going into the village, she had agreed to go to the training field so Faron could teach her some basics in self-defense.

Unlike her usual fine dresses, she'd changed into a pair of comfortable pants and a shirt for the event. While she'd more than likely be dressed in her finery if an occasion to defend arose, she found she'd rather not ruin her clothes during training exercises.

The training ground stood empty when Sabine arrived, a surprise considering the time of day. She found Faron at one end of the grounds, bent at the knees and examining some of the practice swords. A few sat discarded next to him.

She approached, amused by his intent study of the blades. "You look ready to murder the weapons," she observed.

Faron glanced at Sabine, giving her a small but genuine closed-lip smile. His eyes traveled up her body, perhaps taking in her clothes. Perhaps for another reason.

"I keep thinking I've removed all the defective weapons only to find more. They're not the same defects, or I would think someone is putting them back." Faron stood wiping his hands on his black pants. "How's your day been since we last saw each other?"

"I received a summons to go to Coralia," Sabine shared. "And since I am refusing the direct orders from the prince, I imagine our lives are about to become quite interesting."

Faron's confused expression turned contemplative then dark. "We all know who is and isn't welcome in Coralia. You wouldn't take your people with you, and you wouldn't want to go without people you trusted."

"All correct," Sabine confirmed.

"He offered to supply you with guards and the like, didn't he?" Faron asked.

"He did," Sabine said. "And I have a strong feeling I know exactly who he would have assigned."

Faron rubbed his chin. "The order is far too convenient."

"I made the same observation," Sabine shared. "We will need to sit down and discuss some things soon, I think."

"Most certainly. Do you think he will finally come here?" Faron asked.

Sabine could see his mind working through different plans. She once again found herself more than pleased with his presence on her estate. "I think he'll make his way here if I continue to refuse his orders," Sabine said, though she had no way of knowing when Grégoire would make an appearance.

"So, we should prepare for the eventuality." Faron shook his head then grinned. "Any other fun news?"

"None I know of," she said with a playful grin. "But who knows? At any moment, some fun, new, unexpected thing might arise."

"Let's hope it's not as much fun as Avana was," Faron said. "What weapons training do you have?"

"I think it's no secret I've had minimal."

Faron nodded. "I had to ask. For all I know, you could decide to surprise me with archery skills."

"Oh, I can shoot for sport, but it's different compared to self-defense," Sabine said.

"Still, that's a good skill to have. It's something to build on," Faron said. "Would you like to start with hand-to-hand?"

"You are the teacher here," Sabine replied, motioning for him to start.

She heard Faron chuckle softly as he approached her. "Show me how to form a fist and how you'd hold them in a fight."

The fist she formed, though small given her stature, was perfectly formed. "The way I'd hold my hands during a fight would depend on the fight, would it not?"

Faron nodded and moved in front of her. He put his hands up, not in fists but palms out. "Alright, how would you hit me?"

"Oh, I wouldn't," Sabine replied.

Faron gave her a confused look until he found himself on the ground looking up at her.

Faron blinked hard several times as he got his bearings. "How?" he asked as he moved to get back on his feet.

"Your footing wasn't as stable as it would be in a prepared, waiting stance. Most people acting in a physical skirmish have weakened stances. I took advantage of that by hooking your ankle."

"Would you show me?" he asked and took up his stance again.

"Fast or slow?"

"Fast first, please. I want to see how I missed it, then we'll go slow."

"Of course. I'd love to test your idea of slow later," Sabine said. She smiled up at Faron, finding the move as easy and effective as the first time. She stepped back when Faron was on the ground again. "Did you catch it?"

"Sadly, I was a bit distracted." He held out a hand to silently ask for help up, only to pull Sabine down on top of him when she moved to do so. "I'd like to see your definition of slow."

She laughed softly, leaning forward so her lips lingered mere inches above his. "I bet you would," she teased, her voice low. "But showing you isn't training, now is it?"

"Depends on how you show me. Wrestling is good training, you know," Faron teased.

"Somehow, I think you might win at wrestling."

"We might have to see."

"We just might," she agreed. Despite her earlier reference to training, she made no effort to move. From her position, she could feel his growing desire for her, and she couldn't deny the appeal of staying there.

Faron's hands moved to Sabine's hips, grasping them firmly. He ground her down upon him with a wicked smirk.

She sucked in a breath, her own need for him growing insistent. She kissed him, her lips brushing over his in a teasing manner. "Still not training."

"It's a form of training," he leaned up to kiss her. The kisses grew deeper, more needy without much prompting. Sabine didn't care about being outside where anyone could walk up. Faron made it easy to forget the world outside of the two of them. She grinded against him, loving the way he felt and the way he reacted.

There was the sound of loud, purposeful footsteps approaching the training grounds. "Your Grace?" Lisbeth called out, and Faron groaned into the kiss.

Sabine heard Lisbeth, but several seconds passed before the need to separate from Faron sunk into her brain. "Later," she promised Faron after a final kiss. She rose back to her feet, although she doubted it would conceal what she and Faron had gotten up to. "Yes, Lisbeth?" she called back.

Lisbeth came into view, her steps hesitant. She smiled seeing the two of them, Faron still on the ground though slowly rising to his feet.

"Meri sent me to tell you she will have lunch ready in thirty minutes."

"I'm sure she did," Sabine heard Faron mutter.

"Thank you," Sabine said, a little frustrated though mostly amused by Faron's response. "I'll make sure to return in time."

"I'll let her know. Enjoy your training," Lisbeth said and was gone.

"Meri sent her to make sure we were training and only training," Faron said.

"According to you, we were," Sabine pointed out with a grin.

"Well, what we consider training and what Lisbeth considers scandalous could be very different."

"Were we being scandalous, Faron?" she asked, approaching him.

"No, we were just training," he said.

She noted the small raise of his lips and the twinkle in his eyes. Faron was teasing her. She liked him teasing her. Being playful with her. "Shall I put you on your back again, or would you like to be a little more productive in our remaining time?"

"Sadly, I do need you to put me on my back once more, just a little slower this time if you would. I missed your hand placement."

"It works without hand placement," she said. "But of course."

"Show me with the hand placement and then without?" Faron asked and took his stance once more, motioning Sabine forward.

Sabine nodded, and she approached, placing her hand against his arm in a benign manner. The action might be taken as gentle flirting or a subtle request for escorting. Usually serving as a distraction, the move was one she knew Faron would allow in order for her to sweep out his feet, which she did, slowly, so he could study her technique.

Faron made a thoughtful noise from where he'd landed on the ground. Pulling himself onto his elbows, he looked up at Sabine. "I like how you did that. Had I been an upset lord, it would have put me off guard. Made it seem like you were planning to apologize or flirt. I must ask though, what is the follow-up to it? What do you do once they are on the ground? Do you run or pull your dagger?" Sabine could tell from his eyes Faron was extremely curious.

"It completely depends on the situation," Sabine replied. "Sometimes, it makes more sense to flee. Other times, there isn't an option."

"How many times have you been forced to use this tactic?" Faron's voice was dark, as if promising vengeance on any that so much as looked at Sabine incorrectly.

"Maybe five times total since I became duchesse," Sabine replied. "Most of the time, it's because people looking for marriage and power don't think I will protest their advances."

Faron took a deep, calming breath. "I will never understand why some men feel they are entitled to a woman's time, attention, or their person." He gave Sabine a sharp grin. "Hopefully, with your tall scary elf around, men with that mindset will think twice." He moved back into position. "Show me without using your hands, please."

"Oh, so you're tall *and* scary now," Sabine remarked before going through the motions again, this time, keeping her hands to herself.

"I'm only tall and scary when it's needed. Otherwise, I'm perfectly sized and reasonable, as you well know," Faron joked, sounding a bit more winded this time having gone down a bit harder than he'd intended. "Do you prefer using your hands or not?"

"I prefer to not have to use my little trick at all, but either way, it works well."

Faron nodded and held a hand out for Sabine to take, still sounding a bit winded. Sabine took his hand. Faron grinned as he pulled Sabine down on top of him again before rolling them so he was on top, his hair a dark curtain around them. "I think, we still have a few minutes before we are wanted in the kitchen. What do you think?"

"Oh, we definitely have a few minutes," Sabine replied.

"Oh, good." Faron leaned down to kiss Sabine, one hand skimming down her side, to her pants, then between her legs.

Chapter
Twenty-Seven

Faron stood guard at the door of the large meeting room, glad Sabine's time with the guild leaders for the cloth merchants was almost over. Faron had started the afternoon meeting alert and watchful for any possible threats, but he hadn't been able to shake the lingering need for Sabine ever since they're time in the training fields before lunch. Yes, he had managed to bring Sabine to her peak twice before they absolutely had to go for lunch before Lisbeth hunted them down, but it hadn't been enough for him. It didn't help that, as the meeting wore on, it seemed like every movement Sabine made—every gesture of her hand, the way her lips moved as she spoke, how she absentmindedly played with the long braids of her hair—seemed designed to test him, tease him. It seemed like the more he got to be around Sabine, the more he got to know her, the more he craved her, and not just sexually. It was becoming a concern, but one easily pushed aside for now.

Faron glanced around the room once more before looking back at Sabine, who now looked back at him. Slowly, he let his eyes trail down her body, pausing on her lips, her breasts, then lower before making eye contact again, and slowly. By the Spirits, he needed her.

His eyes turned to the last visitor as they left the room, though Faron could recall none of the specifics about him. He'd been all too focused on Sabine. Even now, as she rose from her seat, hands smoothing over the skirt of her dress, he longed to close the distance between them. To feel her soft skin, to taste her desire for him.

Faron joined Sabine as she left the room and strolled down the corridor, his eyes scanning for possible threats, though he struggled to keep his eyes off of her.

"You are quiet," she observed as they walked.

Faron raised an eyebrow. "There was not much for me to say during your meeting, and now, I fear if I say what I wish, you will not make your next appointment."

"Oh, but now I think I should ask just to see if your prediction comes true."

Faron looked at her, meeting her green eyes with his darker ones. He possessed no qualms about what he wished to do with her, nor of sharing his desires. "I wish to remove you to somewhere secluded, strip you nude, and make you scream."

The confession brought an expression of intrigue to Sabine's face. "Then you should make haste and pick a location, lest I miss my next appointment."

Faron looked around, his mind pulling up the servant and guard schedule and the chances of them being seen. He gently grasped Sabine's arm and turned her to face him before pushing her against the nearest column. His body pressed firmly against hers, his arms resting on either side of her head. "I would take you here, where any could stumble across us as you cling to this column, my cock buried deep inside you. I would take you on your bed, your legs thrown over my shoulder as you scream my name. I would take you on your greeting chair, my head buried between your legs while those in your care watched on. Your Grace, I would have you wherever you would let me," he growled, his breath caressing her lips.

She tilted her gaze up at him, closing some of the very minimal gaps between their lips so that they barely touched. "And what is your preference?"

"With you, there is no preference, only need and a desire to please. So, tell me Sabine, where do you want me to take you?"

"Surprise me."

Faron closed the distance between them, crushing his lips to hers, his kiss demanding and needy as his mind thought over where they were and where the nearest safe room was. He forced himself away from her as quickly as he'd pressed her against the column, needing to get her to any private space.

He grabbed her hand as a thought occurred to him, and he had them nearly sprinting down a corridor to the closest meeting room. Once inside, he locked the door behind them. He approached her, an arm going around her waist, pulling her close. His free hand cupped the back of her neck, fingers playing with the loose parts of her silky hair. A low groan of desire rumbled in Sabine's throat, and her lips returned the desperate, crushing kisses. He slipped his tongue into her mouth, thrusting in and out.

A hand went into his hair and tugged at the strands in a needy, desperate way. Sabine only broke away long enough to breathe when her lungs demanded it before reeling him back in. He nipped at her lips while fondling her breast through the layers of her gown. Faron kissed down her jaw, making sure to nip and suck at the spot behind her ear he'd found the other day, as both hands went to the back of her dress, undoing the laces that kept up the top half. He followed by undoing the laces of her corset. He tossed the garment aside as the front of her dress fell down her arms. Faron took advantage of her state of dress, and he fondled her breasts, relishing the feel and weight of them in his hands.

"More," she breathed out, the words floating somewhere between command and request.

Faron obeyed, biting down hard on her shoulder before kissing the tender spot. He pinched her nipple, gently rolling the hard nub between thumb and forefinger. Then he reached down and teasingly pulled up the skirt of her dress, raising it higher and higher until he was able to reach underneath. His hand immediately sought out her warm center, fingers teasing at her folds.

She sucked in a breath, nearly jumping at the contact, and her hips moved forward a little, chasing more sweet friction from his hands. Faron kissed the livid red mark on her shoulder.

"That's it. Enjoy yourself," he whispered as he slid a couple of fingers inside of her. Her hands found his arms, as though she needed to steady herself as he slowly pumped in and out of her sweet sex. His thumb casually circled the little bud of pleasure, and he laughed softly as her grip on him tightened.

"Oh," she groaned softly. "Don't tease."

"I'm not," he promised. He soon felt her begin to tighten around his fingers. Abandoning his quest to leave her skin temporarily branded by his teeth, he kissed her hard as he drew more concentrated circles with his thumb. He wanted her to scream for him, wanted her mind occupied with nothing but thoughts of his touch.

She didn't exactly scream when her limbs started shuddering, and he made sure his fingers kept up their pace until every drop of pleasure had been wrung from her body. She still didn't relinquish her hold on Faron.

Faron smirked against her lips as he removed his hand. With little warning, he nudged her back toward the conference table until she was seated on top with her skirt around her waist. His hands trailed up her revealed thighs and back down. "I'm going to fuck you right here," he told her as the fingers of his right hand plunged back into her warm center. "I think I need to feel you shatter one more time before I enter you, though."

Sabine pressed her forehead against his shoulder as he moved his fingers. He pressed his nose against her hair for a moment, breathing in the sweet scent of her. She came quicker than before, but her soft moans had grown bolder.

Faron licked his fingers as he undid his belt and the lacing of his trousers. "You're beautiful," he whispered reverently. Freeing his hard cock, he stepped forward, a hand going to her hip, while the other helped to guide his straining erection to her entrance. He rubbed the head against her slick mound a few times before pressing forward in one long thrust. He cursed as he held still for a few seconds, enjoying the feel of her around his cock.

"So fucking beautiful," he repeated as he began to thrust rough, harsh movements which caused her to wrap her legs around him to stay put.

Sabine gasped with each movement of his hips. "Harder," she demanded.

Faron obeyed, gripping Sabine's hips in a bruising hold as his pace quickened. "Spirits, you feel so good," he growled again.

His awareness of the pressure building at the base of his spine only forced him to hold back. He needed her to come again. Needed her to, and his fingers returned to her abused clit, causing her to moan and squirm as though she couldn't decide if she wanted more or to back away from him. As she still clung to his body, he decided it must be the first.

She screamed his name, guttural and loud as she came again, her center quivering around his erection. "Careful or you might summon the guards," he teased before he lost all control of himself. Faron's climax consumed him, and he was barely aware of his rapid, uneven thrusts, which slowed until he was spent, at least, very temporarily. He leaned forward and kissed her softly as his breathing calmed.

"Are you satiated for now?" she asked him.

"No," Faron replied as he carefully separated from her. A quick cleanup with a handkerchief, and he tucked himself away. He looked her up and down, skirts still around her waist. "Would you like me to clean you up?"

"I would," Sabine replied, dark lashes lowered. He liked how much she still wanted him.

Faron nodded and went to his knees, then pulled her forward on the table before burying his face between her legs again.

"Faron," she breathed out in weak protest, though her eyes closed.

He knew he could not go as far as he wanted, which was to spend hours like this, hearing her cry out and beg him for more. Still, his tongue thoroughly explored her, swirling around her clit in slow, deliberate moves.

"I can't..." she breathed out, now leaning back on her elbows.

Faron's hands ran up and down her thighs in a soothing manner. He pulled away just longer enough to say, "You can," before diving back in.

When she came for the fourth time, Faron determined she was finally spent. He sat back on his heels, licking his lips before rising to his feet. He stepped between her legs and kissed her gently, letting her taste herself on his tongue. When the kiss broke, he smiled at her. "Let me help you dress."

Chapter Twenty-Eight

My dearest Duchesse Sabine,

What joyous news! Coralia has an heir, and we have been called upon to celebrate! I shall be traveling with my guards and members of staff in the coming weeks. I know the political atmosphere in Coralia is less than ideal, and you have so many members of your own staff who won't feel welcome. Not to worry!

Prince Grégoire has asked me to provide you with the same level of security and care you are accustomed to receiving. I shall visit in a day so we might make adequate arrangements.

Yours,
Tristian Anouilh, Comte du Ciel

Tristian arrived in the early afternoon as promised, looking as pompous and finely styled as he ever did. He brought with him his usual pared-down staff: a man to help him dress, a couple of women to help with other tasks, and a handful of guards to keep him secure on his journey between the estates.

Sabine welcomed him with all the expected grace and warmth. She had Finn escort him to his allotted rooms, and she managed to keep her displeasure at his arrival concealed until she was in the private space of her office.

A knock sounded at her office door, stronger and louder than Lisbeth's and Finn's, two of her most frequent visitors. The owner had to be Faron.

"Come in," she called out after she sat down in her chair. Her relaxed posture had her leaning back in the chair.

The door opened, and it wasn't Faron who stepped in, but Tristian, wearing his ever-tranquil smile. He closed the door firmly behind him, taking in the office with a look of benign interest.

Sabine sat up, her eyes going wide in alarm for a brief moment before turning neutral. "Is there something I can help you with, Lord Tristian?"

"Your Grace," he said with a bow before he approached her desk. "I thought it best if we start planning our trip to Coralia right away. Especially in light of how I will be supplying the personnel coming along."

"Oh," Sabine said. She rose from her desk and made to walk to the side table where a fresh pitcher of wine had been placed along with glasses. She filled both and offered one to Tristian. She remained standing, keeping a bit of distance between them as she contemplated opening the door. "I do not plan on visiting Coralia. I am sorry you were misinformed."

Tristian tilted his head in thanks as he took the wine glass. Sabine watched as he sipped his wine, deliberate and slow as though buying time. "That's inconvenient, Sabine. The prince specifically assigned you the task. Our relationship with our neighbors depends on it, as does the continued safety of our kingdom and your lands." His voice had the same dull, uninteresting tone it always did, though Sabine suspected he was more put out than he let on.

"I understand Prince Grégoire's request, but I am not inclined to go to Coralia for a number of reasons, not the least of which is their poor treatment of those who are not human." She made as though she was casually walking about the room. Her path took her closer to the door without drawing attention to her intention to at least have an escape if needed. Tristian's eyes tracked Sabine throughout the room, making her uncomfortable, though she couldn't pinpoint why.

"It's sweet of you to consider others when it comes to your political dealings. However, I will be informing Prince Grégoire of your unwillingness to work for the betterment of our kingdom because of it. I'm sad to say your actions will harm your position in court. You need someone by your side to help level out your need for whimsy when it comes to your decision-making. A firmer hand if I may. I will inform the prince of that as well."

Sabine raised an eyebrow. "You are, of course, welcome to report any news you deem necessary to his highness, but I think you will find he learns nothing from the report. I have informed him of my intentions, both in travel and in marriage."

"I do not understand why you continue to disregard the wishes of your future king. It makes no sense to me, unless you like being contrary." Tristian held his hands out. "A woman of your age and beauty should be married with a husband and children, and yet, you are content to waste your years. It makes me wonder sometimes…" He shook his head as his sentence trailed off.

Sabine considered her response, knowing she would need to be careful here. "Lord Tristian, even if I were married with children, the title and responsibilities of my position would remain with me. I have always acted with the utmost concern for my people and country, a fact the royal household knows well. One of the duties people in our position must balance is providing advice and guidance to our rulers. If you see my actions as merely contrary, I do not know what persuasion you might require. Either way, I feel secure in my actions and position. I can only hope you feel the same."

Tristian's brows furrowed in thought. "I feel you allow your personal feelings to disrupt your duties even if you think you're doing what's best. What's best, especially considering your status, is for you to carry on your line and follow the orders of your soon-to-be king when you know they would help our country. Coralia is growing in power every day, and they pose a threat to our kingdom, especially considering their alliance with Azmarin. It would not take much for them to learn of your leanings and send even more assassins to kill you, or worse."

His tone remained earnest as if he was concerned about her, but there was something in how he said it which made Sabine's skin crawl.

"A husband could protect you, take care of you, help you share the burdens you have, and children would bring you great joy and a new purpose."

Sabine fought to keep from rolling her eyes. "Perhaps you should consider a husband and children, then, since you so highly recommend them." Her tone was light and teasing, though she wanted to punch him for trying to make her smaller, less competent.

"I have. As long as they are a good fit, I would be happy with either a husband or a wife," he said, as if he missed the point. "As for children, while I am not fond of them, they have their purpose." He moved closer to Sabine. "Is that why you have yet to choose a husband? Do you prefer a wife? I'm sure, even with the preference, you could still marry a suitable man and have your women on the side." The words offered no formal proposal, but the offer was clear.

She took a step back, putting her closer to the door, revolted by Tristian more than she ever had been. "I will keep your words in mind, should I ever need them."

"I'm glad to hear it. I know one day you will recover from these flights of fancy, come to your senses, and agree to marry me. We are a perfect match." For one moment, his dull, unassuming smile turned real, almost sharp, as his eyes trailed down her body before snapping back to her face.

"Given our disagreement just now, I somehow doubt it," Sabine replied shortly. Wasn't she supposed to have a personal guard? She was going to smack Faron for being gone and subjecting her to this bizarre conversation.

"Give it time," Tristian said.

Sabine turned her head to the door as she heard approaching footsteps. "I think time is not on your side in this."

Chapter Twenty-Nine

Faron huffed out an annoyed breath as he left the stables, ignoring the shouts of three of Comte Tristian's guards as Sabine's guards drug them off to holding cells until they could be dealt with. Setting his jaw, Faron headed back toward the chateau. He wasn't looking forward to having to explain to Sabine that less than thirty minutes after the comte arrived, his drunk guards decided to terrorize her horses. He was pondering how their behavior could be used in hurrying along the comte's early departure when raised voices caught his attention.

"What do you think you're doing?" the usually soft voice of Lisbeth was heard shouting.

"We were just looking at the garden, miss. Surely there's no harm?" a slimy voice replied.

Another voice added, "But now, I think I'd like to admire the caretaker of the garden instead."

Faron picked up his pace to a near-run.

"Keep away from me or else!"

"Or else what?" said a third voice followed by a lot of curse words.

Faron sprinted around the corner on the opposite side of the garden to a space Sabine had gifted personally to Lisbeth. Here, Lisbeth grew everything from the traditional beautiful single-bloom roses, medicinal plants, herbs, and a variety of vegetables. She took great pride in her garden, so it was a shock for Faron to see these men trampling through it, pulling at, or maybe kicking the plants. He wondered if they would claim drunkenness as well.

"You will leave my garden and me alone!" Lisbeth yelled.

Faron looked over at her once again, realizing she was glowing green, vine-type plants curling slowly up her legs while the plants around her pulsed and glowed the same bright green color. She made for an intimidating figure, enough so the men might go away on their own even if she couldn't use her powers to hurt them.

Starting her way, Faron spotted movement behind Lisbeth. He couldn't shout a warning before more of Tristian's guards appeared behind Lisbeth, one grabbing her while the other drew his sword. "You're the green witch we've heard about. Our land could use your magic," the one holding her growled out.

"Let her go," Faron said firmly, his voice going deeper with his rage as he drew his long sword.

Everyone turned to look at Faron, Lisbeth letting out a visible sigh of relief.

"Fuck, he's huge," said a black-haired man who seemed to be missing some teeth.

"We can take him. He's not so big," the smaller blond man with the slimy voice said. The group of offending guards exchanged nods and took up fighting stances.

"I will repeat myself one more time." Faron spotted movement behind the two men with Lisbeth and couldn't

help but smirk. "Let her go and walk away, and I won't hurt you so badly you'd wish I'd killed you."

"No. I think we are going to leave here with the green witch, and you can't stop us," the tall, bulkier redhead standing next to Lisbeth with his sword out said.

Faron snorted and nodded to the shadow behind them. The man went down hard as Avana slammed the pommel of her dagger into his temple, moving to place her other dagger at one holding Lisbeth's throat.

"Now you'll let her go," Avana said, and the man released Lisbeth, who quickly moved behind Avana.

"Faron, watch out!" Lisbeth cried out.

Faron, who'd been so distracted watching Avana, barely braced himself in time for the slimy man to body-slam into him, taking them both to the ground. Faron felt the breath leave his lungs on impact, but he still started swinging, his large fists pounding into the man's torso.

"Help me!" the man yelled at the other two as he tried to avoid Faron's fists, failing miserably. The other two tried to jump in, but there wasn't much they could do without hurting their friend.

Pulling back his arm as much as he could, Faron slammed his fist into the man's side just under his ribs. The rogue guard seized up long enough for Faron to get a good grasp on his greasy hair and throw him off of himself. Getting to his feet as fast as possible, Faron kicked the man one more time to ensure he stayed down. He picked up his dropped sword and engaged the other two. The two were ill-prepared for a fight, and with a few quick swings, the guards were on the ground, unconscious and bleeding from several shallow cuts.

Faron turned to the women, only for Lisbeth to run into his side, wrapping her arms around him in a hug. "I had it under control, but thank you," she said with a teasing grin, though he could see the panic and terror hiding behind her eyes.

"I know you did, but five men is a lot," he joked. He looked over at Avana as she cleared her throat.

"Tristian left his room shortly after you were called to help the stable hands. He was looking for Sabine. I thought you'd want to know."

Faron bitterly cursed. Maybe the whole disruption was planned so Tristian could get near Sabine.

"I'll send guards to arrest these men. Will you escort Lisbeth somewhere safe?" he asked Avana, who nodded.

"Oh, no you don't," Lisbeth said, pulling away from Faron. "Avana can stay with me if she wants, but they ruined my garden. I have to fix it."

Faron opened his mouth to argue, realized it was pointless and he needed to get to Sabine. So, he nodded. "Make sure someone notifies their guard captain," he said before he started running for the chateau.

Chapter Thirty

The door to the office suddenly opened, and a very disgruntled and dirt-covered Faron stood there, looming in the doorway. Seeing Tristian, his eyes darkened as he straightened up. "Your Grace, I apologize for the intrusion, but you are needed in the gardens."

Sabine put her cup down on the closest surface. "Of course, Faron," she said. "Lord Tristian, if you'll excuse us."

"Of course. I will see you at mealtime, Your Grace." Tristian bowed but he kept his eyes on Faron as if the man was a problem.

Once Tristian was sufficiently out of earshot, she turned an annoyed gaze on Faron. "Where have you been?"

"I'm sorry. Shortly after the comte's arrival, I was summoned to the stables by one of the younger guards. The comte's guards were causing trouble, and they couldn't find Marcelle. I left to help without checking the door guards were in place. I wasn't informed the comte had left his room until a few minutes ago," Faron explained, looking both pissed off and apologetic.

Sabine nodded. "Is the guard situation handled, or do you need me to intervene?"

"You may need to talk with the comte about the arrest of several of his guards for harassment as well as other things. His guard captain knows already." Faron took a deep breath and looked around before letting his shoulders sag. "Something isn't right, Sabine. Several of them were drunk when they arrived. Others took twenty minutes to become inebriated enough to put their hands on Lisbeth and attempt to fight me. I wish to say the guards were serving as a distraction so he could get to you, but I have no proof, and a senior member of his guard said all the men we arrested are new to Lord Tristian's guard."

"I know," Sabine agreed, taking a deep breath to keep herself calm. Someone putting their hands on Lisbeth crossed lines, and she would use all of her power to make sure the responsible party was properly dealt with. "He's reporting me to Grégoire because I refuse to go to Coralia. He also proposed after telling me I'd be much happier as a wife and mother."

"Is he really so stupid?" Faron moved closer to Sabine, his voice lowering to a comforting, more personal level before he spoke. "Lisbeth is fine. Those men are lucky she can't use her magic to hurt people, though she made a terrible sight when I arrived. I think she's more upset about the garden. They did a good amount of damage to the plants, though she's already starting to regrow everything." He gave her a warm, comforting smile and held his arms open for Sabine.

Sabine stared at him for a couple of seconds, surprised by his silent offer despite what they had shared so far. Something like affection existed between them, she could acknowledge it. They also shared a genuine friendship, but so much of their interactions felt more physical than anything else. She stepped forward all the same and let herself fit into his arms.

Faron held her close, but never did it feel like he was caging her in. "Sorry about the dirt. Hope it doesn't ruin your dress," Faron said softly, resting his cheek on the top of her head. "I'm sorry I wasn't here."

"You were dealing with something more pressing from the sounds of it," Sabine pointed out. "And it's just a dress." Her arms went around Faron, holding him loosely against her, and feeling more at peace than she had since the arrival of Tristian's letter announcing his current visit.

"Nothing is more important than your safety," he replied. "I'll have things better prepared for the comte next time he visits. This shouldn't have happened. You should have never been in a situation where you were alone with him."

"You had other things to deal with," she reminded Faron. "And I'll have to see the damage caused. Then I will approach Tristian about what his people did. I'll have grounds to throw him out of my estate, no doubt." She'd just have to figure out the most appropriate way of doing so.

"We should head outside so you can see what was damaged before Lisbeth can grow it all back."

"Of course," Sabine said, reluctantly letting her loose hold on Faron drop.

Faron didn't release Sabine. Instead, he unwrapped an arm from around her, gently grasped her chin, and lifted her head slightly higher to kiss her. "I'll be right by your side next time," he promised.

"I know," she replied then reached up to pull him back into another kiss. When it broke, she stayed close for just a few lingering seconds. "Let's go to the garden so I can see everything for myself." If she intended to officially address the crimes committed against her people and estate, she needed to witness how bad the damage was.

Faron nodded and pulled away, opening the door for her to step through.

They arrived at the destroyed garden a few minutes later. Sabine walked around, silently taking in a section of crushed wildflowers. Divots in the dirt told her they'd been stomped through with heavy boots by drunken fools. A few feet beyond, a series of prickly bushes known for sprouting gorgeous blooms in the spring drooped with broken branches and wilted greenery.

Sabine took it all in with a grim expression, her lips pressed together in irritation. She looked to Lisbeth, who knelt on the ground, tending to a bush of purple plumage. "Are you well?"

Lisbeth looked away for a moment before making eye contact with Sabine. "I'm alright. Slightly shaken up, but alright."

"Is there anything I can do for you or get you before I go address the heinous acts committed against you?" Sabine asked, her tone much calmer and warm than her angered expression implied possible.

"No, but thank you. Having Avana here has helped make me feel safe, and I know you'll take care of the men who did all this," Lisbeth said, her smile less bright than normal.

"Trust I shall," Sabine promised. "Faron and I are going back inside so I can speak with Comte Tristian. I will return when it is done."

"I'll be here, fixing things," Lisbeth replied. No matter how bright Lisbeth appeared, Sabine sensed fear and irritation. She couldn't blame Lisbeth.

"I'll stick around just in case," Avana piped up.

Sabine nodded in acknowledgment, and she and Faron walked back to the chateau. She needed to deal with Tristian.

Chapter Thirty-One

Faron followed just behind Sabine as she stalked from the almost repaired garden back to the chateau. The fire in her eyes, the controlled rage he saw in them, it did things to him that, had they not needed to deal with the comte right away, would have had him dragging Sabine to an empty room and worshiping her. Sabine did have to handle the comte however, which only served to delay Faron's plans.

Once inside, Sabine sent Finn to fetch the comte. Even in all of her anger, both duchesse and steward agreed she was better served in making the comte come to her. She chose the receiving hall where she took petition a few times a month. She took a seat on the raised chair, the position providing a physical demonstration of their different ranks, while she waited for Finn and the comte to return.

Faron took up the spot just behind Sabine, one hand resting on the chair, the other on his sword. "Are you alright?" he asked Sabine.

"I'm furious," she responded.

Faron moved the hand from the chair to Sabine's shoulder and gave it a supportive, soft squeeze, doing what he could to not think about the amount of affection passed between them today. The hug, the comfort, and now the supportive, not-so-casual touches. Yes, they were having sex on a fairly consistent basis, but today had highlighted how often they were crossing several lines Faron wasn't sure they should be crossing. "Lisbeth is alright," he assured her.

She reached up briefly enough to place a hand on top of his, squeezing it and letting her hand return to the armrest. "She is," Sabine agreed. "But she might not have been, and there are still damages."

"She could have been, yes. I'm going to guess you've never witnessed so much deliberate disrespect on your own property before?" Faron asked, certain he knew the answer already.

She glanced up at Faron. "No. I am second only to the ruling family. No one would have dared before now."

Faron didn't verbally respond, though he placed his hand back on the chair as he listened to approaching footsteps. "He's here," Faron informed Sabine, giving her a moment before Finn opened the doors.

"Your Grace," Finn announced as he and Tristian entered. "The Comte du Ciel." Finn stepped aside, taking up a space near Sabine's chair, though on the opposite side of Faron.

"Lord Tristian," Sabine greeted. "I had you called to notify you of the arrest of five of your guards on the grounds of assault and vandalism."

"I was notified by my guard captain just before your man arrived." Tristian bowed low, and Faron wanted nothing more than to sneer at him. "I apologize for the behavior of my men. There is no excuse for their actions. I will see them suitably punished." The comte's voice wasn't the normal bland, monotone voice but something harsher.

"I should hope so," Sabine said. "And in addition to whatever punishment you give, official charges are being filed. Destroying my gardens and assaulting my staff are unforgivable acts. I cannot imagine how you came into possession of such poorly behaved guards."

Tristian straightened from his bow, and while his expression remained dull and unassuming, something about the gleam in his eye read dangerous. "Your Grace, they were new hires put in place by my guard commander and approved by the captain. I hadn't had a chance to meet them before the trip, but they seemed cordial and well-behaved."

"Be that as it may, your people as they currently stand pose a threat to me, my staff, and my estate. You will need to leave."

The comte's eyes widened then narrowed at Sabine's declaration. "Your Grace, Sabine. I am more than happy to punish those responsible, even to punish them with death should you request it, but asking me to leave? When I've just arrived? Why punish me and the innocent guards? We've only just arrived, after all."

"We shall ignore your decision to come without invitation and focus entirely on your guard's actions." Sabine held up a finger. "You made a poor decision to bring untested guards to my estate." She held up a second finger. "Those guards arrived and got drunk on wine from my cellar." She held up a third finger. "Those guards assaulted a woman in my care." Her hand went back to the armrest. "You cannot guarantee better behavior from your guards, and I cannot provide comfort to my staff members beyond time. I think it best for everyone to bring our visit to an end."

The comte's jaw set, and his shoulders squared before he went back into a more relaxed posture, almost bored. "To address your first point, my dear, I was told to come by our prince, who informed me we were to travel to Coralia together. A request I am now aware you have decided to ignore for your … reasons." Tristian brushed imaginary dust from his tunic.

Faron wanted nothing more than to punch him in the face.

"As for the rest, I am more than happy to send my guards away if it makes your people feel better, but I would like to stay and help in whatever ways I can to make up for what my guards have done."

Faron noted how the comte's eyes flicked to him, and he swore disgust flashed in them. He also noted how Tristian hadn't once touched on Sabine's biggest issues: his men had thought nothing of assaulting a woman.

"How can I make it up to you if you force me to leave?" Tristian asked, his voice almost, but not quite, a pout.

"You can take your leave and trust I will notify you of a period more suited to future visits," replied Sabine.

Tristian opened his mouth to argue more, but his eyes flicked once more to Faron, who made sure to flex the hand resting on his sword hilt. Thankfully the comte took it for the warning it was and instead bowed to Sabine. "Of course, Your Grace." He rose and turned to go, only to look back at Sabine, his normally spiritless smile just a bit sharper than normal. "I am sorry for everything, and you can rest assured I will inform the prince of … everything."

"I genuinely hope you do," Sabine replied curtly. "I look forward to his response."

"Oh, I very much doubt you do, but Mother willing, one can hope." Tristian left the room, the door closing with a firm thud.

"I do not like him," Faron hissed.

"Nor do I," Finn said as he stepped forward. "I will make sure they are packed up and gone within the hour, Your Grace."

"Thank you, Finn," Sabine replied. "And when you are done, please check in on the rest of the household. We need to verify no one else was harassed."

"Of course," Finn replied. He, too, soon exited, leaving Sabine and Faron alone.

Faron shook his head. "There is something not right with the comte, but I can't put my finger on it. Do you think he was dropped on his head as a child?"

"I think he's not as stupid as he lets on," Sabine replied. She rose to her feet, her irritation still present.

"Nor as dull," Faron said as he moved to Sabine's side, offering her his arm, and he felt a frisson of pleasure as she accepted it. They began walking to the exit.

"No. I think he's much more cunning than he wishes us to think. Or, at least, he's being led to think so."

"I dislike how he keeps trying to threaten you with the prince," Faron growled low.

"Let him," Sabine replied. "Eventually, there would be an official split between myself and Prince Grégoire. I think Tristian is acting on his orders. Let them deal the first strike."

"The first strike could arguably have been Avana," Faron mused unhappily. He was grateful to Avana for being there for Lisbeth and him, but he still didn't fully trust her yet. "I worry what the next might be."

"I should offer Avana a permanent home here if she wants it," Sabine said.

Faron let out a deep sigh. He'd known she'd make the offer at some point. Sabine liked to pick up strays it seemed, and Avana was a good addition to the household. "Yes, you should. I think she'd like it here. If only because of the gardens and the chocolate."

"The gardens and the chocolate are half the reason I like it here," she replied, her eyes glancing up at him with mischief.

Faron laughed. "Then we shall have to find a way to ensure you get more of each."

"I think so," Sabine agreed with a chuckle. "First though, let's go check on Lisbeth again."

Faron nodded and they headed back to the gardens where Lisbeth was still regrowing plants to her satisfaction while Avana watched on. Much of the greenery had been restored, although they would still need to clean up the destroyed plants and try to revive those places which could be restored.

"You've made a great deal of progress," Sabine observed.

"Thankfully they didn't do too much damage," Lisbeth said cheerfully, causing Faron to snort.

"Don't lie."

"Okay, fine, but it's not like I can't fix it," she sing-songed. Her arms outstretched in front of her, moving as if to their own music, as a bright forest green light flowed from her fingers into the ground, lighting up the areas she was healing and regrowing.

"Repairing the damage doesn't mean the damage didn't happen," Sabine pointed out. "I think Meri and Avana would agree."

"Avana can agree all she likes, but I've bribed six people to not let Meri know what happened. At least, not yet," Lisbeth said with a blush.

Faron groaned.

"Two she threatened then bribed," Avana added.

"Meri deserves to know," Sabine said, her brows raised. "And she'd probably want to hear it from Lisbeth since she's not been notified already."

"That's why I bribed the others. Imagine how badly she'd react if someone popped into the kitchen and announced 'Meri! Your wife was assaulted.'" Lisbeth made a face as she started talking to herself, saying things like "never allowed to leave my room again, escorted everywhere." Faron wanted to laugh as she continued in a low voice to mimic Meri's, but it really wasn't funny. Meri would be worried and upset, and they all knew it.

Sabine must have agreed with Faron because she ignored Lisbeth's mocking chatter and took a breath. "Avana, I have a question for you."

"Yes?" Avana asked tentatively.

"Would you like to live here at the chateau permanently?" Sabine asked.

Avana took a step back, catching Faron's full attention. He noted Lisbeth had stopped her rambling to listen. "You want me to live here? Why? I tried to kill you!"

"I do," Sabine confirmed. "And you did. You've also helped Faron with training, and you helped protect Lisbeth today. It's my belief you acted as you did the night you arrived because you had little choice."

Despite the strong urge to do so, Faron didn't move his hand to his sword as he watched Avana stare at Sabine. He could see the fight-or-flight instinct fighting behind Avana's eyes as she tried to accept Sabine's genuine offer.

After a few tense minutes, Avana nodded. "Yeah, okay. I'll stay."

"I'm glad to hear it," Sabine replied simply.

Avana nodded then just sat down.

Faron moved to reach out to her, but he realized Avana was okay, just overwhelmed. Faron decided to stay put.

Lisbeth went back to her work on the plants. "Want to raid the kitchens with me when I'm done?" she asked, not looking at Avana but making it clear the invitation was for the petite elf. She seemed even less surprised when there was no answer. Avana just continued to sit there, staring at her hands.

"I shall leave you to your work," Sabine said as though she had not offered Avana something life-changing. "I need to make sure my home is vacated by those who are unwelcome."

"If you need any help blocking the main entrance, I'm happy to grow vines thick enough they can't get back in," Lisbeth offered.

Faron could picture the comte and his men trying to get back through the main gates with flimsy excuses as to why they couldn't possibly leave yet, only to be stopped by vines.

"I shall let you know," Sabine promised with a smile.

"Thank you," Lisbeth said as she went back to her nearly completed work.

As they turned to go, Faron could hear Lisbeth telling Avana about the new confection Meri was experimenting with.

"I think you broke the assassin," Faron said in a low voice to Sabine.

"I saw," Sabine replied as they started walking away. "I thought it best to let her be with her emotions."

"It is. For all we know, her learned response to high stress is to start stabbing things." Faron only half joked. "How are you feeling?"

"The same as before."

"Not even slightly better?" Faron asked, concerned.

"Not really. I'm happy Lisbeth is fine and can repair her garden with not much effort. I'm happy Avana is staying. The rest of it, though..." Sabine shook her head. "It's more than frustrating."

"With any luck, today's events can be used to keep the comte away for some time," Faron said, hoping his optimism might make Sabine smile at least a little bit.

"It's bought us time," Sabine replied. "Which means you need to make sure we are ready for the eventuality of return, and I need to write to Prince Louis."

"There are a few people I met in the village the other day I want to talk to. They look like they might be a good fit for the guard. I had planned to discuss it with you tomorrow." Faron shrugged.

"Then we shall talk about the needs of the estate tomorrow," Sabine suggested. "For now, I need to consult with Finn to make sure the place is free of the unwanted, and after, I plan on relaxing."

Faron nodded, and while he knew he shouldn't, he found himself saying, "Is there anything I can do to aid you in relaxing?"

The corners of Sabine's delectable mouth turned up. "You could try, though I don't know how much fun I might be this afternoon and evening."

Faron nodded. "I will still do my best to help you relax in any way I can," he replied without hesitation.

"Then come along and help me see to things. We'll see what we can get into afterward."

Faron nodded, his heart lighter at Sabine's words. He pushed down another part of him asking what in the Spirit's name he was doing.

Chapter Thirty-One

Dearest Sabine,

I felt the need to write and apologize once more for the behavior of my men and of my own reaction to your very reasonable response to their misdeeds. As a woman living alone in such a large chateau, I can see why you would be angry and fearful about what occurred. Rest assured, I have severely punished the men who touched your lady. I hope the news allows the two of you to sleep better at night. I am aware you do have your own men, and women, protecting you and your lands, but it would make me feel infinitely better if you would allow me to send some of my own, as an apology and peace of mind.

Your faithful servant,
Tristian

Chapter
Thirty-Two

Faron had been on edge since the comte and his guards left the chateau. Telling Tristian and his guards to leave had been the right thing to do, as had Sabine's refusal to answer the sad excuse for an apology letter. She had to set boundaries, and she had to protect the people who relied upon her. Still, Faron worried about what would happen when the comte retaliated, and if not the comte, then the prince.

The lack of communication from Prince Grégoire also worried Faron. He'd never heard of a royal who would just accept a declaration to disobey as Sabine had given, and he still believed all of the small events, like Avana's appearance, the order to go to Coralia, and the sudden appearance of Tristian, were all somehow connected.

So far, each passing day had proven calm and uneventful, but his tension and stress levels had only risen. Faron found himself seeking out Sabine during his free hours and ravishing her until they both felt at least marginally better. However, their increasing personal interactions led to several small complications. Sabine was falling behind on the work which hounded her day and night, adding to her stress levels. In addition, the staff—minus Lisbeth, Meri, Finn, and Avana—had started talking about them as if they were a couple or would soon be.

It was a ridiculous idea considering Sabine's place in the world compared to his own. No, a true relationship between the two of them was a dream neither could entertain. For now, they would enjoy the time they had until Sabine found a suitable husband with a lifespan matching her human one.

Arriving at Sabine's bedroom, Faron took up his place beside it as he waited for her to emerge.

When Sabine emerged, barely a sign of her stress existed. Her light caramel hair sat perfectly arranged. Her smooth skin and vibrant green eyes appeared flawless and warm. Her pink lips... Faron's eyes rose to meet her own.

"Good morning," she greeted.

"Good morning," Faron replied, fighting to keep his voice level and his urge to press Sabine against the door and ravage her lips at bay. He knew he couldn't give in to his desires. Not today. Though, doing so would be so easy. He could just open the door and spend the next few hours taking her apart. Sabine wouldn't complain, but Faron couldn't, not today.

"You're out here early," she observed, looking up at him.

Again, Faron's eyes traveled down, this time, as far as her throat before raising his gaze again. "I woke up early," was the simple answer. The more difficult answer included his Sabine-filled dreaming. Faron didn't remember every dream, but one in particular had started very pleasantly. Then suddenly, it changed.

"I've not been sleeping well, either," she shared.

"Maybe tonight we can try and wear each other out," Faron heard himself say before he could stop himself.

Sabine gave a knowing smile. "Haven't we already been doing as much?"

"Yes, but I'm sure we could do more. I could just not stop. You could sleep then, I'm sure." Faron swore if he didn't stop, he was going to cut his tongue out.

"I doubt I'm quite so adventurous, no matter how much fun we've been having."

"Oh, I believe you are," Faron said, leaning much too close to Sabine. "I would say we test your limits now, but I know you have more important matters to attend to.'

Sabine looked up at him, closing some of the scant space already existing between them. "I do have things I cannot put off, but we always have later."

Faron couldn't help himself as he wrapped an arm around Sabine and pulled her closer to kiss her deeply. Sabine's arms wrapped around him, pulling herself closer against his body, doing nothing to encourage more appropriate boundaries or behavior.

Faron let the kiss go on for far longer than he should have before pulling away, but he didn't let Sabine go. "We should get going, or you're going to be late."

"You're right," Sabine said, her breathing a little heavier than normal. "The Weavers' Guild won't like being put off."

"No, and they do need your attention," Faron said. He mentally kicked himself for leaning down to kiss Sabine again. When this kiss broke, both were left breathless, and Faron's need was firmly pressed against Sabine.

"I'm going to need you to step back, or I am going to miss my meeting," Sabine said, though she stubbornly kept her firm hold on him.

Faron took a deep breath, unable to help the low growl rumbling in his throat. He reminded himself of his resolve and forced himself to step back, though he knew Sabine

could see how much of a struggle it was. "Let's be on our way," Faron said, his voice laced with want.

Sabine didn't speak, but she nodded as her hands dropped from around him. She smoothed her skirt, her hands clearly needing something to do. She began walking, leading him to the meeting room she used to speak with larger groups.

Faron followed behind, his eyes moving across the hall. As they walked, his ears picked up two of the chateau's maids gossiping once more about how handsome a couple he and Sabine made. Snorting, Faron mentally shook his head. The delusions some people had.

When they entered the meeting hall, a bright golden yellow room accented with beautifully colored tile floors and rich furnishing, a group of people ranging in age awaited them. The oldest, a tall woman with long silvery hair and a rich tan, approached Sabine. The two women clasped hands like old friends.

"It is good to see you, Your Grace. It's been far too long."

"Indeed, it has, Elodie," Sabine agreed with a genuinely pleased smile.

Elodie's eyes traveled to Faron, and she took her time letting her gaze travel along his considerable height. "And who is your friend?"

"This is Faron," Sabine replied. "He is my personal guard."

"Handsome, isn't he?" Elodie said, turning attention back to Sabine.

"I think so," Sabine confirmed with a smile. She motioned to the meeting table strewn with refreshments. "Shall we begin?"

Once Sabine and the guild members were seated, Faron moved to stand behind Sabine, closer to the wall so he had a good view of the room, fighting off a blush from the older woman's compliments. Or, perhaps, the public acknowledgment from Sabine had him feeling happy in a way he didn't want to acknowledge. Even as discussions began and guild members and Sabine exchanged concerns and ideas, Faron's mind could not abandon the compliment or the way her lips had felt against his only an hour or so before.

Finally, though, he was able to push both from his mind and focus on what the guild members and Sabine were discussing. It wasn't the most interesting of topics, but he could tell from the way Sabine responded to each member that she truly enjoyed her work with them.

"The weavers from L'Orilan have sent word of unhappiness in the capitol," Elodie said after the final signatures on some ledgers had been exchanged. "The uncertainty of the throne has trade partners worried."

"Many are worried about the uncertainty," Sabine confirmed with a nod. "The princes must work out how they are going forward. The rest of us must maintain patience."

Spirits, he hated politics. Faron wanted to ask why they just couldn't move to put the younger prince on the throne. Sabine backed him, and she wasn't silent in her support. Was she the only one questioning Grégoire's claim? He'd be surprised if so. He assumed the politics were too tangled for them to act forcibly without cause, but given what he knew and how Sabine had been treated, Faron craved action.

"Then we shall be patient for now," Elodie agreed. "If you grow tired of patience, let us know, Your Grace. You have the support of the weavers and many others."

Sabine smiled, and her gaze briefly fell to the table before rising again. "Thank you," she said. "Now, as we have finished our business, can I invite you to have some food and drink before you depart?"

"No, I think we've taken up enough of your time and hospitality," Elodie decided. The guild members rose from their seats, as did Sabine, and a prolonged series of heartfelt goodbyes were exchanged between each member and the duchesse.

Faron waited until everyone was gone before he approached Sabine. "It sounds to me like you have a lot of support for putting the younger prince on the throne."

"I do, and I'm going to," Sabine said simply. "I did mention patience, after all. Grégoire has to strike first. Substantially strike."

Faron thought over the vague plan, his head tilted to the side as he took in Sabine. "Why are you not sitting on the throne?"

Sabine scowled and shook her head. "It is not a position I want to have."

"You'd be a great queen."

"I would," she agreed. "And I'd hate every second of it."

"Then it's something you shouldn't do, unless as a last resort, maybe," Faron joked.

"Depending on how things go, I may have to intervene," Sabine said seriously. "Let's hope for other outcomes."

Faron nodded and looked Sabine over once more, taking in the tightness of her shoulders and the crease between her brows. "You don't have another meeting for several hours, right?" he asked as he reviewed her schedule for the day.

"I don't," she agreed with a nod. "My meeting later may not even happen depending on how late they end up working."

Faron gave Sabine a nod of acknowledgment. Though the first thing he wanted to ask was if she wanted to retire to her rooms with him, he instead managed to ask, "Would you like to go down to the beach? I can grab food from the kitchen."

"I would like that," Sabine agreed with a surprised but genuine smile.

Faron couldn't help but smile back. His suggestion clearly excited her, and Faron's mind now yearned to find more ways to please her. "Well then, I'll go gather some picnic supplies and food. Why don't you change into something more comfortable?" he offered.

"Okay. Shall I meet you in the entryway in a while?"

"Perfect," Faron said, though when she turned to walk to her rooms, he grabbed her by hand and pulled her into a kiss before finally letting her retreat.

Chapter Thirty-Three

Long, caramel locks floated on the wind then fell loosely against Sabine's shoulders as the breeze passed. She'd always loved the beach. Ever since she'd been a little girl, Sabine had loved to spend her free time on the shores just below Vassetre Chateau. Since the age of sixteen, her ability to spend her time down here had diminished day by day. If she were lucky, she could rise some very early mornings to come down for a swim or to sit and watch the sun slowly rise over the gray-blue waters.

Sabine couldn't recall the last time she'd been down here so late in the day, able to experience the earlier afternoon sun as the water retreated further from shore. Low tide left the beach more rocky, and little air pockets between smooth stones bubbled up, telling of crabs and other sea creatures hiding just below.

She glanced over at Faron, smiling gently to herself as she took him in. She couldn't quite explain it, but somehow, Sabine found herself in love with the man. She wasn't even sure when it happened. Sometime after she nearly fired him, of course. But to be honest, she couldn't even say that it had been after they first started sleeping together. Sabine was aware of the very short period in which she'd known Faron and the even shorter period in which they'd become intimate. Perhaps it didn't matter.

Confessing her feelings out loud wasn't possible, at least, not right now. He might not share her feelings, no matter what Lisbeth and Meri thought. The uncertainty was enough of a reason to stay silent, but Sabine feared what might be coming for her. Grégoire grew more frustrated and desperate each day, and desperate people struck out at whatever opportunity they had. She'd rather Faron not be viewed as an opportunity.

So, for now, Sabine leaned back on one arm, enjoying the sound of the waves and the company of her personal guard.

"This place is beautiful," Faron said as he watched the water, a soft, contented look on his face.

"It is," Sabine replied, still watching him. "It is one of the things I love best about my home."

"I can understand why, though I enjoy the general peacefulness of it all, usually, the best."

She nodded. She watched his appreciation for the chateau play across his features numerous times now. "There is much to enjoy here."

"There is. I'm happy to have ended up here," he replied. "I know I've said it before, but I like it here much more than I ever liked Coralia."

"Other than the obvious reason, why?" Sabine asked. Of course, Faron's reason for leaving Coralia would have been enough.

Faron was silent long enough that Sabine thought he wasn't going to answer before he started talking.

"Others I know will disagree with me, but I have never found Coralia, my town especially, to be a good or welcoming place to those considered other. Were things better under King Zephraim the Wise? Yes, but I wouldn't say they were good, especially for city elves. Those of us unlucky enough not to live in one of the elven villages…" Faron looked down at his hands.

"I lost my father to a group of men who decided the city elves were at fault for something they had no hand in. My father stepped in to stop them from harming a group of younger elves. They beat him to death for it, and no one stopped them. The issues Coralia faces today have been there for a long while. They just now have more focus."

Sabine felt sorrow and horror creep up her neck. Faron's story wasn't uncommon or even the worst case she'd heard about. She understood why it struck her. Tragedy always seemed worse when it happened to someone you knew well.

She reached over and put a hand on top of Faron's. "Tell me about your father."

Faron turned over his hand, letting their fingers lace together. "He was a good man, very calm, and he loathed violence. He was a firm believer in talking anything out. He never cared much for my love of swords, but he never discouraged me either."

Faron paused. "He loved my mother with every part of himself. We never had much when he was alive, but he still found ways to bring home the books she loved and small trinkets to make her smile. It broke her when he died."

"I can imagine it would," Sabine said quietly. "It sounds like they were desperately in love."

"They were. I think she was relieved when she got sick," Faron admitted.

She leaned against him, head resting on his shoulder. "Do you look more like your mother or father?"

"My father, though no one knows where the height came from. They were both slightly shorter than the average elf."

"Are you tall?" she teased gently, though by this point, her little joke was recurring. His height could not be missed, but knowing him as long as she had, she'd ceased to notice it as the first and most important thing.

"I don't think so, but for some reason, it keeps coming up," he returned playfully.

"Wonder why," she returned with a gentle laugh.

"No idea." Faron wrapped an arm around Sabine.

They sat together, quietly taking in the crash of waves and the breeze. Sabine closed her eyes, letting herself just exist in the moment with Faron, no matter how brief it might be. He felt warm against her, and even though she knew nothing would come of the spark between them, her treacherous mind kept pondering how perfectly she fit with his arm around her.

"What happened? To your parents? Your uncle? I keep hearing there was an attack, but no one wants to talk about who attacked," Faron asked tentatively.

Sabine took a breath, thinking back to the night she'd lost so much. The memories no longer pained her as a fresh wound might, but she could not deny missing her parents, her family. Even with the chosen family she'd gathered for herself, the loss of her parents and uncle left a permanent hole in her life, and she often wondered how well she lived up to their memory.

"My father was quite powerful and outspoken, as one might expect of the Duc de Vassetre. He was not well-liked by certain people, including friends of the deceased king. Their dislike culminated in his murder while conducting official business for the king. That same night, he sent soldiers to our doors and attacked. Despite Meri's considerable efforts, they forced their way in. They encountered my uncle, the last of the known shifters in Fythias. He was outnumbered, and they left him for dead. My mother they dispatched more quickly. My uncle, while bleeding out, found her lifeless body just outside of my rooms."

"By the Spirits. I'm sorry, Sabine."

She nodded in acknowledgment. "I was in my uncle's room, hidden away by some of Meri's guards. Uncle Alain liked to collect things, so navigating around his belongings would be difficult. Buy time." She'd been hidden inside his large wardrobe, concealed by the clothes inside and numerous boxes, trunks, and trinkets outside.

"I saw none of the violence that night, though the door to the room I hid in opened and closed numerous times. I remember sitting there, hands over my mouth as though it would muffle my breathing. I suppose now, given the screaming and crashes from those outside would have muffled it, it was silly to do. Even after the chateau went silent, I did not emerge."

She opened her eyes to look out at the water again. "Several hours later, Marcelle found me. He'd been at the chateau for less than a month."

Faron let out a harsh breath and kissed the top of her head. "That had to have been horrifying. I'm glad you were safe."

"It was horrifying," Sabine confirmed. "I was basically a child, and not only had I lost my parents and uncle, but Meri was severely injured and I was expected to assume the role of duchesse in the middle of the chaos."

Faron shook his head. "Looking at everything, you did an amazing job. Did they at least give you a moment to mourn?"

"Not in the way people envision in times of grief," Sabine admitted. "Naturally, I grieved, but there was no time to sit with it the way I wanted at the time. I'm still not sure if that's a good thing or not."

"I think it depends on the person. Some people need time to sit and reflect on what they've lost. Others need to keep busy, to do things to process, to function and not break down completely."

"Well, we are talking about me in this case," Sabine pointed out. "But in general, you are not wrong."

"If you needed the time to sit and be with your grief, then they should have given it to you, no matter what else was going on," Faron said, acknowledging her point.

"What did you need when you lost your parents?"

"I don't know what I needed, what I did was pick up a sword and get to work," Faron said as he thought it over. "Might have been for the best."

"Why?"

"My mother had time to sit with her grief, and she never truly moved past it. I worry I wouldn't have either had someone not needed to ensure money was still coming in. It took her a year to realize I'd gotten a job. She was furious, but there was nothing she could do about it."

She nodded, and again, they sat in companionable silence for a long time. She never felt the need to chatter away with him, to keep noise and action present. Sitting with Faron, her head on his shoulder, felt natural to Sabine. She felt Faron give a contented sigh as he relaxed even more, the normal everyday tension seeming to leave him.

After some time, she became aware she'd missed her appointment, but Sabine couldn't be bothered by the slight she'd made. "You are a bad influence," she playfully accused.

"You think so?" Faron asked with a soft smile.

"Oh, I know you are," Sabine confirmed. "Though, I am not complaining."

Faron laughed. "I am sorry you missed your meeting, but at the same time, this has been nice."

"It has," Sabine easily agreed. "And not just because meetings are the bane of my existence."

"You seem to enjoy some of them."

"Some of them I do," Sabine said. "Many of them are just me listening to other people talk so they feel seen and heard."

"I've noticed that with the Jewelers' Guild. It seems they talk to hear themselves talk."

"They do," Sabine confirmed. "They are probably the worst of the offenders."

"I've noticed the others either welcome your suggestions or at least do a better job of pretending to."

"Honestly, it's all very much like children rushing to tattle on a sibling to a parent."

"If I just start throwing them out of the chateau, do you think it will help?" Faron asked as he pressed his nose against her hair.

Sabine sighed contentedly. "I think I'd spend some time apologizing on your behalf," she replied.

"Not if I don't let them back in the chateau until they promise to behave. Meri and Avana would help."

"Probably," Sabine agreed. "But why antagonize people when you can spend your time on more pleasurable pursuits?"

Sabine felt Faron smile against her hair. "Who says annoying people who upset you isn't a pleasurable pursuit of mine?"

"Fair, but when they come to me for apologies, how does it bring me any pleasure?"

"Again. You assume I'll let them near you until they're ready to grovel at your feet for forgiveness. I think you'd enjoy that."

She felt his fingers begin to run up and down her arm from the hand he had wrapped around her. "I might like to see you grovel at my feet," she quipped.

"I think I'd like it, too," Faron shot back, his voice betraying how much he enjoyed the thought.

"Perhaps, one day, we might share the experience."

"Perhaps," Faron replied before his other hand grasped her chin, turning her head toward him and up so he could kiss Sabine.

As they kissed, Sabine felt as though she might melt against him. Every part of her yearned to be closer, to have more, and not just physically. She briefly pondered the idea of bringing up her feelings, of discussing them, but those thoughts were pushed aside as the feel of his mouth on hers overwhelmed her thoughts.

Faron kept one hand on her hip, the other wrapping around Sabine's waist to pull her closer. Sabine could feel his desire for her, something that never failed to excite her. She could not deny wanting him just as much, though admittedly, the beach was not the right place to explore their mutual need. "We should go inside," she said between needy kisses.

"We should. Sand gets in the worst places, after all," he replied, though he made no move to get up, instead pressing her down more firmly against him.

Sabine took in a sharp breath, the feel of his need pressing close against her made her want so many, many things. "You want me," she observed, her voice teasing and a little lustful.

"Whatever gave you that idea?" Faron joked before adjusting his hold on Sabine and standing in one fluid motion.

Sabine laughed as she was lifted. She'd learned to enjoy being in his arms like this, as though she were something he valued. "I couldn't imagine."

"Let's keep it that way." Faron looked at her, the way she sat in his arms, and his expression grew contemplative.

She knew what he must be thinking. Her ears had not been kept from hearing the rumors, nor her eyes from seeing the glances they received from the staff. "What are you waiting for?" she encouraged.

She watched Faron mentally shrug off the indecision before he strode off toward the chateau. "Your permission," he said, only half joking as they went.

Chapter Thirty-Four

Faron got them to Sabine's room in a few short minutes. Almost no one spotted them, as Faron had used his considerable knowledge of the chateau to avoid the watchful eyes of servants and guards. He wasn't embarrassed by their relationship, but he didn't want the already frenzied rumors to spread further and hurt Sabine's chances for a good match with another noble. Eventually, that day would come, even if Faron intended to enjoy every moment with her until then.

It took a bit of skill to get the door open without adjusting Sabine, who had taken it upon herself to distract him with nips and kisses along his neck as they went. Once they were inside, he wasted no time kicking the door shut and striding to the bed.

Faron considered tossing her on the bed, but Sabine read the mischief on his face and smacked his arm. With a laugh, he gently sat her down and took a step back, starting to unbutton his shirt as he watched Sabine.

Sabine took a seat on the edge of her bed, her bright green eyes watching him intently. She shook her head, extended a hand, and pointed toward the ground. "Knees."

Faron raised an eyebrow but asked no questions as he gently lowered himself to his knees as ordered.

She smiled in response, her gaze slowly traveling the length of him. Her hand turned up, and Sabine crooked her finger forward.

Faron kept the corners of his mouth from twitching upward in a half smile as he dropped to his hands and crawled to Sabine, well-defined muscles shifting as he crossed the short distance between them.

When he was within a foot of her, she held her palm out, bringing him to a stop, their locked gazes never breaking. "Tell me what you want," she prompted.

"You," he replied.

"How?"

"Any way you're willing to let me."

"How badly?"

Faron's eyes darkened. "Allow me to please you, Your Grace," Faron requested without prompting.

Sabine leaned forward infinitesimally. "Ask properly."

"May I be allowed to pleasure you, Your Grace? Please," he growled out the last word.

"Yes," she replied. "You may."

Faron's grin went sharp as he finished crawling to Sabine. Upon reaching her, he sat back on his heels and gently placed his hands upon her ankles. He slid them up her calves and to her knees, her dress rising with them. Leaning down, he placed kisses upon her pale, smooth skin as his mouth followed the path of his hands, higher and higher.

Her eyes remained fixed on Faron as he slowly kissed and caressed her skin. As he reached her thighs, her lips parted and her fingers curled into the bedding beneath her. Gently pushing her legs apart, Faron's hands continued upward, pushing her skirts up to Sabine's hips. He used both hands to pull her forward so she sat just on the edge of the bed, granting him easier access to her.

He kissed her knee then her upper thigh. He stopped before he reached her center. Making eye contact, Faron said, "May I please?"

"You may," Sabine consented.

Faron kissed above her clit once before flicking Sabine's clit with his tongue, slowly at first, then picking up speed. Their eye contact remained, and Faron drank in the first signs of pleasure forming on Sabine's face.

A sound of pleasure left her mouth, and her breathing grew quicker the longer he worked. One of her hands abandoned the bedding and found his hair.

Faron made a noise of approval, letting Sabine know he enjoyed her touching his hair. Those long fingers tugging at his curls as he tasted her had kept him up many evenings over the last weeks. He continued licking her clit, finally drawing it into his mouth, causing her to cry out. A beautiful sound.

He could feel the muscles in her legs flex as he continued, as though in preparation for her to fall over the edge. Faron moved a hand up from her hips to her clothed breast as he continued to pleasure Sabine with his mouth. She was soon shaking with pleasure, his name escaping her delightful lips.

Faron abandoned the overly stimulated bud for now, but he continued running his tongue up and down in long, firm strokes.

Breathless, Sabine's hands left his hair, settling on the bed beside her. "Stand," she directed.

Faron did not want to stop, but Sabine had given a command, and so he stood. He couldn't disobey if he wanted to.

"Undress," Sabine said.

"As Her Grace commands," Faron said and started first with his shirt. Undoing the buttons, he then slowly lowered it from his shoulders and down his arms before tossing the shirt aside. Then he bent at the waist, unlacing his boots before tossing them the same way as his shirt. His hands went to his pants, slowly, ever so slowly undoing them and rolling them down his legs.

Their eyes met again, and Faron greedily took in the small reactions playing across her face, the slight tilt of her head as he revealed more of himself. He wanted every reaction he could get from her, every sign of longing. Finally done, he stood there, fully nude and erect, and waited for Sabine's next command.

"Touch yourself."

Faron raised an eyebrow, having not expected the command. He kept his face calm as he ran his flat palm down his torso to his dick, stopping before touching himself. "May I apply some oil, Your Grace?" He let a smile play across his lips.

"I suppose," she replied, her voice warm and amused. "If you beg."

Faron forced the smile away as he considered how best to fulfill her request. "May I please apply oil to myself, Your Grace? Please."

"Surely you can do better than that."

Faron couldn't fathom anything more attractive than Sabine at that moment. "Please, Sabine. Please, may I apply oil to my cock?" He laced his voice with slight desperation as he ran a finger from the base to the tip of his cock, uncertain if he wanted her permission or denial.

"You may," she agreed. "But you must go slowly. Tease yourself."

Faron found the bottle of oil they stored in her bureau which they'd kept since they had started seeing each other nightly. He poured a decent amount into his palm then loosely grasped his cock, slowly dragging his wet fist from tip to base and back up. "Does this please Her Grace?" he asked, his voice husky with need.

"It does," she replied. "Though I think you wish to do something else entirely. Tell me what."

"I wish to bury myself deep within you, bringing both of us pleasure until we fall apart together."

"Then why not ask for it?"

"We will get to that point when you wish it. For now, I am at your command, and this is what you wish." He continued to stroke himself.

"Oh, I did not say you could have it," Sabine replied. "I asked why you did not ask." She was teasing him, her green eyes sparkling with mischief. "Slower."

Faron couldn't help the way the corner of his lips quirked up at her words. As he slowed his pace, he let his eyes slip closed for a second as he tightened his grip, picturing Sabine's delicate fingers wrapped around him.

"You seem to be enjoying yourself," she said, cutting through the vivid mental image he'd conjured. "Perhaps I should leave you to your own pleasure."

"Only because I was picturing you taking me into your perfect mouth."

"Do you deserve my mouth, Faron?"

"I deserve anything you wish to bestow upon me, Your Grace."

She nodded, watching his hand slowly caress up and down. "Stop," she directed.

Faron let out a low groan of frustration, but he stopped immediately, his arm falling to his side. Again, she crooked a finger and beckoned him forward, and he went to her, unable to resist, not wanting to.

When he was within reach, Sabine looked up at him, letting her hand trail down the center of his chest to his stomach. Faron caught his breath, fighting not to touch Sabine as he wanted to. She took his erection in hand, their eyes locking once more, and she began stroking him.

Faron let out a low groan, balling his fists at his side. He wanted to close his eyes and just lean into the feeling, but he didn't dare. Her fingers were slow and careful but knowledgeable in what he liked, what he craved. She brushed her thumb over the head of his cock, starting with the sensitive underside. She repeated the action.

Faron panted as he watched her, enjoying the feelings she brought him. "Sabine," he growled out.

"I like the way you say my name," she replied as she ran her hand down his cock a final time. "Keep saying it," she directed before leaning forward and running her tongue along the head before finally taking him into her mouth.

Faron's head fell back, and her name fell from his lips like a prayer. Her tongue swirled around him a few times before taking him in more deeply.

Faron unclenched his hands and pressed his fingers into the meat of his upper thighs. Short recovery time or not, he would have to beg Sabine to stop soon lest he lose himself in her mouth.

Still, she continued, her head moving up and down his erection, her fingers gently kneading his balls. She glanced up at him every so often, watching his reactions. Faron met her gaze, his eyes dark and voice deeper than normal. "Sabine, I'm going to cum if you keep going." She responded by continuing her efforts.

Faron groaned, knowing he'd last only moments longer, and as she increased her pace, he couldn't hold back.

Faron released a harsh groan as he spent himself into Sabine's mouth, his posture relaxing as he did so. When Sabine pulled back, she ran her thumb along her bottom lip in cleanup.

"I will have to do that more often," she teased.

"I would not be opposed," Faron said breathlessly. He looked down at her, seeing how beautiful she looked, flushed, lips slightly swollen. He wanted more of her.

"You okay?" She asked, just as playful. "I don't think I've ever seen you quite so disconcerted before."

"I just need a moment. I'm okay. It's just been a long time since I trusted someone enough to allow them to be so intimate with me," Faron admitted. He immediately pushed down all the reasons he trusted Sabine and the surge of affection swelling up.

"Of course," Sabine replied. She took his hand and gently pulled him to the bed so he could relax. "You're safe with me."

Faron leaned back on the bed. "I know," he said with a smile. "I think I would truly have to upset you for you to grow violent."

"Oh, I don't think you'd inspire the rage I'd need to be violent."

"I would hope not, but I've been told I'm vexing." Faron gave a small shrug before smiling warmly at Sabine. "May I kiss you?"

"Please."

Faron pulled Sabine across his chest to kiss her. She settled against them as they kissed, her fingers gently trailing along his stubbled jaw. They kissed for several minutes, the exchanges growing deeper and needier, and Faron enjoyed the feeling of Sabine before he rolled them, pinning her under him.

She looked up at him, her breathing heavy from kissing. One hand braced his weight, helping Faron not to crush her, while the other moved down to her hip, dragging her skirts up her body. "May I fuck you?" he asked.

"Undress me first."

"Of course, Your Grace," Faron said, gently kissing Sabine before he rolled off her and sat up, more than willing to do whatever she wanted. "Come here, please," he said, making it clear he was going to undo the laces on her back.

She sat up and turned her back to Faron, sweeping her long hair over her shoulder. Faron set to work, undoing intricate laces with skilled fingers. Only once it was completely undone did Faron slow down, taking his time sliding the bodice down her shoulders, his lips peppering kisses along her neck and shoulder.

She moaned softly as his lips caressed her skin even as she shifted the rest of her top from her body. "Rise for me," Faron said between kisses, and Sabine obeyed, going to her knees so he could carefully remove the rest of her clothes. Once Sabine lowered herself again, he pulled her back against his chest. "What do you wish me to do?"

"To start," Sabine replied, "kiss me again."

Faron gently placed his hand on her chin and turned her head to the side, kissing her deeply. He knew he was being stupid, letting this go on, but he just didn't care at the moment, not when she was near him and he could feel her soft warmth, take in her sweet scent, and her inviting lips.

She pulled him down as they kissed, his body settling on top of hers again. Faron braced himself above her once more with one hand, the other caressing her side as he continued to kiss Sabine. She ran a hand along his back, fingers trailing along his spine. His lower body rested between her thighs, and her right leg bent at the knee, brushing up against his hip and letting him settle against her.

Faron continued to gently caress Sabine, his hand moving up and down her side before palming her breast. The way her back arched up to his touch, the way she moaned his name, all had Faron dazed by his need. The physical part of his desire, which brushed against her thigh as they kissed, only encompassed part of what he wanted from her, and right now, he was in no position to keep pushing aside his thoughts. At least right now.

Faron broke the kiss, resting his sweat-soaked forehead on her own. "May I?" he asked breathlessly, wanting to, no, needing to be joined with Sabine more than anything else.

"Yes," she replied, just as breathless.

Faron closed his eyes and steadied himself. His hand moved from her breast, trailing down her stomach to her center. Taking himself in hand, Faron positioned at her entrance, and keeping eye contact with Sabine, he slowly pushed himself inside her, stopping only when he was fully buried between her legs. Sabine's arm went around him, keeping him close, and Faron stayed still, enjoying the feeling of being one with Sabine. Finally, he moved his hips in, small shallow thrusts which would drive them both crazy wanting more, but it felt right.

"Faron," Sabine whispered breathlessly after the first few movements. Her leg wrapped around his hip, not demanding, but bringing them closer together.

Faron breathed through the slight adjustment, wanting to take his time with her now. He kissed her again, slow and hot, and he groaned as her fingers tangled into his dark curls. "Spirits, Sabine," he groaned as he kept up the slow pace.

"Like you aren't driving me crazy?" she replied with faint laughter.

Chapter Thirty-Four

"I think I'm driving us both a little crazy. Should I stop?" he asked.

"Whatever you do, don't stop touching me."

"I don't plan on it," Faron promised.

"Good."

Their bodies continued moving together in slow, deliberate rhythms, tempting out gasps and groans of need. Faron kept up the slow pace for as long as he was able before the need for more became too overwhelming. He slowly increased his pace as a hand slid between them to caress Sabine's center, prompting her to tighten her grasp.

Faron watched Sabine's face closely, listening to the way her breaths increased. He matched his movements with his hand to his thrusts, determined that she would come undone first. When she finally tipped over the edge, she clung to him as her body shook through her climax.

Faron considered trying to hold back his own release, wanting to bring Sabine to hers over and over again, but with the way she tightened around him and the way she felt, Faron found himself unable to resist and allowed himself to let go as well, spilling inside of Sabine.

As their bodies quieted and Sabine's leg unwound from him, her arms still stayed loosely secured around Faron. She drew him into a quiet kiss. He rolled them to their sides, a hand now in her hair, playing with the long, light caramel strands. "I already want you again," he shared, his voice husky.

"Give me a minute," she replied, her laugh breathy and amused.

"Take all the time you need."

Chapter Thirty-Five

Faron strolled through the town, having decided to take Sabine's advice and spend time outside of the chateau on his day off. Despite living in the Vassetre estate for a few months, he had done everything in his power to avoid going into town more often than required. He wasn't introverted, nor did he feel a need to prove himself useful. Rather, he often assumed the anti-elf sentiments he'd faced in Myrefall, as well as the poverty, would greet him even with Sabine overseeing the village.

Yet, the few times he'd visited the villages with someone else from the chateau, he'd found no children begging on the streets. He'd been greeted by friendly faces. He'd witnessed no suggestion of drunken street fights or evidence of rampant crime. What little he had witnessed in Fythias had not touched Sabine's lands.

The village was simply different, and he wasn't used to it. The shopkeepers and stall merchants were different too. There wasn't the same desperate need to sell their wares here as there was back home where one bad day could see a family starve or be tossed out on the streets. Here, friendly competition was promoted, and Faron wanted to spend the exorbitant amount of coin Sabine paid him.

His good fortune made him feel guilty, and he knew if he asked, Sabine would allow him to go home, gather those in need, and bring them back. Her heart was just that big, as had been proved by the invitation she'd given Avana. Her heart was one of the things he lov... admired about her. Sabine took honest joy out of helping her people, in being out and about amongst them. He couldn't recall the name of the man who was supposed to care for the village he'd grown up in. He didn't recall ever seeing the lord.

Feeling like he'd wandered around idly long enough, Faron pulled a piece of parchment from one of the pouches on his belt and looked it over. Lisbeth had handed it to him when he let her know where he was going. In her neat script was a list of small items she said they were in no rush for, and if he didn't have time to pick up, it was fine. Wandering from stall to stall, he began the search for the items, ignoring a pendant with the sea green stone that reminded him of Sabine's eyes, the vials of bath salts he knew she enjoyed, and more importantly, the stall selling more adult items. They hadn't found time to use the rope he'd purchased not long ago, and they would need to have a more serious talk about boundaries before he bought anything more serious.

Walking as quickly as he could from the stall, Faron found himself in a different area of the market, one primarily made up of vendors selling seeds, plants, and other such items. With Lisbeth's abilities, none of them needed to come to this side of the market, yet Faron found himself drawn to one of the flower stalls. Nestled in between all the brightly colored bouquets was one made up entirely of Gentian, Sabine's favorite flower. That he knew her favorite flower caused Faron to pause. He was sure they had never discussed flowers before, but he somehow still knew those were her favorites, just like he knew her favorite dessert and favorite finger sandwich. Knew which musical piece she enjoyed best when someone played the piano. He knew so many little details about the duchesse, more than was appropriate, but did it truly matter? Wasn't her personal guard supposed to know those things?

Faron shook his head. No, those were not the details he should know as her guard. As her lover, a potential romantic partner, yes, but not as her employee, not her personal guard.

Even as those thoughts settled, Faron wondered if it mattered. He knew they were not meant for each other. She was a duchesse, second only to the royal family, and he was nothing. Any feelings he had for her didn't matter, he told himself. Yet, as he stared at those flowers, thinking over all the time they had spent together, Faron started to wonder if maybe it did matter. His hand was almost to the flowers without his mind telling him to grab them when someone, a male, shouting his name caused him to draw back and turn swiftly, looking for whoever it was that had drawn him from his thoughts.

Looking around, Faron spotted an older elf headed his way, waving with a joyful smile on their face. It took Faron a moment to recognize the elf, and he found himself jogging the short distance as he took in his old friend. Reaching the other elf, Faron wrapped him in a warm hug, lifting him off the ground in his joy.

"By the Spirits, boy! Put me down!" the other elf shouted through laughter. "I'm happy to see you too."

Faron set him down gently, taking in the silver streaks in the man's black hair, the wrinkles and laugh lines, how his deeply tanned skin seemed stretched thin, and the bow in his back. "Phindel. You got old," Faron couldn't stop himself from saying, taking the soft slap the elf aimed his way.

"Well, I am old," Phindel replied with a laugh.

"You're not that old," Faron joked, ignoring the fact that Phindel was, in fact, quite old. He'd known the other elf since he was young. He'd been like an uncle to him growing up and had helped him get his first job after his father died. He and his wife had left Coralia over twenty years ago when Clara had been accused of using her healing magic to injure someone, an accusation no one who knew the two had believed. They'd kept up through occasional letters, but Faron had no idea his old friend resided in Fythias. "Where's Clara?" Faron asked, looking around for Phindel's wife, only spotting a group of children watching them from a few feet away.

A gentle hand on his bicep pulled Faron's attention back to Phindel, and the look in the elf's eyes told Faron everything he needed to know. "She went to the Green Fields several years ago," Phindel said softly, sadly.

Faron had to blink back tears quickly. "But she had magic," Faron found himself saying, as if it would make her death a lie.

"She did, my boy, but the magic only offers humans a handful more years than a non-magical human, and nowhere near as long as an elf. It's okay, though. We had seventy glorious and happy years together."

Faron saw the grin on his friend's face and would have believed that had he not also noted the deep well of sadness in his friend's eyes. Faron couldn't help being reminded once more of Sabine's humanity. She was twenty-six, close to twenty-seven. If they were lucky, she would live another seventy or eighty years at most. He was only sixty-eight. With luck, he would live another two hundred years or so. He couldn't picture starting a life with Sabine only to lose her and have to spend an unknown amount of time without joining her. If he did allow what was between them to become more.

"How are you holding up without her?" Faron asked, knowing it was the wrong question. Thankfully, Phindel knew him better than he knew himself, even after all these years.

"Clara found me a cause before she passed," Phindel said with a smile. He gestured to the group of children Faron had spotted before. "You had kids?" Faron asked in disbelief. He knew human females often couldn't have children after a certain age, and he was sure Clara had been at least fifty-two when they'd left Coralia.

"In a manner of speaking. Just because there are no homeless orphans here doesn't mean it is true of all Fythias. We traveled in the last few years of her life and collected the ones we could find and those children brought other children. I take care of them with help from Her Grace, who stops by when she can," Phindel clarified.

"That sounds like Sab… Her Grace," Faron corrected and ignored the look Phindel shot his way.

"I heard she had a new personal guard—some giant strapping lad of an elf. I guess I should have asked more questions." Phindel laughed and motioned Faron toward the children. "Come, meet my children and have lunch with us. We were going to the new bakery down the street."

Faron didn't stop his friend from dragging him toward the children, the youngest looking to be around four, the oldest maybe sixteen. Before they could get there, Faron found himself looking back at the arrangement of Gentians before pushing them, and Sabine, out of his mind. It was better this way, less painful. He would keep to their current arrangement and not allow himself any more. It was the right choice, for both of them.

Chapter
Thirty-Six

Sabine sighed happily as she settled into the fragrant bath. Hot water rose up to her shoulders, relaxing tense muscles as she leaned back against the cushioned headrest. Her hair was pulled up, preventing her worrying over it soaking along with the rest of her. On a relaxing night, the last thing she wanted to do was spend the next couple of hours contending with her hair.

She closed her eyes, reflecting on the past several days and the reality of the feelings she could no longer ignore. The seismic shift in the way she viewed the world could never return to its former state. Though, Sabine felt she was willing to embrace the old and the new. What other choice did she have, really?

Of course, she'd spent much of her time in meetings and negotiations, the politics surrounding the royal court held a never-ending demand on her time and attention. None of her responsibilities presented new stressors, but the increased demands from the feuding royals, and her direct refusal of Grégoire's demands, had her in great need of time to decompress. These were the problems which would remain with her always.

She smiled to herself as she thought about some of the ways she had been using to relax. Faron's increasing presence in her bedroom did wonders to bring about well-rested mornings. His office visits were another thing entirely. She had well-accepted her feelings for the elf, even if she'd never given them voice. Sometimes, she suspected the feelings were mutual. Lisbeth and Meri thought so, but she respected Faron enough to not pressure him. Sex was not affection, and no amount of suspicion gave her the right to assume more. Her position, both as his employer and her title, also caused her to hesitate in broaching something more. If their positions and roles were reversed, Sabine felt certain she'd have wanted the same consideration.

Besides, Faron had been acting strangely over the past few days. Not impolite, not unfamiliar, but more distant than she liked. As his employer, a fact her mind repeatedly reminded her of, she didn't know how much pressing she could do and remain appropriate. He would speak with her if his worries remained, and if not, he would eventually resume something friendlier and more normal in time. She supposed she could prompt some sort of response from him, something generic, but it felt almost as problematic to treat him as though she were not intimately acquainted with so much of him.

She sighed, sinking deeper into the tub, letting the warm water rise to her neck. She briefly considered forgetting her carefully stacked hair and fully submerging, but she was stopped in those thoughts. Footsteps sounded from outside, and Sabine briefly opened her eyes to peer at the door where the person had paused.

"I can hear you," she called out, now craning her neck to get a better idea of who might be there.

"I was planning on knocking. May I enter? I have towels for when you are done," Faron explained, his voice calm and respectful, but still a little distant with her.

She smiled to herself, despite the formality. She was always pleased to hear his voice, especially when it was unexpected. "You may."

Faron entered, closing the door behind him to keep the heat in, knowing her preference for warmer spaces and privacy. She appreciated the small effort. Walking to the large marble vanity, he placed the towels down then glanced over his shoulder toward her. "Would you like them closer?"

"The vanity should be fine," she decided. She offered Faron an amused smile. "I should be surprised to see you, but somehow, I am not. Have you added laundry delivery to your list of daily tasks?" she asked.

Faron gave her a barely-there smile, though she saw the humor in his eyes. "Perhaps I didn't recognize the servant wishing to bring in towels and decided it would be better if I did. Getting to lay eyes upon you is a privileged part of the job, after all."

"You find reason enough to lay eyes on me," she replied, offering him a warm smile. "And you do so quite often."

Faron didn't blush, but from what Sabine could tell, it was a close thing.

"You are pleasant to lay eyes on. More than pleasant if we are being honest," she replied.

"Am I?" he asked.

"You very much are."

"I shall keep that in mind." Faron bowed, surprisingly. "Should I take my leave?"

"Do you wish to?" she asked, struck again by the distance of the question. She raised a brow, carefully studying him. "I cannot recall the last time you were so formal with me, especially in private. Is everything okay?"

Faron glanced back at the towels, hiding much of his expression from her. "Formality is a good mask to hide behind when one has trouble controlling themselves," he admitted. "I don't want to leave, but I worry if I stay, I won't keep my hands to myself."

"Since when have you worried about keeping your hands to yourself?" she asked.

"Since you have not yet given me permission," he pointed out. "I'm also certain you said you might be too worn out for anything too strenuous when we spoke earlier in the day."

"I am tired," she agreed with a careful nod. "But I do love your company. The rest usually sorts itself out."

"We do spend a lot of time in each other's company." He turned back to her, approached the tub, and knelt, resting on his knees so they were more level. The position brought out something more normal in their exchanges, something friendlier. She relaxed a little.

"You still seem a little distant tonight. What is the cause?" Sabine asked.

Faron hesitated in answering, his gaze cast down at the floor. "I ran into an old friend at the market. It was a good visit, but it brought to mind a lot of things I hadn't wanted to think of."

"Anything you want to share?" she asked, her brows knitted together in concern. "I'll happily listen."

Faron's brow creased as he sorted his thoughts. "I discovered a friend had passed away, leaving her husband behind to mourn her. It gave me some unwanted reminders."

"Oh, I'm so sorry about your friend," Sabine replied, her expression growing more somber. She sat up a little in her tub, the water now only up to her chest. "Was it unexpected?"

Faron shook his head. "I realized after chatting I should have expected the news, but it never occurred to me." He sighed and shook his head before making a sound which came across as a blended snort and scoff. "I also managed to nearly get myself arrested in a tavern for assaulting the head of the Jewelers' Guild. I know it would have displeased you, though."

"Why did you assault the head of the guild?"

"Because he was speaking of you in an ill manner." Faron almost ground his teeth together as he spoke. "Well, maybe not an ill manner, but an inappropriate one."

"What did he say to have you so up in arms?"

"Let's just say it was enough to make me realize you are much more popular with the males of your village than I originally thought, and I am formally putting in a request that you are never alone with him."

She looked over at him again and nodded. "You wish me to only be popular with you?"

"I would like for you to be loved by the people you care for, but otherwise, yes."

"You have always been possessive."

Faron looked away. "I find it worse with you, Sabine."

She raised a brow, curious at the reaction and response. "Why with me?"

"I am not sure, but I believe it started from the moment I first laid eyes on you."

"It started," she repeated. "Elaborate."

"I found you interesting the moment we met. You're playful and cunning, and incredibly beautiful and desirable. You've never shied away from what you are and who you appear to be. You have so many contrasts from not only other noble women but every other woman I've ever met. I cannot help my attraction."

"Your pursuit has demonstrated your attraction. There are days when I find I cannot separate from you at all." She didn't want to separate from Faron, nor did she wish him to separate through any desire or responsibility. Like so many things, Sabine was not afraid to express the desire to be near him.

"I feel the same," he admitted. "I feel drawn to you in a way I have not been to another person before. It makes me want to claim you. It is not love, it is a deep longing, a need to possess and keep you safe."

It is not love...

Sabine felt the hope which had risen in her chest, hope she hadn't even acknowledged before now, dissipate, leaving her hollow and sad. If what he felt was not love, if it was not anything more than base attraction, she did not want it, because she knew she felt so much more for Faron. "I see," she said. "I need to dry off and dress so I can sleep. If you'll see yourself out, please."

Her dismissal surprised him if the slight widening of his eyes and the set of his mouth was any indication. "Sabine," he began, his tone careful and serious. "Are you upset because I said I do not love you or because I said I wish to possess you? I don't believe we have known each other long enough for what we've shared to be love, and I do not believe you love me. But please, tell me if I am wrong or what I have said is wrong. I would not have there be distance between us."

Sabine almost laughed at him, even though she found nothing humorous about his statements. He didn't love her. He'd made his feelings on the matter exceptionally clear, but somehow, he believed he could make demands of her thoughts, feelings, and reactions all the same. He didn't get to do that. He didn't get access to her just because he desired her. He didn't get to take advantage of her vulnerability, something she realized she'd stupidly allowed him to do for far too long.

"I am not leaving Sabine. Not until we've worked this out."

"There is nothing to work out, Faron. I have asked you to leave so I may dry off and dress. You should listen."

"You've never asked me to go before," he pointed out.

"I am now," she replied. "Leave, Faron."

Faron opened his mouth as if to argue more, before snapping it shut with a click of his jaw. Rising from his kneeling position, he said, "As Her Grace commands." He then bowed low, lower than normal, and left, closing the door behind him.

Alone again, Sabine allowed her eyes to sting with furious, heartbroken tears.

Lord Tristian,

After much consideration, I have decided to accept your offer. We may discuss details at your convenience.

Yours,
Sabine, Duchesse Vassetre

A sneak peek from the upcoming sequel,
Vassetre: Heart of a Duchesse.

"Her Grace has decided to visit the Comte du Ciel," Finn said bluntly, keeping his gaze focused on the crowd but no one in particular. "She has her reasons, of course, and she will personally meet with those who need to be aware of her actions and motivations before we set off, which I have been told will be in a few days' time."

"She's not accepted his proposal, has she?" Marcelle asked, eliciting gasps of protest and horrified shock from around the room.

"Not that I am aware of," Finn replied shortly. "But I do wonder if the visit might result in some arrangement. We know the prince has been pressuring her for some time, and the comte had proven interested in Her Grace." Finn held up his hands to quiet the group down, though this took time and an irritated clearing of his throat. "I know," he said bluntly. "I know. This was not an event any of us could anticipate, but she has agreed to visit, and given the state of things, I think it is wise to approach the visit with caution."

Faron felt terribly confused. He couldn't fathom why Sabine would wish to visit Tristian. She disliked the man and all he stood for. She had expressed many times how boring, unintelligent, and potentially dangerous she found him to be. She'd also made it clear there was something about him that made her feel unsafe. She'd had him place guards on the doors to the wing of her side of the chateau, yet she would agree to go and visit the comte? With marriage a possible outcome? No, something was wrong.

"When did she decide this?" Faron asked, suddenly aware that of all the people in the chateau, his position should have made him among the first to know. He was her personal guard, and he had been acting as the guard captain since his arrival. He should have known.

"Late last night," Finn replied with a sigh. "She sent word via letter this morning to the comte's estate, declaring her intention to visit."

Faron's eyes narrowed as he recalled the prior night's discussions between Sabine and himself. He wondered if she's already planned the visit before they had spoken, and if so, had her ultimate coldness before he'd been dismissed been the result? But no. That didn't sound right. Sabine never took her frustrations out on her people. He would have to speak with her when the meeting was done. He waited for whatever else Finn had to say, fighting the urge to get up and go.

"I will notify those chosen to accompany Her Grace to Villa du Ciel as soon as I have been informed of Her Grace's choices," Finn said as he brushed his red-brown curls from his face. "Until then, please proceed with your morning duties."

Faron waited as the staff filed out of the office, noisily chatting and gossiping over the news before striding to the door, purposeful in his steps. That was until his arm was grabbed and he suddenly found himself face-to-face with Meri. Her gold eyes narrowed into fury and her short dark hair seemingly standing on end.

"No," she said, her voice firm.

"No, what?" he demanded.

"No, you will not demand answers from Her Grace, and do not try to tell me you weren't about to do that because I can read it on your face. She must have her reasons to decide on a visit, and your intention to go to demand them of her is disrespectful. Leave it be, Faron." Meri released his arm.

Book Club Questions

1. Would you have forgiven Meri and Faron for their actions on the night Avana arrived?

2. Why do you think Sabine was willing to give Avana a chance?

3. Sabine often makes choices which make her life more difficult, such as defying Prince Grégoire's orders to visit Coralia. Why do you think she makes these choices?

4. Is Faron in love with Sabine, or has he prevented himself from feeling too deeply for her?

5. Why do you think Sabine agreed to marry Tristian at the end of the book? What do you think the consequences might be?

6. How could Faron have better handled his fear of Sabine passing before him?

7. Who do you think sent Avana and why?

8. Do you think Lisbeth, Finn, and Meri overstep bounds in their friendship with Sabine, and if so, how?

9. Sabine acknowledges her feelings for Faron, but she chooses to keep them to herself. Why does she make this choice? Would you have done the same?

10. There are many references to Sabine being cold-natured. Do you think this an important point or just a characteristic she possesses?

Author
Bios

K̲ate Jenkins enjoys writing fantasy, sci-fi, and romance as much as she enjoys reading them. She lives in a small town in Idaho with her autistic teen who is her whole world, her parents, and between them, four dogs and six cats. When not hanging with her son, she loves gaming, especially first-person shooters and asymmetrical horror games she can play with friends. She's a K-pop enthusiast and harbors a secret love of K-dramas and Anime, much to her mother's displeasure, as she's slowly being sucked into them with her. Her favorites tropes are currently enemies-to-lovers, there-was-only-one-bed, coffee-shops, time-travel-fixes-it, and soul mates/soul identifying marks. She is hopeful one day she can talk her co-author into writing these with her.

M̲organ Moreau's literary interests span across various genres, showcasing a love for the realms of fantasy, historical fiction, crime and mystery, as well as contemporary stories. She is an enthusiastic lover of *The Little Mermaid*, as is evident in her vivid red hair, mermaid tattoos, and growing Ariel collection. Morgan also holds a deep affection for pirates, especially those who "wear fine things well," though those in possession of jars of dirt will always hold a place in her heart. She lives in Alabama with her dog, Scarlett, and she looks forward to adopting more puppies in the future. Her current passions include higher education, animal rights, and watching the 1995 *Pride & Prejudice* at least once a month. In addition to her current literary loves, Morgan is a fan of mermaids, vampires, pirates, and superheroes, and she hopes to incorporate this into future works.